THE ORPHAN'S LOST CHRISTMAS

IRIS COLE

PROLOGUE

 858

At six years old, Nora Ellis knew that the bigger children she played with on Sundays did not believe in magic, but she also knew that none of them had ever watched her mother mend someone's shirt in the last light of the day.

She sat on a three-legged stool by the fire, silent and spellbound even though the coals had burned so low that only the barest flicker of warmth escaped them. The light coming in through the cottage's tiny window, there was a big window too, but Papa had boarded it up last autumn, was so grey and grubby that it hardly seemed worthy of the term "sunlight," yet Mama's fine hair still managed to glow in it. She always tried to keep it caught up beneath her bonnet, but after a full day's work, streaks of it fell free and tumbled around her shoulders and captured the light, as though a thousand tiny fairies had woven the delicate golden strands just to catch sunlight in their net.

The reflection of her hair made her gaunt face seem a little softer in those moments, even though long years of poverty had left her cheekbones jutting beneath her brown eyes, which remained fixed on her work.

She draped the shirt over her lap; at this time of day, that last precious light never fell on the kitchen table where she usually worked. Her bruised hand rose and fell, the sewing needle flashing in the light, and with every stitch, she made the broken whole again. The pale threads crisscrossed the hole in the rough spun shirt. When she reached the end, she gave the thread a little tug. Just like that, the hole was gone, as though it had never been there.

"Like magic," Nora whispered.

Mama raised her head. "What's that, darling?"

"I said that you mend things like magic, Mama."

Mama softly laughed. "If only that were true, little one." She tied a quick knot in the thread.

This was Nora's cue. She jumped up and seized the fabric scissors from their place beside her stool. They were Mama's most treasured possession: a pair of fine steel dressmaker's shears with handles of carved bone, worn smooth from years of use. Mama had told her once that they came from a great lady's sewing box, sold off when the lady died. They were the only beautiful thing they owned.

With great care, using both hands, Nora snipped the end off the thread.

"Is that good, Mama?"

"That's perfect." Mama touched her nose with the tip of her finger, making her laugh. "I think that's enough for today, my love. We'd best get these things folded and set aside to take to our customers tomorrow, and then start on supper before your papa gets here. It is Christmas Eve, after all, even if we don't have much to celebrate with tonight."

Nora leaped into action. She carefully returned the scissors to their place on the little shelf beside Mama's needles and thread. She knew how precious they were. Mama always said that a seamstress was only as good as her scissors, and these were the best in all of Devil's Acre.

Then she pushed her stool aside into its corner, and scrambled onto one of the chairs by the tiny kitchen table. As Mama folded the clothes she'd mended that day, Nora stacked them into neat bundles, sorting them by customer; she always made sure to remember which clothes came from which house in the mornings. Then she tied the bundles with bits of string and set them on a barrel by the front door for delivery after Christmas.

"Clever girl," said Mama.

"Don't you mean, 'good girl,' Mama?" Nora asked. "That's what Mrs. Patterson across the street always says to Verity."

Mama chuckled. "You are a good girl, Nora, but you're a clever one, too. It takes more than goodness to survive in London, you know. It takes a good deal of cleverness, too. Lots of people say that girls don't have to be clever, but we know different, don't we?"

Her smile thrilled Nora. She felt that Mama was letting her in on a special secret.

"We know different, yes," she said seriously.

Mama laughed.

"What will we have for supper?" Nora asked eagerly. There had been a heel of yesterday's bread for her at lunchtime, but it felt like an awfully long way away. The lukewarm gruel she'd eaten for breakfast might as well have happened to somebody else for all the satisfaction it gave her now.

Mama hesitated.

"May we have beef soup, Mama?" Nora asked eagerly. "Like we had once before on Christmas Eve? Can we have beef soup again?"

"There's no beef today, I'm afraid. But do you know what we do have?"

"What?"

"We have three beautiful, big, fat turnips. Look at them! They're just about bursting out of their skins. I'm sure there's still a carrot, too. We'll make a lovely soup, beef or no beef."

Nora knew enough to hide her disappointment. "Beef or no beef."

THE STREETS GREW dark long before Papa came home at this time of year. Nora sat by the window, smelling the dense, vegetable scent from the pot sputtering weakly over their last few coals in the fireplace, peering down the twisty street. There were many cobbles missing and the cottages crowded close against the narrow road; there were no gardens here. But there was a lamppost. It stood tall and proud on the corner a few doors down from Nora's house, casting a weak yellow glow in a circle around it.

A wreath hung from the lamppost: a plain circle of holly, their street's concession to Christmastime.

Mama was setting the table with clay bowls for the soup. "Any sign yet, Nora?"

"Not yet, Mama." Nora hesitated. "Wait, do you hear that?"

"Mercy, yes, I do." Mama came over to the window and opened it a little, even though it let the chill air in. "Why, I didn't know the carollers came this close to our street. They must be passing by the little church across the river. I suppose the wind is in the right direction for it."

They sat in silence for a few moments, listening to the distant voices. Nora thought they sounded like angel voices, the words floating into their cottage through the impenetrable dark.

It came upon a midnight clear
That glorious song of old
From angels bending near the earth
To touch their harps of gold.

"I think they are angels singing, Mama," Nora whispered in wonder.

Mama kissed her cheek. "They might as well be, and look at that! Here comes an angel of our own."

She pointed down the street as a shabby silhouette appeared in the streetlight on the corner.

Nora's heart leaped. "Papa! Papa!"

She jumped down from the stool by the window and ran to the door, jumping up and down until her overeager little hands finally found the knob and turned it. Despite the frigid air, Nora bolted into the street, giggling hysterically.

"Papa!" she cried.

The workworn man walking up the street crouched and held out his arms. Nora jumped into them. Papa swept her off her feet and spun her around until she screamed with delight.

"Hello, my little darling!" He gave her cheek a whiskery kiss. "You'll catch your death out here without your coat. Come, come, let's get you inside."

Nora cuddled him, hardly knowing what he was talking

about. There was no place in the world warmer than Papa's arms.

He carried her into the cottage, where he bent to wrap an arm around Mama and kiss her, delightfully squashing Nora between the two.

"You poor thing, you're half frozen," said Mama.

Papa set Nora down. She ran to push his chair nearer the fire, and he sagged into it as Mama pulled off his coat.

"We're having soup for Christmas Eve supper, Papa," said Nora. "Not beef soup, but it still smells nice."

"Your mother could make a soup out of old shoes and it would still taste wonderful." Papa winked.

"Don't worry, John. I've saved all our good things for Christmas lunch tomorrow." Mama gave a brave smile. "There might not be much, but we'll have a bit of roast chicken, at least, and Mrs. Dench paid me enough for a little piece of fruit cake."

Nora busied herself with unlacing her father's boots and pulling them off. "Oh, look! This one's all broken." She pointed to a loose sole at the toe of his left one.

"Never you mind that, darling." Papa chuckled. "Did you hear the carollers, Catherine?"

"I certainly did. They were lovely tonight. I'm surprised they came this far into Devil's Acre."

"Aye, but that's only a name, love. Perhaps they know there are good folks here whose hearts are waiting for Christmas just like theirs." Papa laid a warm hand on Nora's head. "There are them that believe that Christmas is only for rich folks, but that isn't so. Is it, Nora?"

"No, Papa." Nora scrambled into his lap. "You always say that Christmas is for everyone."

"It certainly is. It brings love and light to us all, whether we live in a king's palace or a cottage." Papa kissed her cheek. "I wouldn't take any palace without the pair of you in it."

"Hark at this man!" Mama laughed.

"Besides," said Papa, a secret gleam coming into his eye, "I happen to know that Christmas will be extra-special this year."

"It will?" Nora gasped. "How? Did you buy us chestnuts to roast in the fire again, Papa? Or oranges?"

"There will certainly be chestnuts," said Papa solemnly, "but I'm afraid no oranges. Our surprise is rather nicer than that."

"Nicer than oranges! It can't be."

"What are you talking about, love?" Mama asked.

Papa reached into his trouser pocket and pulled out three little stubs of paper. He waved them with a triumphant grin. Nora had no idea what they were, but Mama's squeal told her that they had to be something wonderful.

"Oh, John!" Mama laughed. "Are they…"

"Tickets to the pantomime!" Papa beamed.

"What's a pantomime?" Nora cried, enraptured.

"Oh, Norey, it's such fun," said Mama. "It's like a play, only it's not stuffy and slow, it's funny and colourful! Which one is it, John?"

"The Boxing Day pantomime at the Royal Victorian."

"The Royal Victorian! My, my. We're terribly fancy, aren't we? I'll have to wear my Sunday frock! John, how on earth…?"

"Old Thatcher at the factory was in a lovely mood today. A bit of Christmas spirit must have come over him," said Papa. "He'd bought the tickets for himself and his wife and mother, but with old Mrs. Thatcher's hip so bad with the rheumatism, bless her heart, they didn't want to go without her. He gave the tickets to me."

"Well, it's about time he showed you a speck of appreciation for the twenty years you've worked in that factory. Why, John, this is wonderful."

"Get your best dresses ready, girls." Papa gripped them both and squeezed them so hard that Nora thought she might explode with happiness. "We're going to the pantomime."

To Nora, it felt as though Christmas that year was twice as long.

When her eyes opened on Christmas morning, her happy squeal was louder than ever, for two glorious thoughts filled her mind at the same moment. The first was that it was Christmas, and that was why the house smelled of warm milk and nutmeg and roast chestnuts from last night. The second was that tomorrow was the pantomime, her first time ever seeing such a thing.

She scrambled from the sleeping pallet on the floor of the cottage's only bedroom and launched herself onto Mama and Papa's bed. Its worn springs creaked alarmingly as she bounced up and down on the tattered blankets.

"It's Christmas! It's Christmas! It's Christmas!" she sang.

Papa groaned and pulled the covers over his head.

"Papaaa!" Nora fell to her knees and plucked the blanket away. "Papa, wake up!"

"Sweetie, five more minutes," Papa groaned.

Mama giggled sleepily. "Five more minutes on Christmas morning? I don't think so, John."

"It's Christmaaaaaaaas!" Nora squealed. "Ooh, Papa, Mama, do you think there's something in my stocking? Do you? Do you? Do you?"

Mama sat up and caught Nora around her belly, tugging her into her lap. "I don't know. Have you been a good girl? Father Christmas only brings presents for good girls."

Papa gasped. "Oh, Catherine, how could you even ask? Of course she's a good girl."

"Good girls let their papas sleep five more minutes," said Mama, but her tickly fingers on Nora's belly told her that she was teasing.

"Oh, please, Mama, Papa, let me see my stocking!" Nora begged.

"All right, all right." Mama let her go.

"Let's go!" Papa swung out of bed in his stockings and nightcap.

Nora seized his hand and dragged him into the room that encompassed the rest of their cottage, and there was her stocking hanging by the fireplace, lumpy with promise.

"Maybe it's coal," Papa joked.

"No, it's not!" Nora jumped up and tugged it from its hook. "It's not coal at all. It's more chestnuts! And look!" She grabbed an orange from the very top and gasped. "Oh, Papa, look! A whole orange!"

Mama padded into the room, a blanket still wrapped around her, and sat on a stool by the fire while Papa added a few more sticks of firewood. "My, my. You must have been a very good girl for Father Christmas to bring you an orange!"

Nora's eager fingers pulled back the peel and exposed

the fruit's sweet, fragrant flesh. After carefully putting the peel aside (Mama would want it for something) Nora raised it to her mouth and inhaled.

Slowly, she lowered the orange. "Why didn't Father Christmas bring you anything?"

Mama lifted Nora onto her lap and cuddled her. "Because he only comes for children, darling."

"But that's not fair. You've been good this year, too." Nora looked down at the fruit in her hands.

"That's all right. We don't want presents." Papa ruffled her hair. "You're our present."

Nora dug her fingers into the orange, separating it into three parts. They weren't quite equal, so she gave the biggest part to Papa, the second-to-biggest to Mama, and kept the smallest for herself.

"Nora, what are you doing?" Mama asked.

"We can all have some," said Nora.

"Darling, no. This is yours." Papa tried to give it back.

Nora wouldn't take it. "Please, Papa."

Her parents exchanged a glance. She didn't know then what the tears in her mother's eyes were for, but in later years, she would look back to know that the expression on her face was pride.

Nora bit into her piece of orange, and it was the sweetest thing she had ever tasted.

THE PANTOMIME WAS everything that Mama and Papa had said it would be.

At first, the theatre made Nora a little nervous. It was a great, tall building, but it had none of the spaciousness of the church she attended with her parents on Sundays.

Instead, the seats were all very close together, and the walls and ceiling crowded near. Smoke from the gallery drifted down to the cheaper seats on the ground floor. When all the lights went out, it was very close and dark, and Nora didn't like the jostle of the crowd so close around her. She clung very tightly to both her parents' hands.

Everything changed, however, when the first gas light fell upon the stage and Nora laid eyes on the character they called Harlequin. His costume was so colourful and his movements so swift and playful that Nora couldn't peel her gaze away from him. He capered and leaped, smiled and bowed, and filled the world with his presence. Papa swept her up onto his lap so that she could see over the heads before them, and she soon found herself laughing and clapping along with the crowd.

The play was Harlequin and Cinderella, and it held Nora utterly spellbound to the very last moment. She thought she had never seen anything as beautiful as Cinderella and the magnificent glass slipper, and the prince was so dashing and handsome and so magnificently vengeful upon the evil stepsisters that she clapped until her little hands were raw.

The whole theatre trembled with cheering as the cast took their final bow.

"Again, again!" Nora cheered. "Oh, Mama, can we watch it again?"

Mama had to shout to make herself heard over the hubbub of conversation. "No, darling! For a start, it's high time you were in bed. Besides, listen to that crowd outside. There are more people coming in for the evening performance."

Papa lifted Nora onto his hip and cradled her as the crowd began to move away from their seats. As soon as she looked away from the stage, the magic seemed to have gone. Even the holly wreaths hanging from the railings and the Christmas tree all aglow at the edge of the stage suddenly looked shabby and dowdy, and the theatre was once again a stifling, overcrowded building.

Nora suddenly realized how very tired she was. She rested her head on Papa's shoulder and draped her arms loosely around her neck.

"My, what a lot of pushing and shoving!" said Mama.

"Stay close, Catherine," Papa called. "Hold onto my coat, that's right, hold tight. We don't want to be separated."

They made slow progress toward the doors, pausing to allow more people to flow downstairs from the gallery.

Nora was almost drifting off on her father's shoulder when the sudden cry split the air.

"Fire!" somebody screamed, their voice hoarse. "Fire!"

Nora's head snapped up. "What?"

"Don't panic," said Papa, but it was too late. Screams echoed through the dark space.

"Fire! Fire!" people shrieked. "Fire!"

The air filled with the thunder of feet. A tide of people spilled down the gallery stairs, pushing and shoving.

"Easy!" Papa called. "Easy now!"

Somebody shoved past them, almost knocking Papa onto the seats. Nora cried out and clung to him.

"Slowly, everyone!" Papa shouted.

Nobody took heed of him. Nora looked around frantically for smoke and flames, but she saw only panicking people running and shoving their way to the exits.

"John!" Mama screamed.

"Hold tight, Catherine!" Papa clutched Nora close.

There was a deafening crack. The railing of the stairs

shattered in a spray of pale wood splinters, and people leaped from the stairs, heedless of those below.

"John!" Mama wailed.

"Take Nora. Quickly! I'll make way!" Papa thrust Nora into her mother's arms.

Mama clutched her tight, and Nora clung to sweaty fistfuls of her dress as Papa held out his arms, fending off the people who now scrambled over the seats and leaped from one aisle to the other like rats climbing over one another to escape a terrier.

Someone thumped into Papa, and he stumbled, almost falling.

"Papa!" Nora cried.

"No!" Mama yelled.

The big man came out of nowhere. Nora caught only a brief glimpse of a round, sweaty face before he barrelled headlong into them, and Mama fell.

Nora's head struck the ground with a thump that echoed through her entire body. She heard Papa calling her name and somehow rose to her hands and knees. When she looked around, she saw only feet and legs everywhere. There was no sign of her mother.

"Mama! Papa!" she shrieked.

A hobnailed boot descended on her splayed fingers with a horrible crunch. Nora shrieked in agony. The pain drove her to her feet despite the crush around her. She jumped away from the trampling feet, and a knee slammed into her back, throwing her forward. Her outstretched hands found a dress and clung to it, but its owner pushed her away and rushed on.

"Mama!" Nora sobbed, even though part of her knew that Catherine had gone down in the chaos. "Papaaaaa!"

The inexorable tide of humanity pressed her forward.

She staggered, looking around wildly, but the world was full of strangers who cared nothing for the tiny creature in their midst. Their panic was as thick as smoke in the air. It was choking.

"Mamaaaaaa! Papaaaaaa!" Nora's screams burned her throat.

Then, suddenly, an ease in the crowd. Nora staggered into a few yards of open space. She saw the outline of the door, the streetlamps glowing golden through it.

There were people lying on the ground around her. None of them moved. One had blood coming out of his mouth and ears and eyes. Everything in her shuddered at the sight, but the golden door beckoned. Her instincts told her to move toward it, and she did.

The sound was like dull thunder. Another railing snapped, showering the air with wood splinters. Nora jerked her head up as the railing fell and a tide of young men poured over it, screaming and shoving, stampeding for the exit.

None of them looked twice at the tiny girl standing in their path.

"Nora!"

Nora spun. "Papa!"

He reached her moments before the young men did. His strong arms surrounded her, pressing her face into the wonderful familiar scent of his chest. She tangled her hands in his chest and clung to him. He bounced as though he was running, and then the crush hit him, and he went down.

The trampling went on for a long time. Papa grunted and gasped at every blow that shook his body. Nora clung to him with all her might, sobbing, listening to the steady thudding of his heart against hers.

That heartbeat raced faster and faster. The grunts stopped. The trampling did not.

Then, suddenly, the heartbeat was no more.

THE TIME that passed could have been a few minutes or a hundred years for all Nora knew. She might have fainted. The next thing she knew, it was bitterly cold, and there were no sounds.

And Papa's arms were no longer tight around her.

She rolled back. Papa didn't move. His eyes were closed, and his face was so bruised and swollen that she hardly recognized the man lying there.

In that moment, like a thunderclap, Nora understood that her father was dead. She had seen dead rats and dogs on the street before, and she was there the day that the rag-and-bone man's donkey dropped dead in its shafts. She remembered how still the poor little animal lay, how its tongue protruded between its teeth, swollen and purple.

Papa looked just like the dead donkey.

The realization was like lead in her veins. She felt almost too heavy to stand. She wanted to scream, to run, to explode, but it was as though her body no longer belonged to her. Everything felt muffled and far away.

Somehow her legs were walking out of the theatre. There wasn't any smoke or fire. Only the bodies. They lay here and there, some of them in pools of dark fluid that smelled like metal.

The golden doorway was still wide open. Nora staggered through it.

Outside, there were crowds of people. Lots of them were

shouting. Bells rang and whistles blew, but it all felt a long way away. No one looked at Nora or spoke to her.

It all felt like a dream.

Nora wanted to go home. She wanted her mother. She called out to her once or twice, then turned and looked back at the motionless bodies lying in the theatre, and she knew that Mama was one of them.

She could not bear to go back and look, to see her shining, angelic mother bruised and bloated like poor, poor Papa.

She hardly knew what to do except to get away from the horrible sight and the appalling smell and the shouting. So Nora wandered down the street, alone, and into the cold night.

The cold only worsened.

Nora had never been awake all night before. She hadn't realized how inexorably long a night could be. This one seemed to stretch on and on, and no matter how far she wandered, the dawn wouldn't come.

Instead, snow came. It started to fall in fat flakes from the pitch-dark sky, sparkling when it tumbled through the golden beams of lampposts, but ice cold and damp when it met Nora's coat.

She walked. At times, she thought she recognized the streets in which she found herself, but every turn seemed like a trick. It wasn't long before she was hopelessly lost in the careless madness of Devil's Acre.

Dogs barked at her sometimes. She ran from them, and also from rats, and from men with hollow eyes glowing out at her from dark alleys. But as the night wore on, her limbs grew too tired to run any farther, so she walked.

And when her little legs could not walk another step, Nora dragged herself to the lee of a lamppost on the edge of a ramshackle market square and sagged down beside it.

It was still snowing. The flakes piled up on her lap and around her legs. They melted on her cold hands, which only made them colder. She tucked her hands into her coat and watched the snow grow deeper around her as the night wore on and on.

The cold hurt at first, but soon it made everything simply numb. Nora began to feel utterly tired, more tired than she had ever been, more tired than she knew it was possible to be.

All she wanted was to close her eyes and rest. Her fingers had gone blue, but at least they had stopped hurting.

She was about to close her eyes when she heard it: a cheery whistle, in a familiar tune, bright and piercing in the dank air. The tune brought Nora back instantly to the window with Mama a few nights ago, listening to the carollers. It came upon a midnight clear...

She raised her head and gazed in the direction of the whistle, and saw a scruffy man strolling down the street, whistling. He was bundled up in coats and scarves and a big woolly hat with a fluffy pom-pom on top. Everything was rather tattered, but his whistle was so cheerful that it hardly seemed to matter.

He carried a long stick in his hand with a hook on the end, swinging it cheerfully as he walked. Nora watched as he paused by a lamppost a few yards away, lifted the pole high up, and used the hook to turn a valve near the top. The lamp went out.

She blinked. Somehow, the night had passed. It was morning; the day was grey and cold, but it had come at last.

Yet she still had no strength to do anything about it.

The lamplighter kept coming, still whistling. Nora gazed at him mutely. He stopped only a foot away from her and raised the hook to the lamp. He had been smoking something, and his tobacco smelled rather strong, making her sneeze.

"Cor blimey!" The lamplighter leaped back. "What on Earth! Where did you come from, you wee mite?"

Nora didn't have the strength to say anything. She merely stared at him.

"Land's sakes!" The lamplighter tossed his stick aside and knelt next to her. His gloved hands brushed the snow away that half-buried her, and he cupped her face in them, the fabric rough on her skin. "Say something, little one."

"Hello," Nora croaked.

"You're alive. You poor little scrap! Look at your blue hands." The lamplighter plucked off his coat and wrapped it around her. It was gloriously warm, like stepping into an oven, and he tucked it snugly around her arms and legs. "Where are your parents?"

Nora knew she should be sad, yet somehow she couldn't seem to cry. "Dead," she told him.

The lamplighter's face fell. "Where do you live?"

Without Mama and Papa, there was nowhere to live. Nora shrugged, this time, her little face crinkling up .

"Poor lamb. Poor lamb!" The lamplighter wrapped her in a snug bundle in his coat and scooped her into his arms. "Look at you, blue with cold. It's a wonder you're still alive. A Christmas miracle, I'd reckon."

Many things had happened to Nora that Christmas. She could hardly think of any of them as a miracle.

"Now what are we going to do with you?" The lamplighter tucked his coat more tightly around her face.

Nora didn't care. The coat was wonderfully warm, and she wanted to sleep, so she closed her eyes.

"No, no, no! Don't you go to sleep, little one." The lamplighter gave her a little shake. "That's how you freeze to death. Stay awake, now. I'm taking you somewhere safe."

He kept talking to her as he walked quickly through the streets, and Nora listened to his voice as she lay in his arms. He had such a nice voice, and a nice face, too, even if his white beard was patchy and his teeth were yellow. There was kindness in him.

"Wish I could take you home with me, poor lamb, but my sweet Marjorie is sick as it is and we've barely got a crust of bread to share between us." The lamplighter sighed. "But you'll be all right here. I know you will."

Nora raised her weary head. They were going up a flight of steps toward a very big, very dark building with almost no windows. Its walls went straight up and down, like a giant box.

The old man pounded on the door. "Oh, do hurry!" he called. "Wake up, wake up!"

He pounded on it several more times before it finally opened to reveal an elderly woman in a nightcap, her eyes still puffy with sleep.

"What's the meaning of all this, then?" she barked. "It's the third day of Christmas. Some of us are resting."

"Aye, aye, I'm sorry, but I found this wee one in the cold. She's half frozen, she is."

The old woman looked down at Nora, her mouth puckered in distaste as though she'd tasted a sour lime.

"Where are her parents?"

"She don't have none. They're dead."

The woman sighed. "Very well. Give her to me."

She held out her arms, but the lamplighter clung to Nora for a moment, his kind face shining down at her.

"You'll be all right, little one," he said. "They'll take good care of you here in the workhouse."

The woman took her. Nora closed her eyes, weakness overcoming her. Her last thought before she drifted away was that the old lamplighter sounded like he was trying to convince himself as much as her.

PART I

CHAPTER 1

1865
Seven Years Later

There used to be a time when moving from the sleeping pallet to the door had been like running a gauntlet. Limbs were always outstretched to trip one, and hands ready to pinch or pull hair. But now, Nora marched across the dormitory with her head held high, the ugly grey-and-white stripes of the workhouse skirt swirling around her knees as she strode to the door.

On either side of her, narrow beds squeaked, each holding two or three little girls in the same ugly dresses as hers. There were pallets, too, with little louse-ridden children huddled on them. They all knew better than to rush to the door at the breakfast bell: reaching the hallway, and thus the dining hall, first in line was the privilege of the oldest girls in the group.

At thirteen, Nora had finally become one of those girls.

"I hope it's bread-and-butter today," said the girl on her left. Betsy was her own age, with a pug nose and black hair in two stubby braids.

"Anything but gruel," Gwendolyn agreed from Nora's left. "I'm so tired of gruel."

Nora laughed. "Do you remember when we didn't care at all what breakfast was? The only thing that worried us was getting to eat it in peace without the bigger girls taking it."

"Now we are the bigger girls." Betsy grinned.

Nora didn't quite like the sharp, wolfish edge to Betsy's grin, but she didn't say anything. It wasn't always easy to get on Betsy's good side, and Nora tried her best to stay there. Betsy could be cruel and frightening, but she was powerful.

And in the workhouse, power was everything.

They were the first to step into the dining hall. The long, cold, shadowy room had only a single fireplace at one end, which did little to heat the frigid air. Their breath still steamed despite the leaping flames. Four rows of tables stood bolted to the floor down the middle of the space, and on one side, there stood a disinterested-looking woman by a cauldron of gruel, judging by the smell.

"More gruel," said Gwendolyn with a sigh, reaching for a wooden bowl.

Nora did the same.

"Oh, look." Gwendolyn slowed and pointed to the corner of the room. "They're putting up a tree!"

Nora didn't want to look, but she couldn't help it. She turned, bowl in hand, and beheld the tall, unadorned pine propped up against the corner.

There were no ribbons or tinsel yet. The paper ornaments it would eventually gain, Nora knew, would be tatty and colourless. Yet the sight of it transported her instantly back to seven years ago, as a tiny child, gazing up at the Christmas tree on the corner of the stage as

Harlequin leaped and danced and Cinderella mimed her joy at the glass slipper sliding so effortlessly onto her foot, all mere minutes before the entire world fell to pieces...

Nora jerked her gaze away and held out her bowl to the woman by the cauldron, who ladled a careful portion of the tasteless grey sludge into it.

"Will they decorate it?" Gwendolyn asked. "This is my first Christmas in here. I didn't know they cared about Christmas at all."

"They will, but let's not talk about it," said Betsy.

Gwendolyn prattled on, ignoring her. "Oh, do you suppose Christmas lunch will be any different? I heard from someone that they give you plums sometimes, or oranges. Maybe even..."

"Gwendolyn, for goodness' sake, shut up!" Betsy snapped.

Nora trudged across to the nearest table and sagged onto it. Hunger drove her to take a bite of the gritty gruel even though she felt sick to her stomach.

"What is it?" Gwendolyn asked. "Nora, you've gone so pale. What's the matter?"

Nora stabbed her spoon into her bowl. "I hate Christmas."

"But why?"

Nora's head snapped up. She glared at Gwendolyn. "Because my parents died on Boxing Day, you stupid girl."

Gwendolyn ducked her head. "Sorry, Nora."

Nora wolfed down the lukewarm gruel, trying not to think about it, but it all came rushing back with such intensity. She so clearly remembered the light and warmth and music of the show, and then the devastating cry, the panic, the cold. Seeing Mama go down under those heedless, crushing, trampling feet. Papa's tongue, puffy and bloodied against his lips.

"My parents died of the cholera," said Gwendolyn softly. "Two days apart. I know how it feels."

Nora glared at the girl. "Mine were trampled at a Christmas pantomime. People panicked and crushed them. They didn't care that they were crashing into living people. They just killed them."

Gwendolyn and Betsy both said nothing.

Nora cast a last savage glance at the pine tree leaning against the corner.

"So if I don't believe in the Christmas spirit," she spat, "that's why."

It was the Devil's Acre Workhouse belief that fresh air was good for inmates, even though the running joke among the girls was that the air outside in the exercise courtyard was far more foul than the air inside could ever be. A steady stench rose from the miserable slum huddled around the workhouse, sometimes harsh and chemical, sometimes nauseatingly organic.

With only one outside yard, the inmates had rotating hours. Nora's group, the girls between seven and fourteen were the unlucky souls who had their exercise hour right before dusk.

The cold was always bitter, though the matron maintained it was character-building and forced the children to move around. After hours of mind-numbingly dull lessons, and subsisting on the colourless and meagre meals the workhouse supplied, moving around was the last thing that any of the girls really wanted to do.

Nora remembered skipping in circles simply to keep her toes and fingers warm and pink. She could never forget the terrible colour her fingers had been the day that the old lamplighter had saved her. Since then, she had seen other girls' fingers go that colour, when they were very, very sick, or that one winter when the matron wouldn't listen when everyone told her that the dormitory had a draft.

None of those girls had survived.

Now, though, being the oldest, Nora had the best spot in the yard: a corner between a pillar of the palisade fence and the wall. It kept her out of the wind and mostly out of the matron's eye, and it even offered a little view down the street.

She couldn't see much from this spot, but her hands stayed pink if she tucked them inside her coat, even though the lowering grey sky threatened snow. Besides, the strip of view, a few shops, the church across the street, a stretch of cobbled road, and a few lampposts, was as much variety as Nora ever got. Watching wagons or pedestrians go by was one of the few pleasures in her austere workhouse life.

The days were still growing ever shorter as December loomed. Though the bell had not yet struck half past three, already the long shadows had blended into growing dusk.

Exhaustion tugged at the corners of Nora's eyes. She found them closing.

Christmas… the pantomime… the panic. Wandering in the cold. The soft kiss of snowflakes on her hair.

The flare of golden light jerked her from the nightmare. For a confusing instant, she thought she was back under that lamppost beneath a blanket of snow. It took her a moment to realize that she was in the workhouse exercise yard, that she'd only nodded off for a second, but the golden light was the same: it came from the lamppost down the street.

She shook herself as the scruffy figure of a lamplighter came nearer. Dream and reality blended for an eerie instant before she realized that this lamplighter was far shorter and younger than the old man who'd saved her from the cold that frigid morning. He, too, wore a thick coat and scarf and woolly gloves, and she could almost swear that the knitted hat with the pom-pom on it was the same as the old lamplighter's. But that was where the similarity ended. This lad had a thatch of red hair poking out from beneath his hat and a sprinkling of freckles over his youthful nose. He could hardly have been any older than she was.

He hummed to himself as he strolled to the next lamp, turned the valve, and cautiously lit it with a wick attached to his pole. She thought it had to be a difficult job, lighting lamps; after all, the wind must be ready to pounce on the little flame and put it out at any moment. But the boy made it look easy. He closed the lamp's glass with a little click and strolled on to the lamppost nearest her.

She didn't realize that she was staring until the boy turned to go past her and their eyes met. His were startlingly green. Not bright, but deep, like pine needles.

"Oh!" The boy grinned, displaying a merry collection of crooked teeth. "Hello, there!"

Nora glanced around, confused. No one ever spoke to the workhouse inmates. In fact, sometimes she had to be careful with sitting here against the fence; passersby would spit at her sometimes.

"Ain't it a little cold for you to be out?" the boy asked.

She realized he was talking to her. "I don't know. The matron thinks the fresh air is good for us."

"I s'pose." The lad seemed to be in no great hurry. He leaned on his pole and tugged down the sleeves of his coat to meet his gloves. "It doesn't look like much fun, living in that huge old place."

"No. It isn't."

"I was born in one, you know."

"A workhouse?"

"Aye. But I didn't stay there long. I hardly remember it. My mama left when I was a little scrap."

Looking away, Nora suddenly didn't want to talk to him. "My mama died when I was a little scrap."

The boy didn't seem bothered. "So did mine. I'm sorry."

She glanced at him.

He seemed to take it as an invitation to keep talking. "My grandpapa raised me. He was a lamplighter too, you know. Worked this same beat. I took it over when he died last year, God rest his dear soul."

"A lamplighter?" said Nora.

"Aye."

She thought of the sweet old man who'd saved her and said nothing.

"What's your name?" the boy asked.

"Why are you talking to me?" Nora demanded.

"Why shouldn't I? You looked cold and lonely, like you could use a little chat. Grandpapa always said that saying a kind word didn't cost nothing."

The words spilled out of Nora before she could stop them. "Did your grandpapa ever tell you about a little girl he found in the cold and brought to the workhouse?"

The boy's eyes widened. "Aye, he did! The morning after Boxing Day, 1858. He always talked about it so fondly. He always wondered what happened to that little girl."

Nora shrugged. "Well, now you know."

"Oh! You're her?"

"Your grandpa saved my life." Nora sighed. "It's Nora. Nora Ellis."

The boy touched his forelock. "Bobby Tibbett at your service, miss."

His gentlemanly manner made her giggle despite herself, the type of laugh she hadn't given in a long, long time.

The sunny afternoon was unseasonable, and Nora knew the warmth would not last long. It had not yet snowed, and though the world was icy and covered in frost every morning, by afternoon much of that ice had melted.

It was nearly pleasant in the exercise yard as Nora, Betsy, and Gwendolyn headed outside. Bright colour caught Nora's eye on the church across the street. It had hung its Christmas decorations: a wreath decked out in bright holly and colourful ribbons on the front door and candles in all the windows.

She hastily looked away, stomach churning. It was getting harder and harder to ignore the advent of Christmas. Quickly, she pushed the unhappy memories away and reminded herself that her favourite time of day was fast approaching.

Stepping away from her friends, Nora headed toward the corner.

"Where are you going?" Betsy asked.

"To sit over there," Nora said.

"But why?" said Gwendolyn. "It's a nice day, for once. Don't you want to play a skipping game with us in the sun? There's no reason to hide over there, out of the wind."

"I'm too tired for that."

"Too tired!" Betsy chuckled. "I know there's more to it than that."

Nora felt her cheeks grow warm.

"It's that boy, isn't it?" said Betsy. "The one you've been talking to every day for more than a week now."

"I don't know what you're talking about, I'm sure." Nora brushed her hair behind her ear.

"I've seen him, too. The lamplighter," said Gwendolyn. "He wears that silly hat with the pom-pom on top."

"We've both seen you talking to him," Betsy added.

Nora hugged herself. "What's it to you if I talk to him? He's sweet."

"The matron would have your guts for garters if she saw," said Betsy.

"That's why I make sure she doesn't see."

"Leave him alone for today, Nora," Gwendolyn urged. "Come and play with us."

"Come and speak to him yourself if it troubles you that much. You'll like him, Gwen. He's always funny and kind."

"No, thanks." Gwendolyn shivered. "I won't take the risk of getting in trouble with Matron!"

Nora left them to go off to the sunniest part of the courtyard, a prickle of nervousness in her belly. She knew that her friends were right to fear the matron's wrath if she ever found out. Talking to a boy on the street would be considered an appalling offense.

But the matron had never spotted Nora in her sheltered corner before, and of course, her friends would never tell her. Betsy and Gwendolyn betraying her was simply unthinkable.

She was nearly late. Bobby came down the street right as Nora tucked herself into her corner. He wasn't whistling today, and his steps had a slower pace to them, almost a shuffle. Even his face seemed pale and drawn.

She waved to him. His face brightened as though he'd been looking for her.

"Hello!" he called softly as he neared her.

"No whistling today?" Nora smiled. "Normally you're always whistling or humming a Christmas carol as you go."

"You like carols, then?"

"No." Nora looked away quickly. "But your whistling sounds nice."

"I'm afraid I don't have the strength today." Bobby sat on the lip of the wall.

"Why? Whatever is the matter?"

"Well, one of the other lamplighters is ill, and our overseer has given us all an extra few blocks of lamps and hardly any extra time to do it in. They don't like it when we do the lamps too early, you see. Uses too much gas, they say. But I have to walk all the way out to the Strand to start this route, then all the way back here to get these lamps lit before dark, then back down to Westminster to do a few streets there. The trouble is all the fancy gas Christmas lights they've put up on the well-to-do streets. They take ages to light. Then people complain when I'm late to light the streetlamps. Why, I hardly know how I can keep up with it!"

"Perhaps the other lamplighter will be well again soon."

"We all hope so, but the way the overseer shouted at us today, I fear that one of us will be dismissed when he's well again." Bobby's lips turned down. "If I'm always the slowest one, perhaps that one will be me."

Nora's heart gave an unexpected little jolt. She hadn't realized how much she had begun to look forward to

Bobby's visits every day. Would he still come by if he didn't have lamps to light on this street?

He hung his head, and a pang of guilt ran through Nora. All she was thinking of was herself.

She reached through the palisades and let her fingertips touch his sleeve. "I'm sorry, Bobby. That must be frightening."

"Aye, a little, but I shouldn't burden you with such things." Bobby straightened, his smile bouncing back. "Have they started any decorating in the workhouse?"

"They have, but I'd rather not talk about it."

"Of course." Bobby's smile slipped. "It must be a hard time for you, seeing what happened to you on one Christmas Day."

"I'll never forget that day," Nora whispered. "The tree on the stage, the lights..." She straightened. "That's it. The lights!"

"What?"

"I know how you can make your route work better." Nora grinned.

"What are you talking about?"

"You said that all the fancy Christmas lights on the Strand slow you down. Well, those don't need to be lit before the sun goes down, do they? They're for show, not for safety."

Bobby frowned. "I suppose."

"If you start your route with all the streetlamps, you can make one circuit and finish them quickly, before dark. Nobody will complain. Then you can go back and do the Christmas lights when it's properly dark, and everyone will love that, seeing them go all bright against a dark sky."

Bobby tugged at his pom-pom hat, a slow smile spreading over his features. "Why, Nora, aren't you clever? I hadn't thought of that. I dare say that would work ever so well. I'll try it. My overseer will be pleased."

"You might get compliments instead of complaints."

"That's always good for business, that is. I've never met someone so clever." Bobby looked at her with sparkling admiration in his eyes.

Nora felt a flush of warm satisfaction. "My mama always used to say that it takes more than goodness to survive in London, you know. It takes a good deal of cleverness, too."

"Well, you have it in spades," said Bobby.

He was still looking at her with that awe in his eyes, as though she had done something magnificent. No one had looked at Nora like that in a long time. It seemed to wake something in her heart, something that had been asleep for far too long.

CHAPTER 2

Someone had decorated the Christmas tree. It stood proudly in the corner of the dining hall now, all hung with cheap paper ribbons, a yellow cardboard angel dangling from the top. Nora purposely sat with her back to it, but she could almost feel it mocking her despite this angle. Every time she turned her head, she caught a little glimpse of it, and each one threatened to drag her back to that night in the theatre, to the tree on the stage, and to the horrors that followed.

She turned her attention back to her supper instead. It was stew, of a sort, with the greyish and gristly lumps of meat drifting in a listless, watery concoction of slightly-too-soft vegetables. As she ate, she was aware of hungry little eyes on her.

She looked down the table at the spot where a smaller girl sat, her bowl licked spotless, spoon in hand, staring hungrily at Nora's meal. Nora merely narrowed her eyes and the frightened little girl scampered off to another table.

"I hear we're having soup tomorrow," said Betsy. "I hope they put a little meat in it this time."

"You know they won't," Gwendolyn scoffed. "You know it'll be nothing but turnips and beets, as usual."

"I hear that when you turn fourteen and go to the women's dormitories, you help with making the food. Maybe then we could find a little more."

Nora was aware that by find, Betsy meant steal, but she didn't protest. Why would she ever stand against getting a little more to eat?

The dining hall door opened with a long moan.

"Oh! What's this?" Betsy looked around.

Nora raised her head as a girl stumbled into the room as though she'd been pushed. She was tall, tall enough to be Nora's age, and she had the pink-scrubbed look of a new intake. They had shaved off her hair completely, leaving only a dusting that suggested blonde. Her frowsy dress was still new and stiff, and her skin was flushed with cleanliness.

The girl's eyes, however, caught Nora's attention at once. They were pitch black, and they glittered around the room with a cold and calculating look in them.

The matron shooed her forward. The girl strode to the table with bad grass and seized a bowl. With a sigh of annoyance, the woman at the cauldron scraped the last bits of stew up and dumped them in the bowl.

"A new girl," said Betsy.

Gwendolyn shuddered. "She looks mean."

Nora didn't care how she looked. She took another bite of her cooling stew.

The table and bench shuddered as the girl flung herself down in the spot recently vacated by the hungry little one. Nora ignored her. New intakes were beneath her notice.

Gwendolyn, however, made a bid for friendliness. "What's your name, then?"

"Felicity Trapp," the girl barked, "and I suggest you shut yours, or I'll shut it for you."

Gwendolyn winced.

The girl ate with the huge, ravenous gulps of someone familiar with starving. Nora had not yet finished her meal when Felicity's bowl was spotless.

She was spooning up another mouthful of the tasteless, chewy meat when a sudden pain stung her arm. Nora gasped and opened her mouth, and the pain intensified sharply. Felicity had seized the soft skin of Nora's forearm in hard, calloused fingers. Her knuckles were bruised and broken; there were not only fresh scabs on them, but half-healed ones as well.

"If you scream," she hissed, "I'll tear your arm right open."

Nora stared at her, trembling. The strength of Felicity's grip made the words fully believable.

"Give me that." Felicity gestured at the few bites of stew remaining in her bowl.

Nora gripped it tighter.

Felicity's fingers hardened, and the pinched skin turned from red to ashy white.

"All right!" Nora pushed the bowl across. "Let me go!"

"Quiet!" Felicity commanded, but she released Nora's arm.

Nora snatched her hand to her chest. It throbbed ferociously, and a red welt was already forming where the other girl had pinched her.

Felicity smirked as she gulped down the last of Nora's stew. Gwendolyn and Betsy merely stared at her in horror.

"You lot had better understand a few things." Felicity pushed the empty bowl aside. "I ain't no soft workhouse whelp like the lot of you. I didn't grow up with my three meals given to me on a platter every day. I had to scrounge for them, I did. Steal for them. Fight for them. Them coppers caught my gang and sent me here, but you better know something."

Nobody said anything.

"I was in charge of them streets. I was queen of Devil's Acre." Felicity's grin held no mirth. "And now I'm the queen here, too."

Nora cupped her pinched arm. Gwendolyn tentatively put her hand on Nora's shoulder, but a swift glare from Felicity made her drop her hand very quietly into her lap.

Everything in the life of every girl in their age group changed overnight, although for Nora, one thing stayed the same as the week dragged by, each day dragging her closer to the dreaded prospect of Christmas Day. It was Bobby.

Felicity had no interest in the quiet corner into which Nora tucked herself every evening during their exercise hour. The big girl preferred to spend that time terrorizing the smaller children and asserting her dominance. She hardly noticed Nora squeezed into her corner out of the wind, and that afforded her an hour's welcome peace each day.

And every day, as dusk fell, Bobby came by to light the lamps. Somehow, he always seemed to have time to stop and exchange a few words with Nora.

No snow had fallen yet the week before Christmas. Instead, the slate-grey skies offered the threat of sleet. Nora hoped it would hold off until their exercise hour was over; there was no chance that the matron would let them stay out if it was too wet outside. She tucked her measly coat tighter around her shoulders and wedged herself a little deeper into her corner, listening to a little girl scream as Felicity pulled her pigtails.

Bobby's whistle cut through the cacophony of Nora's life. She found herself smiling, an expression so unfamiliar her face almost felt too stiff for it, as he kindled the lamps along the street. There was something strangely tender in the way he handled the wick on its long pole, fussing over the little yellow flame so that it remained strong enough to brave the wind, leaving a trail of golden light in his wake.

"Evenin', Nora!" he called as he closed the shutter on the nearest lamp.

"Hello, Bobby." Nora maintained the smile as long as she could.

Bobby wandered over, the pole over his shoulder, his free hand in his pocket. "My, what's the matter?"

Nora shrugged.

"You're awful pale. Are you ill?" he asked.

"No. Not ill."

"Something's wrong, though." Bobby perched on the low wall supporting the palisade fence, resting his feet. "Your face is all pinched. You look like you haven't slept well."

"Sleep!" Nora shook her head. "How can I? I'm so hungry it feels as though my stomach is eating me alive at nights."

"Nora! Don't they feed you?"

"They do. But she takes it all." Nora directed an acid look across the yard at Felicity.

"Oh. The new girl. You told me about her." Bobby scowled. "She sounds like an awful bully."

"Bully! She's a monster! We all eat as fast as we can, but it's never fast enough. She takes everything you have left."

Nora's voice cracked. "There...there were bullies before, but never, never like this."

"Oh, Nora. I'm awfully sorry. That sounds terrible."

"Look." Nora pulled up the sleeve of her dress and showed Bobby the blue and red welts along the insides of her forearms. "Look what she does."

Bobby pawed through his pockets. "Here. Have this. I was saving it for supper, but I'll get something else." He pulled out a greasy little bundle wrapped in newspaper and handed it to her.

Nora unwrapped it and stared at a piece of dried fish a few inches long. She looked from the fish to Bobby, mute and astonished.

"Go on. Quickly. Before she sees it," said Bobby.

"But... why would you give me this?" Nora asked slowly.

Bobby stared at her as though the answer should be obvious. "Because you're hungry."

"You're hungry, too."

"Aye, but like I said, I'll get something else. Quick, Nora, eat it before somebody sees."

The fish was salty and chewy, but after losing half of her lunch to Felicity, it tasted like sweet nectar to Nora.

"Why don't the matrons stop her?" Bobby asked.

"The matrons! They hardly care what we do, and she's clever. She pinches you where nobody can see and makes you give her your food so that there's no fighting. If you fight back, she finds you at night and pulls out your hair or tears up your blankets. Then the matrons are angry at you for destroying things."

Bobby shook his head.

"I don't know what to do." Nora broke off half of the fish and carefully re-wrapped it in the newspaper. Her friends were as hungry as she was. "I'm so afraid of her, Bobby."

"Then come with me," said Bobby suddenly.

Nora gaped at him. "What on earth do you mean?"

"There's a spot in the corner of the yard, over there." Bobby pointed. "The bricks are a little loose, and there's a rusty gap in the palisades. We could easily take out a brick or two and there'll be enough room for you to squeeze out of the yard."

Nora gasped. "You mean...leave the workhouse?"

"Exactly."

Nora hugged herself, frightened. She'd only ever seen children leave the workhouse when they died or when someone purchased them as an apprentice. That happened with the younger girls, the ones who were fresh for the work. At thirteen, Nora knew she had little chance of being chosen.

"But where would I go?" she whispered.

"There are ways of staying alive on the streets. The Gas Light and Coke Company gives me a tenement. There's room in the building's basement. If you were quiet, you could hide there a while before you find a job."

"A job!"

"You can read and write, can't you?"

Nora shrugged. "A little." The lessons were poor in the workhouse, but she had been attending them for six years.

"Then you'll find work somewhere. Or you could sing on the street corner or sweep crossings. It'll be hard, but there won't be any Felicity."

Nora gazed across the yard at the huge girl, who stood over a sobbing smaller child. The other children formed a silent, horrified ring around her. The fear shining in all their faces echoed in Nora's heart.

Gwendolyn and Betsy stood side-by-side, clinging to one another's hands. Betsy had been her friend for years, and Gwendolyn had stuck close to her since she arrived. How could she leave them?

"I don't know," she said softly. "I don't know if I can."

"It's up to you," said Bobby. "All I'm saying is that if you need to get out, I'll help you."

Nora tucked the remnants of the fish away in her dress. "Thank you, Bobby."

He smiled and went on his way, his cheery whistle fading into the distance.

CHAPTER 3

Smoke. Shouting.

Mama's screaming face as she crumpled beneath the crushing, charging feet.

Papa's crushed cheekbones, his eyes swollen shut.

Then Nora was falling.

She struck the dormitory floor with real force, ripping her from the nightmare with a little shriek. Her blanket landed on a pile on top of her, and there was a clatter as several other small objects rained down beside her.

A comb, two hard-boiled sweets from a donation to the workhouse earlier that week, and the little newspaper-wrapped bundle of fish she was saving for her friends.

Groggy, her shoulder aching from contact with the floor, Nora lunged for the fish. Felicity's bare foot came down on her hand with enough force to make her scream.

"Let's see!" Felicity cackled. "What have we here?"

It was so dark. Only a scrap of light from the street outside entered through the chink in the curtains, but it was enough for Nora to see the horrible sneer on Felicity's face as she bent down and seized the fish.

"No," Nora whimpered.

Felicity's heel ground harder on her fingers. "Be quiet!"

Nora bit down the squeal of pain as Felicity scooped up the two sweets she'd hidden in her mattress and popped them into her mouth. She chewed them loudly with her mouth open as she peeled back the newspaper.

"What's this you were hiding, eh?" Felicity hissed. "I knew you had something with you, the way you kept touching your dress, right where it's easiest to hide something in your sleeve. Ha! Don't you know that everything in this workhouse belongs to me now?" She leaned close, close enough that Nora saw the crunched bits of sugar between her teeth. "I am your queen."

The whisper came on foul breath. Nora gagged, partly from the smell, partly from pain and terror. Where were Betsy and Gwendolyn? Betsy shared her bed.

"What have you done to my friends?" she whimpered.

Felicity removed her foot from Nora's hand and seized her by the hair. Nora squealed as her head was wrenched back. She heard the pops in her scalp as a few hairs came out.

"You don't have friends," Felicity snarled in her ear. "Not anymore."

She released Nora's hair so quickly that she had to brace her hands on the floor to keep from hitting her nose on it.

"Open that curtain," Felicity barked.

A familiar voice said, "But..."

"Do it!"

The curtain hissed open, and Nora looked up, blinking in the sudden light, at the familiar form of Gwendolyn standing beside it. The girl's eyes were full of tears, and she wouldn't look at Nora.

Disbelief and pain flooded her as though her blood had

become acid. Her head swivelled, and she saw who was standing beside her upturned sleeping pallet.

It was Betsy.

Neither of her two friends, the people for whom she'd been saving that fish, said a word to her. Neither of them apologized. When Felicity turned and stomped away, Betsy and Gwendolyn simply followed.

It was up to Nora to turn her pallet upright and replace the straw mattress. She curled up underneath the blanket, cradling her bruised hand against her chest, and cried. But she did so quietly.

She would not give Betsy and Gwendolyn the satisfaction of knowing how deeply they had broken her heart.

The day dragged. Nora's hand stung so that she struggled to form half-hearted letters on her slate as the teacher shouted against the general undisciplined cacophony of uncaring students during lesson time. She didn't even try to hold onto her breakfast or lunch; as soon as Felicity approached, she abandoned her bowl and went to sit at the back of the dining hall where no one would bother her.

It seemed to take an eternity for the day to pass and for exercise hour to finally come. Nora hurried at once into her corner. She kept her sore hand close to her chest; it had turned blue and purple during the day, and there was a puffy swelling that obscured the small bones at the back of her hand.

The minutes ticked by. The church bell struck the quarter hour, then the half-hour. At last, as dusk settled over London, Nora heard the welcome tune of Bobby's whistle. The sound was like a sip of hot tea on a freezing day. She shivered, suddenly cold and weak, desperate for him to come.

His whistle stopped as soon as he saw her.

"Oh, Nora!" He leaned the pole against the nearest palisade. "What's happened?"

"I need to get out," Nora whispered, her voice cracked from crying. "Please."

"What's happened to your hand?"

"It was Felicity. Please help me, Bobby. She'll hurt me again, I know it, and..." She bit her lip. "And I don't have any friends here anymore. Not one."

Bobby held her gaze for a long moment, then nodded. "All right. Come along the wall. Don't let anyone see you, especially not that Felicity girl. I've loosened two more bricks. I did it early this morning, before anyone could see. Wait a little first. Let me get there; if we walk together, people will notice."

"A little? How long?"

"Until I put out that lamp on the corner. See it? When it goes out, you'll know I'm ready for you."

Nora nodded. "All right."

"All will be well, Nora. I'll get you out of here," said Bobby.

He whisked off, and Nora waited, trembling, in her corner as a few interminable seconds passed. From her vantage point, she could not see the outside of the other end of the yard. It seemed to her that the next few minutes passed like days.

What if those sweet words were a lie, and Bobby didn't help her?

A hot tear traced down her cheek, cooling fast in the cold wind. She huddled deeper into her corner, resting her aching head on the wall. Bobby had always seemed so sweet... yet so had Gwendolyn and Betsy. If they had betrayed her, why wouldn't he? Her final hope flickered, a candle flame in a cruel wind.

She had just begun to think that she was a fool to ever trust Bobby Tibbett and that all this, their supposed friendship, the escape plan, all of it, was nothing but an elaborate game he'd played to make her look like a fool when suddenly the lamp went out. She could not see the lamp itself, but knew at once it was out when the light changed.

Hope and terror clashed in her. Nora slipped from the corner and warily eyed the group of girls. Felicity had tired of terrorizing her unlucky victim; the little girl had gone off to weep in a corner. Instead, Felicity now taunted another girl in a high, singsong voice, mocking her straw-colored hair. Betsy and Gwendolyn followed her wherever she went and added their snickers to her cruel remarks.

She turned away from the infuriating sight and reached the corner Bobby spoke of without being seen. He was crouched beside the palisades, and as he'd said, there were several bricks missing from the top row beneath the iron fence with its cruel, spiked tips. The resultant gap was only a few inches wide.

"Here. Quick!" Bobby whispered. "Do you think you can fit?"

Nora doubted it instantly, but she had no choice. "I'll have to."

"I'll help. Hurry, before anyone sees!"

Nora dropped to her knees and pressed her arms through the gap, then her head. The rough bricks scraped on her chest as she tried to follow with her body. It was broad enough for her shoulders, but the rusty iron palisades pressed into her back, forcing her to squeeze against the bricks with all her weight. Crushing pain filled her chest.

Bobby seized her arms. "Keep going!"

Nora dug her toes into a gap between the paving-stones of the yard and pushed. She felt skin scrape from her back, but made a few inches of progress.

"Only a little more," Bobby urged. "Come on!"

He leaned back, pulling, and Nora felt the strain deep into her armpits and upper back. She grunted, not having the breath to tell him to stop, but it was working. She was moving.

"Oi! Look at that!" Felicity's unmistakable voice ripped across the exercise yard. "Nora's makin' a break for it!"

One of the smaller girls screamed. Bobby pulled harder, but all he achieved was agony in Nora's shoulders.

"Hey! Hey! Somebody, come!" Felicity shrieked. "Matron! Matron!"

"No!" Bobby moaned in dismay.

Nora braced her feet harder and thrust her body forward with all her might, but the palisades only dug all the more sharply into her back.

She would have screamed if she had the breath, but she could take only the briefest sip of air. Bobby's face was inches away from hers. Real tears shone in his eyes, and his cheeks turned purple as he struggled to pull her feet, effort written in the veins standing out on his face and neck.

She knew in that moment that Bobby tried to free her with everything he had, but it was not enough.

A shriek tore across the yard. "Let her go! Go away! Winston, run, run, and catch him!"

Then hands closed like shackles over her ankles and yanked.

Nora's wrists slipped through Bobby's sweaty grasp.

She shot backward and landed hard, face-down, on the paving. Her chin struck the unyielding ground with enough force to fill her mouth with blood.

The matron grasped her arm and plucked her upright despite the blood dribbling from her lips. "Seize him!" she shrieked. "He was trying to take her!"

Bobby froze on the sidewalk, wide-eyed, his expression filled with dismay.

"Bobby, run!" Nora choked out.

The matron shook her so hard that her teeth chattered. "Silence, you wretched girl!"

The workhouse porter was running around the outside of the yard, nearing Bobby.

"Run!" Nora cried.

This time, the matron slapped her hand, hard. Nora yelped, but Bobby listened at last. He turned tail and fled into the streets, running much faster than the porter could hope to catch him.

The matron uttered a foul oath.

"It's all right, ma'am," the porter called. "I know that boy. He's a lamplighter. I'll be having a word with the Gas Light and Coke Company about him. They've got an office not far from here."

"You do that," the matron barked. "I will deal with this."

She spun on her heel, yanking Nora after her, and stormed into the workhouse.

Nora was crying. The salt tears running over her cheeks burned her scuffed face, yet she couldn't stop them.

"Stop that racket at once," the matron commanded. "Have you no shame, girl? We've fed and clothed you all your life, even attempted an education, a fool thing, I say, teaching paupers to read! Whatever next? And yet this is how you repay us! By trying to run off with that boy from the street!"

"I'm sorry," Nora whimpered.

"No. You certainly aren't sorry yet, but I will see to it that you will be."

Nora's tears dried in terror as the matron marched directly past the hallway leading to the girls' dormitory. She left the hall that went to the offices, too, the place where girls usually received their stripes as discipline.

Nora knew instantly where they were going. In her years at the workhouse, she had managed to avoid infractions serious enough for the worst punishment possible, but she had heard the stories about this long, windowless hallway where her footsteps echoed in unrelenting silence.

"No," she gasped. "No, please, please!"

"Silence," the matron barked. "You will accept your just punishment with grace!"

It was out of terror and not obedience that Nora fell silent when the matron pushed open a narrow door and she glimpsed the place that the other inmates spoke of with such dread. The cell was tiny, barely any wider than the door. A stone bench formed something like a bed that took up almost all of the space, with a blanket neatly folded at one end. There was barely enough room to stand beside it; a bucket occupied part of that space.

There were no windows.

Nora wanted to scream, but she didn't have the strength. The matron propelled her inside and slammed the door, sealing her in semidarkness; the walls did not quite reach the ceiling and a few stray chinks of light seeped into the tiny space.

It felt at once as though the walls would collapse and

suffocate her. When she stretched her arms out to the sides, her fingertips touched the walls.

She squeezed herself into a corner of the stone bed, wrapped in the blanket, shaking violently from the cold and terror and the pain in her chest and chin.

Once the matron's footsteps had faded away, there were no sounds. All the other people in this workhouse might as well be on the other side of the world for all the contact Nora had with them.

She was the most alone she had ever been.

CHAPTER 4

Nora could not begin to guess how long she spent in the refractory ward. Time lost all meaning faced with those four walls and that faint half-light. Occasionally, someone came by with meals, if one could call them that; half-rations of cold gruel, dry bread and cheese, or broth so watery she could see through it.

She ate the meals slowly, trying to make them last. At least they gave her something tangible to concentrate on.

The rest of the time, she lay on the stone bed, staring at nothing. There had to be a fire nearby, for the cold was uncomfortable but not intolerable. Yet it added another layer of discomfort to a body filled with pain.

The pain was all she could think of for the first while; she tried to sleep and forget it, yet her back soon ached from the hard surface, and she woke with dried blood crusted on her lip. After that, she sat propped in the corner of the bed and slept only in brief naps. Her hips went numb and her legs tingled from the uncomfortable position.

There was nothing to distract her from thoughts of Christmas and memories of her parents. She wondered if there would be roast chestnuts and oranges for the workhouse paupers as there sometimes were on Christmas Day. The thought only made her feel bitter, almost sick with rage.

It was the rage that changed everything.

As she sat with her anger in the dark, Nora felt the burning heat of injustice. She felt the sting of her friends' betrayal and the hopeless agony of Felicity's cruelty.

When her rage blended with nightmares of her parents, it changed into an awareness that this was not what Mama and Papa, dear souls that they were, would ever have wanted for her. They wanted a better life for Nora. They dreamed of a brighter future.

In the cold and dark, Nora's pain and anger slowly dissolved into something far greater.

It became absolute resolve.

And in that resolve, in the long, silent hours, a plan was born.

They were singing Christmas carols in the church across the street when the matron finally released Nora from the refractory ward.

She heard them faintly as the matron silently led her through the hallways toward the dormitory. It must be evening; someone had served her a bowl of thin broth only a short while earlier. The lights were dim, the curtains drawn, but as they neared the dormitory, Nora heard the singing all the more clearly. It gave her goosebumps, stirring up the dark memories of that terrible Christmas seven years before.

The matron stopped outside the dormitory door. "I

hope you learned your lesson, but if you didn't, I'll certainly conduct you back to the refractory ward the moment you put another foot out of line. Do you understand?"

Nora nodded. "Yes, ma'am."

"Good. That's a far better bearing for a girl of your station to have. You are a pauper. You owe me your very life. No cheek will be tolerated. Is that clear?"

"Yes, ma'am."

The matron opened the dormitory door, and Nora stepped inside.

"Nora!" Gwendolyn gasped.

The girls were preparing for bed, settling under musty blankets on their hard sleeping pallets. Nora's had moved across the room, nearer to Felicity's. Felicity enjoyed a bunk to herself; Gwendolyn and Betsy were now perched on Nora's pallet.

Betsy wouldn't meet her eyes. Gwendolyn looked as though she wanted to come toward her, but a single glance from Felicity froze her in place.

"How was the lock-up?" Felicity leered. "Teach you a lesson, did it?"

Nora ignored the bigger girl.

"Lights out in five minutes," the matron barked, and shut the door.

Nora moved stiffly across the dormitory. Only one space was open; the foot of a sleeping pallet containing a new child, tiny and wide-eyed, her cheeks streaked with tears. She cowered when Nora sat at the end of the pallet.

The talking died down, and in five minutes, the lights went out.

Nora sat in silence, waiting for the last few murmurs to settle into the deep breaths of sleep. Outside, the carollers sang on. In the dark, with the familiar hymn soaking through the workhouse walls, Nora felt so close to the memory of her parents that she could almost reach out to touch it. She thought of sitting by the window with Mama, hearing those angel voices.

Still through the cloven skies they come
with peaceful wings unfurled
And still their heavenly music floats
o'er all the weary world.

The sound gave her the courage she needed.

She edged to the single window in the dormitory and squeezed herself between the curtains and the glass. The window directly overlooked the street. Right across, the church was all lit up and golden, and the streetlights shone in the dark.

There was no fence separating the wall from the street here; the palisades of the exercise yard started at the corner of the dormitory. If she could slip through the window, then nothing stopped her from reaching the street.

The carollers sang on. Wreaths decorated the doors and windows of the church. From this height, through one of the dormer windows, Nora could glimpse the splendid Christmas tree in the corner, all wrapped in bows and tinsel. It had just begun to snow. The flakes sparkled in the streetlights, settling like stars on the dark church roof.

She tried the window. It was not locked, and it slid open easily, bringing a gust of breathtakingly cold air.

It did not surprise her that the window was unlocked. She was two stories above the cobblestones of the street.

Only a fool would jump from this height. A desperate fool, she thought.

The cobblestones seemed to get farther away the longer she stared at them. The cold had not woken anyone yet. She could still retreat, shut the window, and live out her days in this workhouse. Always, always knowing that the refractory word was waiting for her if she did anything wrong. The darkness. The silence.

She gazed at the church, all alight with Christmas, and a sudden surge of courage seized her.

Nora grasped the windowsill and pulled herself onto it with a grunt until she was straddling the sill, one foot in the dormitory, one dangling over the drop. She had to squeeze herself through the open pane.

"Oi!" Felicity barked. "What's all this, then?"

There was scuffling in the dormitory. She was coming for her!

"Matron! Matron!" someone screamed.

There was no more time to hesitate. Nora swung her other leg over the edge and pushed herself over the drop.

The frigid wind caught her skirt and wrapped around her legs. She knew a moment of breathtaking cold and a lurch of fear as she plummeted, and then she hit the ground, feet first. Something wrenched horribly in her ankle and agony speared up her leg.

A scream tore from her. She crumpled to the ground, curled around her ankle, shaking violently. Pain consumed her world. The church, the snow, the cold all faded away compared to it.

Dimly, she heard shouting. Then running feet.

Nora forced herself onto one knee, still clutching her ankle. Tears of pain washed over her cheeks as she stared helplessly at the form of the workhouse night porter crashing through the gate nearby, rushing toward her. He would drag her back inside, and this time her stay in the refractory ward would be even longer.

Warm hands closed around her arm. "Hold onto me!"

"Bobby!"

"Hold on!"

Nora's frantic fingers found his scarf. She wrapped her arms around his neck, and with a grunt of effort, Bobby hoisted her into his arms.

"Hey! You! Stop!" the porter roared.

Bobby bolted. Every step he took jolted Nora's ankle, drawing cries of pain from her, but she clung to him with dear life.

"Stop!" the porter yelled.

Bobby swerved hard toward the church. For a despairing moment, Nora thought he would run directly into the hedge. But at the last second she saw a gap, and he squeezed through, twigs seizing her hair and tearing at her face. She yelped, and Bobby was sprinting across a graveyard as the snow fell faster. The carollers sounded far away now; the lights and candles were a blur.

He dived behind a large gravestone. They fell, pain lancing through Nora, and slithered into a drainage ditch at the bottom of the hedge.

Nora was crying.

"Shhh!" Bobby squeezed himself underneath the hedge and pulled her after him. "Shhh, shhh. They're coming."

Nora clasped both hands over her mouth and forced her sobs to grow quiet. They lay against the freezing ground. Nora's ankle stabbed with fierce pain and the hedge dug into her back, but Bobby's hand was on her shoulder, warm and steady, and it gave her the strength to lie motionless and soundless.

Footsteps came and went. Nora hovered at the edge of fainting.

Then Bobby was tugging at her sleeve. "It's all right. They've gone. Let me help you."

He tugged her gently out of the hedge and onto the

street behind the church. It was narrow and grubby, the edge of Devil's Acre. Tenement buildings with sheer walls and tiny windows lined one side of it.

Nora draped an arm over his shoulders and he helped her to her feet.

"How..." She sucked her teeth at the pain in her ankle. "How did you find me?"

"Providence, I suppose. I was in the church, listening to the carols. They let me sit quietly near the back. But I kept looking at the workhouse, wondering what happened to you... what they did to you. You didn't come to the exercise yard yesterday. I was afraid for you."

"They put me in the lock-up."

"I hoped they wouldn't, but..." Bobby shuddered. "I'm sorry, Nora."

"Did you see me jump?"

"I saw you in the window at first. I came out, and then you jumped, so I ran to you."

"I'm glad you did."

"Are you?" Bobby groaned. "I'm the one who told you to escape, and then you were locked up, and now you're hurt."

Nora said nothing. She realized, with piercing terror, that everything depended on what Bobby did next.

"It'll be all right, though," the lamplighter said quickly. "I didn't lose my job. I feared the workhouse folk would talk to the company I work for, but they never did. I have a tenement. It's in the cellar, but it's all right. It's dry. There's a curtain, too, closing off one side of it. You can come there with me, if you like. You'd be safe there."

Nora met his eyes. They were soft as ever above his freckles, and the look in them stilled something in her.

She had been ready to trust him before. She was more

ready than ever to trust him now. And anything was better than the workhouse.

"Please," she said quietly.

"Come along. We'll get you home."

They limped slowly through the streets together as the snow fell faster and faster until it formed a sparkling blanket over the world, muffling all to silence as the church services ended and the carollers faded away, leaving only cold and stillness on that Christmas Eve.

Nora woke the next morning to a steady, sharp ache in her ankle and to strange silence.

The stillness startled her at first. There had been no such thing in the workhouse dormitory. Even at night, the snores and grunts and sleepy whispers of the several dozen other girls had always been there. But here in Bobby's tenement, a scrap of cellar in the bowels of a large building, there was no sound at all except for the distant rumble of the street above.

Nora sat up. She had slept on a straw mattress on the floor; Bobby had insisted on giving it to her. She twitched the threadbare curtain aside and peered into the rest of the tenement. A few coals smouldered in the pot-bellied stove in the corner. There was a table with two upturned buckets for chairs. Bobby's bed, which he'd made of a pile of newspapers and rags, was in the opposite corner.

An old woman sat hunched over a table in the corner.

"That's Fran," said Bobby. "Hello, Fran!"

The old woman grunted.

"She doesn't talk much," said Bobby, "but we help each other with the rent."

The old woman returned her attention to the bit of sewing before her.

A knot in Nora's belly loosened. At least her honour would be intact; Fran was the perfect chaperone.

The most surprising thing she saw was the wreath. It hung on the cellar door: a modest collection of dried holly leaves, several of them bending at wrong angles, others missing. Nora guessed that he'd scrounged it from a rubbish heap, yet there it was, a little nod to the existence of Christmas.

It reminded her of something her mother would do.

She rose slowly, gingerly. He had bound up her ankle the night before, and despite the swelling that strained against the makeshift bandage, it felt a little better. She tested her weight on it; it ached, but she could walk. It wasn't broken, she guessed.

No bell had woken her that morning. No matron shouted. No other girls pushed.

It was like a different world.

There was a soft knock on the door that startled Nora. She spun, not knowing what to say, then heard, "It's only me!" and the door swung open.

Bobby entered the cellar, brushing snowflakes from his pom-pom hat and scarf. His cheeks were bright red with cold, but his eyes danced.

"Oh, good!" he said. "You're up. How is your ankle?"

Nora perched on one of the buckets, trying not to stare at the brown paper parcel Bobby held in both hands. "It's all right. No worse than yesterday. I can walk on it a little."

"Good. Then I can say to you, 'merry Christmas!'" Bobby beamed. "I've brought you something. Do you think you could climb a few stairs, if I help?"

Nora hesitated. "Why?"

"I want to show you something."

She eyed him. No one had ever said such a thing to her in the workhouse. There was nothing to see there; only the drudgery of moving from one moment to the next, hoping for the next meal, avoiding Felicity.

"It's all right if you don't want to come," he added.

"No... I'll come."

Bobby held out his hand. Nora took it and leaned on his arm, finding it much easier to move than she'd feared. Still, she found herself holding his arm a little more tightly than she really needed. Feeling its strength, its sureness.

He smelled a little like lamp oil. Nora found that she liked it.

They climbed the cellar steps together, but Bobby didn't turn toward the front door. Instead, they mounted the dusty stairs of the tenement together. She paused twice to catch her breath, but the movement seemed to be making her ankle feel a little less stiff instead of worse, and she was almost stepping on it when they reached the third floor.

"Don't worry. Nobody lives up here," said Bobby. "Not right now, in any case. There used to be more people in Devil's Acre. I suppose this floor was abandoned."

Nora could see that. Black streaks of mould marred the walls, and she heard the distinctive scratching of cockroaches hiding in every crevice. It made her skin crawl.

"Don't think about them. Come over here." Bobby led her across the floor to a large window, a board leaning in front of it. He must have come up here earlier; there were two stacks of newspaper serving as seats on either side of a few sticks of firewood merrily burning. "I've gotten it ready for us. It'll get chilly, but we have the fire."

Nora heard distant music. "What are we doing here, Bobby?"

"Celebrating Christmas, of course."

Bobby led her to one of the newspaper stacks. Nora sagged gratefully onto it, relieved to have her weight off her feet. Bobby placed the parcel nearby, then approached the board over the window.

"Ready?" He grinned.

Nora shrugged, not knowing what she was meant to be ready for.

Bobby moved the board aside. "Look!"

Nora gasped despite herself.

The view from this window overlooked a market square below, and at the centre of the square, towering high into the sky, was the biggest Christmas tree she had ever seen. It so thoroughly dwarfed her memory of the pantomime tree that she barely connected the two. A huge gold star decorated the top, and ribbons and tinsel wrapped the rest, sparkling in the sudden sun. There were no clouds, yet the air was so cold that last night's snow had gone unmelted; it lay thickly on the roofs of the businesses surrounding the square and in tall piles where folks had shovelled it away from the tree.

"It's beautiful!" Nora cried.

"Wait till you hear them. They stopped to drink some hot tea, I think. They were singing earlier."

"Carollers?"

"No." Bobby grinned. "Just happy children on Christmas morning."

A moment later, they were flooding from the cottages near the square again: an assortment of children from big to small, all cozy in their scarves and hats even if their coats had been mended many times over and were mostly far too large for them. Their little voices floated through the still air to the broken window, and Nora couldn't quite make out the words, only snatches of laughter.

Then their voices came together, and they began to sing. It was "It Came Upon a Midnight Clear." Nora knew every word; it had been Mama's favourite.

Bobby sat down beside her and unwrapped the parcel. "We were lucky today. The baker was in a generous mood. I got these for only tuppence."

The glorious smell of fresh bread rose on clouds of steam from the parcel. It contained two whole white rolls, still piping from the oven, and Nora's jaw dropped at the sight. She couldn't remember when last she'd tasted soft white bread.

Bobby handed one to her. "Merry Christmas, Nora."

She slowly took the bread, meeting his eyes. "Merry Christmas."

And in its way, strange though it was, it was a merry Christmas after all.

PART II

CHAPTER 5

*N*ora spotted the older woman even before she reached the door of the toy shop. She wore a headscarf and a voluminous dress, and the parcels in her arms were even more voluminous: paper-wrapped bottles on a string around her neck, a great box under one arm, and a stack of smaller boxes clutched under another.

She hurried toward the door, but didn't reach it quite in time. The older woman stepped through the door and gasped in surprise as the wind snatched at her dress. She staggered, almost dropping her parcels.

"Here, ma'am!" Nora rushed up to her and grasped two parcels before they could fall. "Let me help you!"

"Oh!" The woman blinked in surprise at the grubby street girl who had chosen to help instead of running off with the parcels. "Oh, thank you. My cab is right over here."

"I'll help you," Nora repeated, quickly taking the entire stack of parcels from under her arm.

The wind howled, blowing her skirt around her legs, as she crossed the sidewalk and tucked the parcels into the carriage that the woman had indicated. More traffic rushed up and down the street; the shops here were always busy, even in this appalling weather. The sky was dark grey, and there was a dampness in the wind that made it even colder.

The woman put her box inside on the seat. "There we are."

"Lots of shopping to do, ma'am?" Nora asked hopefully.

"Well, yes. I have a very large family. Christmas shopping is quite an expedition."

Nora grinned. "You're getting an early start, ma'am. It's not quite December yet."

"Like I say, it's a large family." The woman clambered into the carriage.

Nora kept her big grin in place and held out a hand encased in a grimy glove, the fingertips missing. Her fingers were white with the cold.

The woman sighed, but she reached into her purse and withdrew a sixpence, which she dropped into Nora's palm before ordering the driver on.

Nora whisked the sixpence into her apron pocket with a sigh of relief. It was a lucky thing she'd seen the woman when she did. Her usual efforts on this street, begging, singing, or going from one shop to the other, looking for odd jobs, had been unproductive today, yielding only tuppence.

The sixpence was an inconvenience to the woman with the many parcels, but to Nora and Bobby, it was a hot dinner.

She hurried down the street to the fishmonger's. She looked after his children sometimes when his wife had errands to run, and the wife slipped her a goodly piece of fish for a penny less than she usually would. A quick stop at the greengrocer's earned her two potatoes with only a little softening on one end, and then Nora was on her way again.

It was only five minutes' walk to the tenement. She let herself into the cold, grimy cellar, noting the lit streetlamp on the corner nearby, which told her that she would not be alone when she reached home.

"Bobby!" she called, striding inside. "I'm here!"

The dour old woman who shared their tenement was in the corner, doing piecework, her only hope of an income. Even after two years, Fran hardly ever said anything. She gave Nora a grunt and a nod.

"Evening, Fran," said Nora.

"Hello, hello!" Bobby was washing his face and hands in a bucket of cold water from the pump. He'd gotten the stove going; its warmth filled the cellar. "There you are, then, you pretty thing."

Something in the way he said it sent a delicious little flutter up Nora's smile. He had started saying it a few months ago, and each time he did, she found it even more delightful than the last.

He turned to her, his water-darkened hair falling over his forehead. Part of Nora wanted to brush it out of his eyes for him. The thought made her blush.

"I've got fish and chips for supper," Nora announced. "At least, I will have soon."

"Ah! Wonderful. I was hoping you'd bring supper."

Nora tilted her head. "They docked your wage again?"

Bobby's mouth turned down at the corners. "They're always looking for a reason, Nora. Seems I used too much waxed string for the wicks this week. But there's enough for our share of the rent, so that's something."

"I'll say," Fran grunted.

"That's more than something. Maybe we'll find another odd job tomorrow."

"Aye, though those are easier to find in the spring."

Bobby smiled. "Never mind that. We can eat well tonight, at least."

Nora still had a little lard put away from yesterday, and she warmed it in their chipped cast-iron pan on the stove while she cut the potatoes. She had to hold the knife carefully; they'd scrounged it from a rubbish heap, and the handle was a little loose. There were some beans, too, thanks to Fran. Nora cut them up as well.

"Can you believe I helped a lady doing Christmas shopping today?" she said.

"Christmas shopping!" Bobby chortled. "In the end of November?"

"Isn't it mad? These rich folks seem to think Christmas lasts forever." She dropped the potatoes into a pot of water to boil. "Thank you for pumping the water."

"Of course. Couldn't let you carry the bucket down them steps. They're slippery at the best of times." Bobby sniffed. "Why, smell that lard! I think Christmas does last forever when you've got somebody to make you delicious dinners like this."

"Hark at you." Nora laughed, but she enjoyed the flush on her cheeks.

"Perhaps we'll get more work now that people are doing more shopping." Bobby sat on one of their upturned buckets and pulled a broom nearer. He added a few twigs to it. "We might have the money for oranges this Christmas."

"Oh, maybe. That'd be lovely. Perhaps even a few sweets."

"Yes! Or even plums."

"Then I'll make plum pudding, and we'll eat like royalty," said Nora.

His eyes sparkled. "Aye, that'll be something."

Fran scoffed, incredulous as ever.

Nora giggled as the smell of boiling vegetables filled their cellar. "It could happen. We have a good patch now for crossing-sweeping and odd jobs. In between your lamp lighting, why, we might do better than ever this Christmas."

"Well enough for plum pudding, like we're a king and queen!" Bobby guffawed.

Nora laughed. She didn't know how to tell him the truth: that when he looked at her like that, she felt like a queen anyway, plum pudding or none.

Beef or no beef.

It was a good day for road apples.

The street passing by the row of businesses was bustling with traffic. Carriages, wagons, donkey carts, the odd horse and rider, they rattled this way and that, hooves clattering, leaving behind their own unique and pungent debris.

Nora gripped her broomstick a little harder. Across the street, Bobby gave her a cheerful little wave.

She returned it joyfully, something leaping in her at his smile. He was right. As traffic around the businesses picked up with the approach of December, they'd been doing better. Her pocket jingled promisingly with pennies.

She spotted a carriage slowing near them and hurried toward it. The hansom-cab disgorged a young gentleman, a foppish creature with a plum-coloured suit and top hat that put her in mind of the fruits they so dearly hoped for their Christmas treat.

"Good mornin', sir!" Nora called brightly.

The young man barely glanced at her, but his lip curled as he surveyed the manure-ridden street.

"Don't you worry, sir. We'll keep them shiny shoes of yours spotless." Nora waited for the crossing to quiet down, then hurried across the cobblestones. She worked her broom swiftly, whisking the lumps of horse manure from the stones.

The young man followed her sedately, swinging his cane and holding his top hat against the wind. Nora chatted brightly to him for a few more moments, then fell silent. Some gentlemen didn't appreciate her talking.

She brushed a last bit of filth from the road as they reached the sidewalk. "A very good morning to you, sir." Without much hope, she held out her hand.

The young man didn't give her a second glance. Shoes spotless, head high, he strutted off to the shops, leaving her empty-handed.

Nora waited until he was out of earshot before she muttered, "Toffs!"

"Don't you mind him," said Bobby. "We've already got a few pennies today."

"We haven't done badly." Nora smiled. "You're right. This is a good patch."

The church bell chimed a quarter to two.

"Another forty-five minutes, then I'll need to start my beat." Bobby raised his broom. "Let's make it count, eh?"

"Let's make it count," Nora agreed.

They were about to split off and go to separate crossings, hoping to maximise their chances of a profit, when Bobby suddenly gripped her arm. "Oi, that's not good."

"What?" Nora looked around.

She quickly spotted the trouble he was talking about. A gang of three boys, all Bobby's age or older, congregated on the corner across the street. They each held a broom, the sticks still white with newness.

Nora's heart sank. "No, no... not again."

"This is our patch," said Bobby firmly. "We'll hold onto it."

"There's three of them, Bobby."

"Aye, I see that. Don't you worry about them. You keep doing what you do. I'll make sure they don't harm you."

It was very gallant of him, but Nora felt a familiar sinking sensation in her belly as she reluctantly left him and headed to the next crossing. She'd seen this happen before.

If you were a street child in London, and you weren't part of one of the urchin gangs who carried knives or bits of sharp glass, getting pushed off your patch was inevitable.

She swept the crossing for a well-dressed woman who barely acknowledged her existence, then helped a little old lady in rags across. Nora didn't expect anything for the latter, but the old dear scrounged up a half-penny from the bottom of her purse and pressed it into Nora's hand.

One more half-penny. A little closer to plums for Christmas. She slipped it into her pocket, and when she turned around, the boy with the broom was only feet away from her.

Her heart dropped. She wanted to back away, but stubbornness kept her frozen in place.

The boy wasn't looking at her. Instead, leaning on his broom, sucking a matchstick between his teeth, he scanned the crossing. Like her, he was waiting for his next customer.

Nora's palms sweated. This is our patch, she repeated to herself. We'll hold onto it. But she had little faith in her own silent assertion.

The splendid clatter of a pair of carriage-horses

announced the arrival of a fancy brougham, a gilded crest on its door. Nora immediately stood to attention. When a young lady with a sweet visage disembarked, Nora stepped forward, and her shins rapped against an outstretched broomstick.

She tripped, barely managing to keep from falling. The boy with the broom was already ahead of her, sweeping the crossing.

It was one of his cronies that had tripped her.

Nora spun around, holding the broom like a shield. The boy was big, with a hard-bitten look in his little black eyes. A scar marked his jaw.

"This is our patch," Nora snapped. "Leave us alone!"

The boy laughed at her impudence. "I could knock your teeth out right this minute."

"Well, I won't go." Nora raised the broom.

The boy sneered. He lifted his broomstick as if to strike her, then stumbled forward.

Bobby was behind him, his hand still outstretched from where he'd shoved the other boy. "Get away from her!"

The boy spun. Without warning, he rammed the butt of his broomstick into Bobby's stomach, forcing a grunt from his lungs. Bobby doubled over in agony and the boy raised his stick, ready to deal a mighty blow to his head.

"No!" Nora shrieked.

She swung her broom in a wild arc. The brush smacked against the bay of the boy's head, and he bellowed with rage.

"Run, Nora!" Bobby was suddenly beside her, grabbing her hand.

They had no choice. The other two boys were on their way, eyes murderous. Nora tried to bolt, but Bobby was still bent over, struggling to keep up.

The first boy caught up to them in a single bound. He kicked at Bobby's legs, and he went down hard, letting go of Nora's hand.

"Bobby!" she screamed.

One of the other boys reached her before she could go to Bobby's defence. The boy lunged as if to grab at the front of her dress. She turned with a yelp, and his fingers caught in her pocket, the one containing the coins.

The stitches tore with a dismaying pop of thread, and coins littered the pavement.

"Hey, boys!" Her assailant pounced on them. "Look at this!"

Bobby was on his feet. "That's ours!"

"Bobby, no!" Nora shrieked.

The first boy, their leader, swung a wild blow with his fist. It landed hard on Bobby's face, and he reeled back with a cry.

Nora seized his arm as the three boys scrambled to grab the money she'd dropped. "Come on!"

He didn't resist. They bolted, Nora's shins stinging, her heart aching for the precious copper coins that now littered the street.

Bobby knew the streets well. In a few quick turns, he led them well away from the row of shops, and they reached the muddy streets of Devil's Acre. They took shelter in the lee of a grimy tenement building, breathing hard.

"Are you all right?" Bobby asked. "Did they hurt you?"

"I'm all right." Nora sighed. "Except that they tore my pocket. Look! I lost every penny we'd earned today, Bobby, every last one." Anger made her eyes burn with tears. "They didn't work for that money. I did. I worked honestly, and they took it. Thieves!"

"Boys like them are no good at all," said Bobby. "I'm

sorry, Nora. I shouldn't have said we'd stay and fight. If we'd left when we first saw them..." He sighed.

Nora touched his cheek. She hardly knew why, but it felt good to rest her palm on the side of his face, feeling the faintest bristle of hair against her skin.

Bobby's eyes found hers. One was already swollen almost shut, but the other, soft and brown, filled her world.

"You did your best to protect us, Bobby. It's not your fault."

"It'll be all right," he told her. "I saw another patch when I was out lighting lamps on the other side of Devil's Acre. It's a bit of a walk, but we could do well there. A market square, right on the edge of Westminster. Plenty of well-to-do folks there. It'll be worth the extra time to reach it."

"Then we'll go there tomorrow," said Nora. "For now, let's go home, and I'll put something cold on your eye, you poor thing."

The church bell chimed.

"There's no time for that. I need to stop by the company, get my things, and go light the lamps. But don't worry about me, Nora. Go home. There's still a little bread from breakfast. I've got tuppence in my pocket from that last customer; I'll bring supper."

"Bobby..."

"Go home." He lowered their hands, but didn't let go of hers. "I'll be back. Stay warm."

"Your eye."

"I'll be all right." He squeezed her hand. "Everything will be."

She watched him go, arms wrapped around herself against the rising wind. When he said it, it was so easy to believe him.

CHAPTER 6

Bobby was right. The new patch was perfect.

Nora could hardly contain her delight as they walked across the square. It had even, well-maintained cobbles, not a single one loose or missing. A row of businesses lined it, each one with a brightly painted sign and colourful gas lamps in the windows: there was a tailor, a butcher, a shop that sold sweets, an apothecary…

The clientele were even better. Even this close to Devil's Acre, Nora saw no one in rags, except for the odd urchin lurking in the shadows of an alley. These were smaller than Nora and Bobby, and when they came nearer, the urchins melted silently away.

Everyone else who hurried from the carriages waiting in patient rows at the square's centre wore beautiful, warm clothes and carried silver pocket-watches. Many of them would be snobs, of course, but they also looked as though they wouldn't think twice about a sixpence.

The same sixpence that could feed Nora and Bobby for an entire day.

"Oh, Bobby." She gripped his hand tightly, wrapped around hers. "It's perfect!"

He grinned, eyes dancing. "What do you think? Should we start with sweeping?"

Nora looked critically over the square. "No. There's not quite enough traffic for that. Besides, your broom was broken in the fight, and we haven't time to look for a good stick to make another. Let's try for jobs instead. Look, the brewer's dray just pulled up outside the pub. Maybe they'll need a hand unloading the barrels."

They crossed the square to the cheerful little public house on the corner, where a quiet hum of conversation came from the well-lit interior and the smell of frying sausages made Nora's mouth water. There had been no money for breakfast, except for a cup of hot, weak tea with only the faintest splash of milk. Not if they were going to afford their share of the rent—and miserly Fran wouldn't allow them to contribute even a penny less than agreed, or she would have them out on their ears.

The dray was a large wagon stacked with barrels of ale, drawn by a pair of great horses. Its driver stepped down from the wagon and approached the pub, while the boy accompanying him scampered around to hold the horses.

"Good morning!" Bobby called.

The driver turned, a scowl on his face and his hand going protectively to his pocket-watch, but the scowl dissolved into a smile. "Ah, Bobby! Mornin', lad. I saw you early when I was harnessin' the horse, puttin' out lamps."

"Aye, sir. I always love passin' by your brewery. It's always got a lovely smell about it." Bobby nodded at the barrels. "Need a hand unloading?"

"Why, lad, that'd be capital. There's a penny in it for you. I was just about to ask old Mrs. Peggs if any of her guests could help, since I know her son's all laid up with consumption."

"I could hold the horses, sir," said Nora. "I'm not afraid of them. Then your boy could also help."

"Charming! We'll be done in no time." The brewer winked. "Make it a penny and a half, then."

Nora went up to the horses. They were giant creatures, their limbs hairy, their hooves seeming as vast as manhole covers, but their big dark eyes were gentle.

"They won't do nothin' to you, miss," said the boy.

Nora gripped the reins. One of the large creatures pressed a silky muzzle against her hand; the other dropped his ears to the side and went to sleep.

The men got to work. Nora exhaled, hope lifting her chest. Bobby was right. This patch was as good as any they'd ever had, and that penny-and-a-half would already be enough for a loaf of bread and a cup of milk for breakfast.

The horses stood patiently, requiring little of her attention, apparently content to rest after drawing their heavy load. Nora looked about the square, hoping to spot their next opportunity.

Her eyes alit on a shop in the corner. The space was large, easily outdoing the neighbouring apothecary, and the door was glass, with spacious windows shedding warm gas lightning into the grey day. It caught her eye because of the brilliant colours in the window. Wooden dummies within displayed glorious dresses in the most vibrant colours: sapphire blue, royal purple, rich scarlet, emerald green, butter yellow. The dresses had beautiful, elegant forms, and were decorated with sparkling glass jewels and feathers, or merely with sophisticated pearl buttons and lace trimmings.

Nora gazed at them, enjoying their beauty. The sign over the door read, C. Whitmore, Milliner.

A pair of well-dressed young ladies disembarked from a nearby brougham and strolled into the millinery. At once, a handsome older woman appeared in the window to attend to them. Nora couldn't help staring at her. There were no men in the store; no sign of a male proprietor or owner to command the older woman, the milliner, Nora presumed.

Instead, C. Whitmore attended to the ladies, showing them different dresses and bolts of cloth. She smiled widely, and her cheeks held a healthy colour. Her dress was not as extravagant as those on display in the window, yet it draped her figure with a flattering form, and the dark green fabric looked warm and lush.

Nora stared at her in fascination as the ladies placed several gold sovereigns into her hand.

"There we are, then!" The brewer came out of the pub, slapping his hands clean. "Thanks very much, Bobby, and here's your penny and ha'penny."

Bobby accepted them with a little bow. "Thank you, sir."

"Keep warm, now." The brewer hopped into the driver's seat.

Nora released the horses, and Bobby took her hand as the dray clattered off.

"We've enough for breakfast," he said. "That's a good start, isn't it?"

Nora couldn't tear her eyes away from the millinery. The milliner didn't look as though she ever had to miss breakfast because of money.

"Nora?"

"Yes," she said. "Yes, it's a good start." She blinked. "You know, Bobby, there's another way we can make money. It doesn't all have to be odd jobs and begging."

"Oh? How, then?"

"Well, look at everyone on this square. They all make their money the same way, by selling things."

"Mm, that's right." Bobby led her toward the nearby bakery. "But we don't have anything to sell, do we?"

"Not yet, perhaps." Nora looked around the square, an idea formulating in her mind. "Do you know what you can't buy on this square?"

"I'm not sure. Seems like it has everything one could need."

"Almost everything, but not a fishmonger."

Bobby looked about. "Why, you're right. There's a butcher and a greengrocer, but no fishmonger."

"But we're not far from the river. Why, do you remember when we had a patch near the river, when we used to see the fishermen loading their catch onto carts to go deeper into the city?" Nora grinned. "What if I bought fish from them, and brought them here, and sold them in this very square, more expensively than I'd bought them?"

Bobby looked down at the penny-and-a-half in his hand, then up at Nora.

"People would buy fish," she said eagerly. "I know they would."

"But we don't have a stall."

"Perhaps we'd make enough money to get a cart. That's cheaper than a stall, and better besides, because it could move around and help me to bring more fish from the river to here. People would gladly buy it here rather than having to go somewhere else."

Bobby smiled.

"It could work. I'd start with only a little. Three or four

fish. Enough that we can dry and preserve them to use at home if they don't sell. I might make only a ha'penny on each one, but the next day, I could buy more. More the day after. Then more still."

His hand tightened on hers. "All right," he said. "Let's do it. A pennyworth of bread will do us for the day, don't you think?"

Nora hesitated. "We'd have no meat for supper."

"What does it matter? Your plans sounds so wonderful that we'll have all the meat we need soon." Bobby pressed the ha'penny into her hand. "Everything else we make today, we keep for fish."

Nora searched his face. "Are you sure about this?"

"I don't know anything about business. Not a thing. I only know how to light lamps. But your eyes are shinin', Nora." His smile filled the world. "That's quite enough for me."

She knew from his tone that he meant it with all his heart, and perhaps that was the moment that the coal that had been quietly smouldering in her chest for the past two years at last became a little, dancing flame.

The basket Nora carried on her back had been heavy when she left the riverbank that morning, but now, it contained only the small piece of chicken, a few potatoes, and the leeks she'd bought for supper.

And there would still be plenty left over.

She listened to the jingle in her apron pocket as she strode toward the square's corner where Bobby always met her on his way back home from the evening's lamplighting. Every streetlamp on the square and its warm light reminded her of him, and added to the warmth she felt in her own chest.

She had so much good news for him.

Sure enough, Bobby reached the corner a few seconds before she did, right on the stroke of six. He always did, and the sight of him made something merry and bubbling fill her heart, as though she were a snow globe all shaken up when she saw him.

"Evenin'!" he called. "Why, aren't you all smiles!"

"Why shouldn't I be?" Nora gave a delighted laugh. "Bobby, I sold every last one!"

Bobby gasped. "Again?"

"Every last one," Nora repeated. She plunged a hand into her apron pocket and showed him the fistful of coins she'd earned. "And I already bought all we need for supper!"

Bobby folded his soot-blackened hands around Nora's. "My, Nora! Look at that!"

"I'll take every penny to the docks tomorrow, Bobby. I'll buy a little more than I did today. It's only been a week, and already, each day is a little better."

"You're doing a wonderful thing," said Bobby.

Nora felt as though the words lit her up on the inside. He could always brighten her just as he brightened the streets of Westminster and Devil's Acre. "You're so good to me."

She slipped her hand into his as they turned away down the narrow alley that led back to their home. It was such an easy motion, one that she once performed simply to keep from getting separated on a busy street. But now the alley was empty, and their fingers laced between each other in a new way that made her tremble a little.

"Who would be anything but good to something as lovely as you?" said Bobby softly.

The gentleness in his tone reached into the deepest part of her, waking something that had been sleeping for a long time, since the days of wonder when her parents were still alive. She found herself looking up at him in awe, and their eyes found one another. Suddenly he was both too close and not nearly close enough.

"Bobby..." she whispered.

Footsteps echoed in the alley. Bobby's face changed, the smile vanishing. His grip on her hand became hard enough to be painful, and he pulled her against him as two boys appeared in the alley ahead of them.

Nora's skin prickled at once. The boys walked casually, hands in their pockets. They were ragged creatures, like her, but that was where the similarity ended. Dirt smeared their cheeks, thick and crusted as though they never bathed. Their hair stood in tufts from the holes in their caps, and their eyes were cold and hard, like the eyes of a rat.

Bobby pulled her behind him and moved backward, almost treading on her.

"Go," he growled. "Go!"

She turned, but there was another boy behind them, and he was somehow worse despite the wide and crooked grip on his face. A few wisps of dark hair clung to his chin. He wore what might have been a top hat once, but it was so battered and wrinkled and crushed that it teetered precariously to one side, and the brim was folded in at the front.

"Ain't nowhere she can go," he called. "Nowhere for you to go, neither."

Bobby spun. His grip never eased on Nora's hand.

"Leave us alone," he shouted.

"Now why in the Queen's name would I do that?" said

the boy. "I saw you flashin' your copper about, little missy. That was a silly thing to do, don't you think? Yes. A very, very silly thing."

Nora swallowed hard and hoped the jingle of coins in her apron pocket was less conspicuous than it seemed.

"You know, anyone might see you do such a thing," said the boy, "anyone, and there are them roundabout here who might not have the nicest intentions."

He reached for Nora's face. Bobby pulled her behind him, shielding her. "Don't touch her."

The boy smirked. "You're a fiery lot."

"We don't want any trouble," said Bobby.

"Aye, of course, you don't. But don't feel too bad, little missy," said the boy. He was a little older than Bobby; seventeen or eighteen, perhaps. "After all, I am Jack Ketch, King of Devil's Acre. I know everything that happens on my patch. Sooner or later, I would have found out. It's not hard to keep my eye on a pretty little thing like you."

The boys behind them cackled like wild animals in the dark. Nora squeezed herself against Bobby's back.

"Now you'll soon learn that there are easy ways and hard ways to live here," Jack Ketch went on. "The easy way is to do as I tell you. The hard way? Well, that's everything else."

"Everything else," one of the other boys hissed, so close that Nora felt his breath on her neck. It made her skin crawl.

"So here's how this'll go. You can hand over them pretty, shiny coins," said Jack, "and then you can be on your way, happy as can be."

"Nora worked hard for that money. You can't have it, thief," Bobby spat.

Jack's eyes narrowed. "What did you just call me?"

"I called you a thief, and it's what you are!" Bobby trembled with rage. "A thief, a scoundrel, and a bully!"

Jack moved so fast that Nora barely saw the blow coming before it fell. His punch landed in Bobby's mouth with a horrifying crunch. The boy's head snapped back, and he went down backwards, almost knocking Nora over with him. She grabbed his arm and tried to slow his fall, but he still struck the ground with a nasty thud.

The other boys moved in. One aimed a kick at Bobby's head. Nora slammed her hands against his chest and pushed him away, forcing him to stumble back several steps.

"Leave him alone!" she shrieked.

Jack grabbed her arm. "Now you're mine."

Nora twisted, somehow breaking free. She almost tripped over the groaning Bobby as the boys closed in.

Her thoughts moved fast. Without hesitation, she plunged her hand into her pocket and seized a fistful of those hard-earned coins. Then she flung them away from her as hard as she could.

All three boys turned their heads to watch the money fly.

Jack laughed. "Clever move, little girl."

The boys lunged for the money, and Nora grabbed Bobby's arm. He was trying to get up, blood pouring from his mouth. She draped his arm over her shoulders and staggered from the alley, half dragging, half supporting him with her.

Jack didn't give chase. He only shouted after them, his words hounding them to the alley's end.

"Let that be a lesson to you both!" he shouted. "It's always best to give Jack Ketch whatever he wants!"

Bobby sipped the tea gingerly, wincing. His upper lip had already swollen into a tight purple sausage.

"You poor thing." Nora sat on the bucket beside him. They had safely made it to their tenement, and the chicken and vegetables were boiling on the stove, filling the room with the comfortable scents of a hot supper. Fran had contributed a loaf of stale bread. "Is it still very sore?"

Bobby gave her a valiant smile. He'd washed off the blood, but the gap in his mouth where his front tooth used to be, was still disconcerting to look at. "It's getting better. Thanks for the lovely tea." His words sounded thick and slurred through his swollen lips. "It's helping so much."

"I'm sorry, Bobby."

"Nora, there's no reason for you to be sorry. That boy is a bully and nothing more."

"If he hadn't seen when I showed you the money..."

"It's not your fault," said Bobby firmly. "Do we have anything left?"

Nora pawed through her pocket, searching for the pennies in the corners. She withdrew them and sighed against the tightness in her throat. "A shilling."

Fran spoke up for the first time since they'd returned home. "Don't go thinkin' you can skimp on the rent." She didn't look up from her mending.

"We wouldn't dare, Fran," Nora muttered.

"If you think you can crook me by a ha'penny, I'll cast you both into the streets, d'you hear me?"

It was true. Nora knew it. Fran could find a dozen desperate youngsters like them to share her tenement.

"Yes, Fran," she said obediently.

The old woman grunted and returned to her work.

Bobby lowered his voice. "Only a shilling! They took so much."

"It's all right. We already have supper, and there's a bit of bread left over for breakfast. I'll use it all to get more fish tomorrow and I'll still make something." Nora kept her tone cheerful for herself as much as for Bobby. "It'll be all right."

Bobby took another painful sip of the tea. "It's a pity. It was such a good patch, too, especially for the fish."

"It's still a good patch, Bobby."

He looked up from the mug. "You want to go back?"

Nora thought of the millinery, warm and bright, sturdy and immovable. She remembered the milliner's calm movements and easy smile. That was the face of a woman who stood firm, who did not allow herself to be pushed around by every bully that came along. If Nora wanted what she had, that steadiness, that structure, that freedom she realized that she had to do the same.

"I'm not giving it up," Nora said firmly. "Not this time."

"Nora..."

"No, Bobby, listen to me. We'll run out of places to look for work soon, do you know that? We've been running from every gang that frightens us, and it's no good. None at all. This time, I have a good patch, and I know it. We need to be careful. We should take the main street back to our building instead of the alley, and we'll have to keep our eyes open for Jack and his friends. But I'm not leaving." Nora raised her chin. "Not this time."

"We are doing well there," Bobby acknowledged.

"We'll continue to do well there. It's time we stood our ground, Bobby, or we'll keep on losing everything."

Bobby lowered his mug and studied her. His swollen lip gave his mouth a downturned appearance that stung

Nora's heart, and he couldn't quite smile with his mouth, but his eyes could.

"All right," he said. "Then we stay."

"Bobby… thank you."

"No." Bobby held out his hand. "Thank you."

Nora glanced at it, but it seemed so simple to let her hand rest in his, even though they'd never held hands except on the streets before. It was somehow different here, even though she took care to keep her hand before here, where Fran couldn't see. A gentle thrill warmed her blood at the touch. "We won't regret it. We'll make more money, you'll see."

She thought of the milliner again as she stirred their simple supper in the pot. One day, she thought. One day, she, too, would sell her wares from a warm building instead of the windswept square, and she, too, would move with calm confidence in a shop that was her own realm.

That would never happen if she kept running from the likes of Jack Ketch.

CHAPTER 7

*N*ora had found the perfect spot for the day's sales, yet it had done her little good.

The precipitation trickling down from the dark grey sky was not snow, yet it made the air feel frigid. The sleet came down softly but gathered in puddles of grey slush, outlining each cobblestone of the square with liquid. Carriages splashed up sheets of water from their wheels. The well-to-do clientele of this square moved carefully, picking their way between puddles, their umbrellas held protectively over their heads.

The overhang beside the millinery sheltered Nora from both wind and sleet. She stood with her basket on her back, feeling its depressing fullness as it tugged on the straps around her shoulders. In each hand, she held a string of fish.

The traffic was limited today. Customers darted from one shop to the other, then rushed to scramble into the shelter of their cabs or carriages. Only a few dashed past Nora.

She held up the fish hopefully. "Fresh fish! Caught overnight! Lovely cod! Fat trout!"

So far, she'd sold only a few. She hardly knew if they would go bad overnight or not. Would this all be a dead loss?

Not so soon, she pleaded silently. Not right as I've started to recover from the money Jack Ketch stole.

The memory sent a shiver down her spine. She scanned the square, checking the shadows as she always did, but there was no sign of Jack or his cronies.

Not this time.

Another gentleman headed in her direction. She stepped forward, ignoring the sleet that pounded her face, and held out the strings. "Fresh cod! How about a bit of fish for your supper, my good sir?"

The gentleman brushed past her and hastened to a waiting carriage.

With a sigh, Nora retreated to the lee of the millinery. If the milliner minded having a smelly little fishmonger beside her shop, she hid it well. Nora gazed longingly through the window at the cozy interior.

The milliner was showing pieces of cloth to a young lady. An older woman, the girl's mother, Nora guessed, hovered nearby.

"This is Persian silk, m'lady," said the milliner, holding out a bolt of wonderful, glossy blue fabric. "The finest of the fine. Go ahead, feel it!"

The words were muffled through the glass, but Nora heard them clear enough to follow the conversation.

"Oh, that does feel lovely," said the girl.

"Do you have any other fabrics in this colour?" her mother asked.

"Certainly, madam." The milliner picked up another

bolt and showed it to them. "This is plain cotton, coloured with a similar dye. Sturdy and cool, it is, and half the price."

The mother looked much happier about the cotton, but the girl's lips turned down as she felt it. "It's not as soft."

"That doesn't matter. You'll look fine in the cotton," said the mother.

"My dear lady, your daughter is so fetching, she'll look fine in any colour or fabric in the world!" The milliner beamed. "Why, look at this." She turned the girl around and held the bolt of cotton beside her. "She'll light up the room in this. It certainly looks lovely on her. But if you don't mind my saying so, m'lady, your eyes are the most wonderful blue I've ever seen. They have such a light in them." The milliner set the cotton bolt aside and held up the silk beside the girl. "The lustre of this silk, why, it awakens something in your eyes, makes them seem ten times the brighter."

The girl touched her face. "Oh, it surely does!"

"She has your eyes, madam," the milliner added.

The mother beamed. "I think you're quite right, Mrs. Whitmore. The silk is far lovelier. I think we've made our choice, haven't we?"

"Yes. The silk!" the girl cried. "Thank you, Mama!"

"The dress will be beautiful," the milliner crooned.

Nora watched as the mother counted out money and gave it to the milliner, who noted it down in a ledger. She wondered how much more expensive the silk had been than the cotton, and yet the milliner had so artfully persuaded the mother to purchase it.

An idea formed in her mind. She scanned the streets, waiting until another woman headed in her direction: a sturdy-looking, businesslike person in a dress.

"Good afternoon, ma'am!" Nora held up the fish. "Why, you look like you know a good piece of fish when you see one! You must be a cook for a fine household with such a long shopping list in your hand. Can I interest you in a good bit of carp? Some bream? All fresh-caught!"

The woman slowed. "Why, yes," she said, puffing out her chest. "I do work for a very fine household."

"And your masters deserve only the finest and freshest catch for their supper!" Nora enthused.

The woman inclined her head. "They certainly do." And she bought six of Nora's largest trout on the spot.

Nora's heart pounded with excitement as she whisked the coins into her pocket. She held up her remaining string of fish.

"Finest fish for the finest folks!" she called. "Lovely and fresh! You there, sir! Your son is a fine, strapping lad! How about a nice hearty bream for supper?"

The gentleman she'd called out to came over, beaming in pride with one hand on his son's shoulder, and he was not the only one. As Nora flattered and complimented the passing crowd, the fish flew from her basket until every last one was all gone.

She waited for Bobby by the butchery; the butcher had a flat over his shop, and the gas light over the door was always on, his angry dog always growling in the back garden. It was a good spot to avoid Jack Ketch and his like.

At the same time as always, Bobby came by. His head hung today, and he didn't see how intently Nora gazed at him, how she enjoyed the strength of his silhouette and the tumble of his hair over his forehead. Nora read weariness in every step he took. He'd carried the heavy fish basket to the square for her that morning as he always did, long before dawn broke the horizon and negated the lamps he was to extinguish, and she could tell that his limbs had carried him many long miles that day.

His lip was less swollen, and she had almost grown used to the gap in his smile, which he always seemed to find for her no matter how tired his body appeared. "Evening, Nora-dear!" he called.

Dear! The sweet nickname made her heart flip in her chest. It made her wonder if there might be times when he gazed at her when she wasn't looking, just as she gazed at him.

"Bobby, look!" Nora swung the basket from her shoulders. "I sold them all. Every last one! We won't even have fish for ourselves for supper tonight. I've bought us a bit of beef instead."

Bobby looked into the basket and gasped. "Beef! My, I can't remember the last time we tasted beef."

"In the workhouse a few Christmases ago for me," said Nora.

Bobby beamed, eyes shining. "This is wonderful! How, how did you sell so much fish? And you must have gotten a better price, too!"

"I certainly did. I was watching the milliner."

"Who?"

"You know... the lady who owns the millinery."

"Oh, yes. I've seen the dresses in the window." Bobby took the basket and carried it for her. "They're so pretty." His tone softened. "I wish I could get you one just like those for Christmas."

Nora blinked. "You... you do?"

Bobby's eyes darted away, his cheeks reddening. "Sometimes I wish I could bring you the moon and the stars, Nora."

The silence between them held no discomfort; it was gentle, filled with hope. Nora hardly knew what to say, but she was aware that his words made her feel warm on the inside.

"You said you were watching the milliner?" Bobby quietly prompted.

"That's right. I saw how she talked to the customers, how she convinced them to buy things, giving them compliments, and I tried it. It worked, Bobby! I did better than ever today. Why, I made up all the ground we lost when those villains took our money!"

Bobby shuddered. They passed the alley where it had happened; they never took that shortcut home anymore, walking the long way round instead, where the roads were busier.

"If things keep going this well," said Nora eagerly, "then I'll be able to buy a cart next week."

"A cart?"

"Yes! A handcart, like the ones the other peddlers have. I spoke to the old rag-and-bone man this morning while you were out lighting lamps. He told me that he bought his cart from the carpenter down on the street by the river, and it cost him three shillings. I've been putting by a few pennies each day that goes well. I'll have the money by next week."

"My, Nora, that would be wonderful. I feel so sorry for you, carrying this heavy basket on your back," said Bobby. "A cart would be so much better."

"I could carry more fish, too, Bobby. The more fish I sell, the more profit I make. Beef might not be something we have only once in a few years," said Nora eagerly. "We could get a better tenement, warmer clothes. Why, we could even have a Christmas tree one day!"

Bobby smiled. "A Christmas tree?"

The words still always held a note of sadness for Nora, but now, instead of thinking at once of the tree on the stage at that deadly pantomime, her heart took her back to the great tree in the square on that cold Christmas Eve two years ago when Bobby had first brought her to the tenement building that had become her home. They'd long since given up on searching for work or food on that specific square as it was the home of a particularly ruthless gang of beggar urchins, but she would never forget the magic of the falling snow and the shining tree that night.

She wanted to bring that magic home, capture a little of it in a pine tree wrapped in splendour.

The gentle look in Bobby's eyes told her that he was thinking of that night, too. Their hands found one another, fingers interlocking, and they walked home with hearts full of Christmas dreams.

"Catch of the day, folks! Beautiful big bream! Delicious baked with a bit of garlic and herbs!" Nora held up the string of fish on an arm that trembled with weariness. "Hurry, this is the last one! What beautiful children you have, ma'am. You must feed them well!"

The woman hurrying toward her, a boy and girl clinging to her skirts, laughed as she pulled her purse from an apron pocket. "I certainly do, miss, and I know a nice bit of fish when I find it. My neighbour told me that there's a new fishmonger in this part of town. I was expecting a few sad little sardines, but look at this bream! It's fresh as can be."

"Caught last night, ma'am," said Nora, "and only sixpence for these lovely big bream."

"Sixpence!"

"Feel them, ma'am!" Nora held out the string. "They're heavy fish, they are, juicy and fresh."

"I can see that. I suppose it's a better price than I'd get at any shop." The woman held out the precious coin. "I'll take them both."

Nora wrapped them in newspaper, something she'd only been able to afford recently, and the woman gave a grunt of satisfaction as she tucked the resulting parcel under her arm. "I'll certainly be back. It's nice to find a fresh fishmonger in this part of the Devil's Acre."

"I'm here every day, ma'am. Have a lovely evening," said Nora.

The woman left, children in tow, and Nora joyfully tucked the sixpence into her pocket. She couldn't count her money in public, but she'd done her sums the night before thanks to the education she'd eked out in the workhouse, and she was almost certain she had her three shillings saved up.

It was time for a cart to ease her aching back and carry yet more fish to this lucrative little spot.

Nora was humming with pleasure as she swung the empty basket onto her back. She turned, ready to go the baker's to find some bread for dinner, but she must have worked later than normal; Bobby was already waiting on his customary corner, the bright light from the nearby streetlamp reflecting golden on his hair.

Nora almost skipped across the square to him. "I did it, Bobby!" She seized his hand; the motion was automatic now, effortless. "We have enough."

"Oh! For your cart?" Bobby smiled.

"I think so. I'll count it tonight."

"You are wonderful, Nora. Absolutely wonderful." Bobby squeezed her hand.

She realized that she was standing very close to him. He smelled like lamp oil, and something stirred in her heart.

Then Bobby's eyes widened. He ducked away, tugging her after him, and dived behind the cover of a wagon standing outside a nearby shop.

"Bobby..."

"Shhh!" Bobby hissed. "Get under the canvas! Quickly!" He lifted the wagon's cover.

"But..."

"Quick!" Bobby pushed her toward it.

Clutching her basket, Nora scrambled into the wagon. Bobby joined her a moment later and pulled the flap down behind him.

"What's happening?" Nora whispered.

"It's him," Bobby breathed. "It's Ketch."

Jack Ketch. Fear stung all the way down Nora's spine.

"I don't think he saw us," Bobby whispered. "We have to stay still."

A few long moments passed. Nora heard nothing but the general hubbub of the square, the stamp of the horse's feet, and the soft squeak of harness as the animal shifted around, waiting for its owner to return.

She was aware that they were very close to one another, elbows and hips touching as they crouched side by side, and wondered if Bobby could hear the mad thunder of her heart. Its acceleration was not entirely due to fear.

Then she heard it: the ugly, braying laugh.

Her breath caught. She glimpsed a scrap of light nearby, a hole in the canvas, and peered through it.

Jack roamed across the square, his dark eyes darting everywhere, his hands buried in the pockets of his many-patched greatcoat. A gaggle of younger boys followed him, all scarred and bruised, their faces tough, their eyes cold and hard.

"Where is she, boys?" he hissed.

"I saw her over there only a few minutes ago." One of the boys pointed. "She was with that lamplighter. She has to be close by."

"She came here with a full basket of fish and had none left tonight," another boy said. "She's got to have a good haul on her, Jack."

"Then we'll find her." Jack laughed again.

They were so close now that Nora could see the streaks of filth on Jack's face, the tattered hairs clinging to his upper lip. He turned his head suddenly, and for a breathtaking instant, she looked directly into his heartless eyes.

Nora barely managed to stop herself from gasping. She drew back, her heart slamming in her chest, and footsteps drew nearer. For a terrible moment, Nora thought that Jack was upon her.

Then the footsteps went past. "Here, they must have gone down this alley. Let's go," Jack called.

The boys drew away. Nora exhaled, her body trembling.

"Shhh. It's all right." Bobby wrapped an arm around her shoulders. "It's all right. They've gone."

They waited a few moments more before creeping off the wagon. Bobby kept his hand firmly on hers.

"That was close," Nora whimpered.

"Did you hear what they said? They've been watching you all day." Bobby shuddered. "Waiting for you to make your honest money so that they could steal it all. Nora, I don't think it's safe here for us anymore."

Nora shook her head. "We can't leave, Bobby."

"But if they try to steal from you again…"

"Then we'll still have more than we did anywhere else.

We can't leave. This is the best chance we've ever had. We can't let someone like Jack Ketch take it from us!"

Bobby's lips pressed together, displeasure on his face. "I don't think it's worth it."

"I do." Nora clutched his arm. "Please, Bobby. This is working. Please… please don't make me leave."

He let out a shaky sigh and wrapped an arm around her shoulders. "I won't make you do anything, Nora. Come. Let's go home."

CHAPTER 8

The old carpenter's shop was really only a shed at the back of the tiny cottage where he lived by the river. Everything smelled of fish here; the air, the water, and the dingy little shop, where labour had bent the old man's back double over many hard decades. A single oil lamp glowed in the grimy rafters; not everyone could afford gas.

He was a snuffling creature, dirty grey stubble clinging to his weak jaw, breathing loudly through the gap where his bottom teeth used to be.

"You brought the money?" he rasped.

"That's right, sir." Nora had carefully counted and re-counted the shillings she'd so carefully saved. "It's all here."

She gave him the coins, and he stared at them dimly for several long moments before shuffling into the shop.

A few seconds later, the old man returned, pushing a handcart. He had cobbled it together from old bits of wood, and one of the wheels already squeaked, but in that moment Nora had never seen anything more wonderful, because this was hers. She took it by the handle and pushed it into the street, marvelling at how easy it felt compared to the heavy basket she'd always used. There were bars over the top for her to hang her fish from, and a compartment in the middle that she could fill with ice or snow to keep them cold. The four wheels rattled easily on the pavement.

"It's perfect!" she cried. "Oh, Bobby, look! Isn't it wonderful?"

Bobby's smile curved and glowed like a half-moon. "Why, look at that, Nora! You'll be the talk of the town with it." He swung the basket of fish from his shoulders. "Come on! Let's see how it works."

Nora selected several of the best fish from the basket and strung them up, then hung them from the bars. Bobby tipped the rest into the central compartment along with the snow they had packed in with them.

She stepped back to admire her handiwork. In the lantern's watery glow, the fish's scales shone as they swayed gently from the cart. It looked official and real, very different from selling scraps on the corner. Nora felt the ground grow more solid beneath her feet.

Bobby's fingers wrapped around hers. "I'm so proud of you, Nora."

She looked up at him, the lantern glow turning his eyes soft. He smelled of lamp oil and the river, rough, familiar, and better than any fine gentleman's cologne. The street was empty; the carpenter had gone back inside, and at this early hour, no one yet stirred.

She found herself staring at his lips, smoothly pink between the freckles. They looked wonderful to kiss...

His hand tightened on hers. "Promise me you'll be terribly careful."

"I'm always careful."

"I know, but this cart..." Bobby sucked his teeth.

Nora let go of his hand. "What about the cart?"

"I'm pleased for you, Nora, but I'm worried that Jack will think you're easier to steal from with it. Don't keep your money in it, all right?"

"I won't. And Jack won't get to me. I'll be careful. I promise."

A bell chimed the half-hour, and Bobby stepped back. "Time to go, or I'll be late for the lamps on the Strand."

Nora smiled. "Be safe, Bobby."

"You too, love."

He froze for an instant, as though he hadn't meant to call her that, yet she saw it shining in his eyes: the truth that he felt that way about her. She opened her mouth to say something, but a church bell chimed and Bobby only smiled and then ducked away.

He went off whistling, his pole on his shoulder. The whistle was a cheerful Christmas carol: "I Saw Three Ships." Nora hummed it too as she pushed her cart through the streets, revelling in its effortless motion over the pavement. Revelling still more in the echo of that gentle word in his voice: Love.

She felt one step nearer to the milliner in her warm shop, whatever Bobby's fears might be. The admission he'd so nearly made left her feeling invincible.

IT WAS STILL a little more than two weeks to Christmas, but the folk of the market square seemed ready to celebrate early.

Nora stood beside her cart, proudly gesturing at her fish as she cried her wares. The cries had become so habitual that she barely needed to think about them. Instead, she watched the Christmas tree rise in the middle of the square.

A team of young men were hauling it upright with ropes, laughing and cheering each other one as they heaved its green crown heavenward. It was a beautiful thing even without its adornments, its green vibrant against the snow-capped rooftops and slumbering stores, and several excited children emerged from the nearby homes and businesses to watch it rise.

"Lovely fish!" Nora called. "Ask your mama for a bit of fish for supper! Battered and fried, perfect with chips!"

"Excuse me, miss." A small, hollow-eyed child appeared beside the cart. "Don't you have a very small piece? A piece nobody else wants?"

Nora understood the pinched, pale cheeks at once. Not so long ago, she had looked very similar.

Quietly, she reached into the cart and withdrew a smoked kipper. "Here."

"How much is it, miss?"

"Just take." Nora pressed it into the child's hand.

The little girl's eyes widened. "Thank you, miss! Thank you very much!" She touched her cap and took off, thrusting the precious food into her mouth.

It warmed Nora's heart to be able to do such a thing. She glanced over her shoulder into the millinery and smiled at the beautiful woman within, laughing and singing as she wandered among her dresses.

When I'm like you, I'll give money to the church, she thought, and oranges to the workhouse, and candy to the children on the street. When she gripped the wooden handles of her cart, it felt as though that cart connected her to the warm reality within the millinery, like a golden thread drawing her closer to a brighter future.

A shadow flickered in the corner of her vision. Nora turned her head quickly and thought she saw someone duck behind the corner of the millinery, into the alley on the other side.

Her belly tensed. Were Jack's boys watching her again?

Don't be silly, she told herself. It had to be the little urchin, maybe hanging about to see if she might get lucky with another kipper.

"Fresh fish!" Nora called. "Christmas is coming! Why not celebrate the tree going up with a fat bass for supper?" But her voice sounded flat and worried even to her own ears.

Something moved again. This time, Nora was sure she saw someone quickly darting behind a nearby stack of barrels.

Her skin crawled. She tucked herself nearer to the milliner's door, its gas lamp giving her a feeling of safety.

Two more women stopped by and purchased fish from her as the evening settled. Nora fancied she heard laughter coming from the alleyway. It sounded coarse and masculine, and strangely familiar. As though Jack Ketch himself was watching from the shadows.

She tried to tell herself that she was being ridiculous, but all the same, when the first lamppost on the street approaching the marketplace flickered to life, a rush of relief ran through her. Moments later, Bobby rounded the corner and lit the lamp in the square.

Every time she saw him since the day she'd bought the cart, she heard those words in her again—you too, love.

Nora pushed her cart across the cobbles toward him. The square had grown quiet, most of the shops already closed.

"Evening!" Bobby called on a curl of steam. "Isn't the tree lovely?"

Nora hustled the cart to him and grasped his hand. "I think they're watching."

Bobby's smile vanished. "Come. Let's go. Quickly." He seized the cart.

They hurried toward the street, but Nora heard the laughter all around them and knew it was already too late. The moment they turned onto the quiet side street away from the market square, two boys appeared before them, quick as shadows.

"Get behind me!" Bobby hissed.

Nora tucked herself behind his broad, strong back. Bobby lowered his pole like a lance.

"Get away from us," he ordered. "Now!"

"Oh, Bobby, Bobby, Bobby." Jack Ketch laughed. "Do you really think that's going to work?"

Nora whipped around. Bobby did, too, holding out the pole to defend them. Jack was behind them, a group of boys fanning out around him. His crooked smile curved as cruelly as a sickle.

"We've been watching you, Little Miss Fishmonger," said Jack. "Done well for yourself, haven't you? Gotten a cart and everything. My, my. Perhaps honest work is worth it after all."

The boys laughed as though they'd never heard anything so ludicrous.

"Did you think we'd forgotten about you?" Jack taunted. "Of course not. We've been watching. Waiting. Seems you had a good day today, what with everybody coming to see the Christmas tree go up."

"You stay away from her," Bobby barked.

"Oh, Bobby. I'm not afraid of you. Nobody is," said Jack.

He reached into his pocket and pulled out a knife. It was a simple thing, short and stubby, its cracked handle held together with a bit of string. But the edge shone as viciously as a monster's fang.

The sight made Nora give a little scream. She ducked behind Bobby, her heart hammering.

"You know how this goes," said Jack calmly. "Give us your money, or feel the knife. Simple as that. Ain't no need to make this hard or painful."

"Or you could fight us." One of the boys laughed, a low, deep sound, like a bull snorting. "We like a fight."

The other boys joined in the laughter.

"Bobby," Nora whimpered.

Bobby's eyes flashed. "No. You're right, Nora. We can't let them take everything."

"Bobby, no!"

It was too late. Bobby lunged, swinging his lamplighter's pole. Jack jumped back and another boy lunged at him. Bobby spun around and the pole hit the boy squarely in the ribs, knocking him sprawling on the cobbles.

"Get him!" Jack yelled.

Bobby spun again, the pole swinging with vicious force, and knocked another boy on the head. The group scattered.

"Run, Nora!" Bobby shouted.

She grabbed the cart's handles.

"No! Leave it! Just run!"

"I can't!" Nora cried.

Bobby gave a grunt of pain. One of the boys, the big one with the bull-like laugh, had grabbed hold of the pole. He jerked it from Bobby's grasp and Jack moved in, knife flashing.

"No! No!" Nora screamed. "Take the money. Here! Take it! All of it!"

It was too late. Jack had made up his mind. Bobby threw his hands up to protect his face, and the knife found the soft flesh of his forearm and tore a long red gash in the pale skin.

"No!" Nora shrieked.

Bobby fell to the ground, clutching his arm. Dark blood dripped between his fingers and coursed over the cobblestones.

"Take it!" Nora had pulled two fistfuls of coins from her pocket. "Take it all! Only don't hurt him. Don't hurt him!"

Her scream resounded through the street. Jack gestured fiercely. The other boys stopped, warily watching, as Nora stood over Bobby, holding out the money.

Blood still gleamed on the edge of Jack's knife.

"I think you've learned your lesson now," he hissed. "When we want money, you'll give it to us."

"Don't hurt him," Nora begged, tears pouring hot down her cheeks. "Please."

"Take the money," Jack ordered.

Another boy came forward, hands cupped, and Nora dropped the coins into them as though they were hot enough to burn her fingers.

Somewhere, a policeman's whistle sounded.

"Time's up, lads." Jack touched his cap and gave Nora that awful grin. "Thank you kindly, Little Miss Fishmonger. It's always a pleasure doing business with you."

Then they melted away into the streets like smoke.

Nora fell to her knees. "Bobby! Oh, Bobby, your arm!"

Bobby gritted his teeth with pain. "I'll be all right."

"You need a bandage... a doctor." Nora gripped his good arm. "Can you walk?"

Bobby tried to rise, then sagged to his knees. There was so much blood on the cobblestones.

Nora ripped at the edge of her apron and tore off a strip of linen. She wrapped it swiftly around his arm, her heart thudding as the slick blood slid between her fingers. When she pulled the bandage tight, the ooze slowed.

"I'm all right," said Bobby again.

"I'm so sorry." Nora realized that she was crying. "I should never have let this happen to you. I should have listened… we should have left… I shouldn't… the cart…"

"Nora. Nora, stop."

"This is my fault. This is all my fault!"

"Nora, no!"

Bobby reached up and wrapped his hands around her face, staining her skin with mud and blood. His gentle eyes found and held hers.

"None of this is your fault," he told her. "None of it. You didn't do this. Jack Ketch and the other boys did."

Nora's breath caught in a sob.

"They are bad and evil, not you. You've only ever tried to help us." Bobby grunted and rose to his feet, clutching his arm. "Come, love. Let's go home."

CHAPTER 9

Two days passed in relative normality. Nora had a few coins left, even after the theft; enough that she could buy a few fish and bring them to the square in her cart. She made only a few pennies each day, but it was enough for food and water, and Bobby, his arm in a makeshift sling, still went out to light the lamps every day.

But it all changed on the morning that it snowed. Nora woke to the new chill in the air despite the stove burning low in a corner of their cellar. She drew the curtains to the diminutive window on eye level with the street and saw the sparkle of snowflakes tumbling through the streetlamp's glow.

"It's snowing again, Bobby," she said. "We'll have the most beautiful white Christmas at this rate."

Bobby didn't respond. He lay on his sleeping pallet, wrapped in blankets, unmoving.

Nora slipped the kettle onto the stove and stoked the fire. "Time to wake up. I'll have a cup of tea ready for you, even if it is a little weak." They hadn't had the money to buy more tea this week.

Bobby only let out a sigh.

"Bobby, darling?" Nora's heart gave a painful skip. She hurried to his pallet and crouched beside him, laying a hand on his shoulder. "Wake up!"

He jerked at her touch, and his eyes snapped open, but she knew at once that something was wrong. They were red-rimmed and unnaturally bright in a face the grey colour of window putty.

"Nora," he moaned.

"What's the matter?" she cried.

Bobby let out a long groan, his eyelids fluttering.

"Bobby! What's wrong?"

"Just need a little more sleep," he mumbled. "Not to worry. A little more sleep."

Nora pulled back his blankets. He drew back, shivering, and she saw that he'd put on his coat sometime in the night.

"So cold," he mumbled.

"You're sick." Nora grabbed at his buttons.

"No... please. Too cold."

"Let me see your arm." Nora tugged the coat off.

He cried out when she touched his arm, and she immediately saw why. The night before, she had carefully wrapped it in strips of clean bandage. Now, something yellow and brown soaked through the bandage, streaked with blood. The skin was scarlet and grotesquely swollen. It almost burned her fingers when she touched it.

Bobby gritted his teeth and lay back, agony on his face.

"Oh, Bobby," Nora whispered.

"It's all right," he mumbled. "I'll be all right."

She reached out and laid a hand on his cheek, and his skin blazed against her palm.

Everything inside her froze. The thought of losing him

flashed through her mind, and it felt as though it disembowelled her, leaving her bleeding and empty. She realized like a thunderclap that he was her entire world, that if she lost him, she lost everything.

"Fran!" she cried.

The old woman, as usual, was already at her mending work by the light of a candle stub. She looked up from her needle for a moment.

"He's ill," Nora hissed. "What—what shall we do?"

But the old woman's face remained as hard and cold as stone. "You won't skimp on your rent. Get him back to work."

There would be no help from that quarter, Nora realized. There would be no help from any quarter. She was alone.

"Need to go to work." Bobby tried to sit up, then groaned and sagged against the pallet.

"You're not going anywhere. I'll tell Master Lawrence you're ill. He'll understand." Nora tugged the blankets around him, leaving his arm free.

"Nora... we need the money."

She inhaled, a steadying breath, and the knowledge that he had to help him filled her with strength. "Don't you worry about the money. I'll take care of you. Everything will be all right."

As Nora peeled back the strips of bandage from the oozing wound, her belly somersaulting at the sight of the diseased and suppurating flesh, she prayed that it was true. It had to be true.

Bobby had to get better. He was everything she had.

She had to save him.

All that day, the fever raged.

Nora knew she had to go, to get fish to sell. First, she nipped out for some milk at the market square. When she returned, Bobby was burning up and barely conscious, and she understood that she couldn't leave him.

When the fever raged so that his breathing grew ragged and his limbs twitched with bad dreams, she peeled off his clothes and sponged his thin arms and legs with cool water. Then the chills would come, goosepimpling him all over, and he would shake and shake. Nora wrapped him in blankets then, yet he felt scorching even as he trembled.

Fran said nothing, did nothing. She finished her mending and went off to deliver the clothes to her customers, stepping past Nora and Bobby as though they did not exist. Nora didn't know what suffering had hardened this old woman into the stone shell she had become, but she hated her for it.

She begged him to eat something, but could only persuade him to sip a little milk and tea and to drink a tiny portion of the bone broth she made that evening. Bobby had never not been hungry before. The thought of leaving even a scrap of food on a plate was alien to them both, yet he seemed incapable of persuading himself to do more than take a few sips of something before he drooped on the pallet.

All that day, and all the next night, the fever gripped him. His arm swelled to a caricature of its former self, twice its usual size and as brightly scarlet as the flesh of a trout.

Nora plied him with food and water, but she knew that what he truly needed was medicine. They had a few drops of laudanum left from the time when Nora broke her toe running from some other gang last winter. It did little for him, and when dawn broke, their last food and medicine was all spent, and Bobby shook uncontrollably, his eyes rolling back in his head.

Somewhere, a bell chimed eight. Nora could hardly believe the night had passed except for the leaden exhaustion in her limbs.

She ran a damp cloth over Bobby's face and neck. Her hair accidentally brushed his wounded arm, and he let out a long moan.

"You're not getting any better, Bobby." Nora lowered her hand. "I'm going for the doctor."

"N-no." His head lolled on the blanket she'd rolled up as a makeshift pillow. "No money."

"Don't you worry about the money." Nora looked at her cart standing the corner, the cart of which she'd been so very proud. "I'll find it."

"You'll have to," Fran growled.

"Nora..."

Nora took his good hand and wrapped both of hers around his, seeking his fever-bright eyes. "Nothing matters except for you, Bobby." Her voice cracked. "I owe you everything. Everything. I would never have survived on these streets without you, and I..." The words came with the realization of how true they were. "I love you."

He reached up with trembling fingers. Their tips caressed her cheek, their gentleness breathtaking, before his hand fell onto his chest with a thud and his head lolled back in a dead faint.

There was no time to lose. Nora threw his blankets over him and rushed across the cellar.

She seized her cart and wrestled it up the stairs to the cold outside, where snow covered everything and landed in cold stabs on her hands and face.

Her heart ached as she wheeled it toward the pawnbroker's on the street corner, but she knew she had no choice.

The Christmas tree towered on the square above her. Squinting against the snow, she saw the golden cardboard angel perched at the top, wings and arms outstretched as though to shelter the world. It was so very bright in the still, dark night.

Let him live, Nora prayed silently. Let him live.

THE DOCTOR HAD ASKED Nora to wait outside. Fran, too, had gone out to make her deliveries. Her absence felt like a mercy.

Nora seen the surprise in the doctor's eyes when she came to his house, clutching the precious shillings that the pawnbroker had given her for the cart. They were the last hope she had: she'd tried to pawn the cart, but he hadn't given her enough money for it. If she would sell it, he'd said, he would give her three whole shillings. He had a buyer for it.

Her beautiful cart was already gone. It was a small sorrow compared to the ferocious ache of her worry about Bobby, but it dug into her chest, as insistent as a splinter.

Nora sat on the steps down to the cellar, her head leaning against the mould-streaked wall with little care for its grime. She thought of the milliner in her warm and well-lit shop. If someone in her life was ill, Nora was certain, the milliner would be able to help them at once.

She wouldn't have hesitated the way Nora did. Bobby was so still and pale when she brought the doctor to their tenement. Was it too late?

A tear escaped her eyes. She clenched them shut and

closed her fists, fingernails biting into her palm. It can't be too late. Oh, Bobby… Bobby!

The squeak of the door startled her. She flew to her feet as the doctor emerged: a slight man, stooped, his bowler hat unable to hide his thinning hair.

"D-Dr. Martins," she croaked.

He studied her through a monocle for a second, then removed it, polished it with a handkerchief, and replaced it.

"Please…" Nora whispered.

"It's a very bad wound, Miss… what did you say your name was?"

"Ellis, sir. Nora Ellis."

"It's a very band wound, Miss Ellis. You should have called me the moment it happened. Why, he's laid open nearly to the bone."

Shame drenched her. She hung her head, staring at her feet.

"It was very bad, yes, even before the rot set in. The infection is throughout his body now, not only in his arm."

Nora was shaking. "Is he… will he live?"

"If you had waited another hour, young lady, he would not have lived. Mercifully, you called me in the nick of time. I cannot promise that we can save his arm, but he has responded to the medicine I gave him, and is sleeping comfortably now. I have cleaned and covered it well with carbolic acid. If the acid can stop the infection, then he has a chance of keeping his arm."

Keeping his arm! The thought of losing it was shocking, but there was nothing more shocking than losing him.

"He'll live, then?" she asked.

"He is young and strong. You are lucky. He should live, yes, but I will be back every day to dress the wound," said Dr. Martins sternly.

Nora nodded. "I'll pay, sir. I can pay." She couldn't, not now, but she would find a way.

"Yes, well. Your payment covers tomorrow's visit. After that, I expect a sixpence each time I trek out here to this hovel in this weather, and with the family in town for Christmas, too." Dr. Martins shuddered. "Here, this is laudanum. Give it to him anytime the fever rises. If the bandage loosens, soak a rag in this, carbolic acid, and place it over the wound. It's imperative that the acid keeps on working."

"Yes, sir."

"I'll be back in the morning." Dr. Martins brushed past her and was gone.

CHAPTER 10

Nora didn't mean to fall asleep. She lay half on the floor, half on the pallet beside Bobby, her eyes never leaving his face. The dreadful flush had left his cheeks and the doctor's neat, precise bandages made his arm look almost normal. Even the appalling smell was gone, replaced by something sharply chemical.

He breathed slowly, eyes closed, and somehow those breaths lulled her away into a doze of her own.

A stirring against her cheek woke her. Nora sat up, gasping.

"Nora... I didn't mean to wake you," Bobby whispered.

Nora touched his face and found the skin deliciously cool. "Oh, Bobby! Your fever... it's gone."

"I feel better." Bobby blinked. "The doctor... he was here. He was cleaning my arm. It hurt very much... but then he gave me something that made me sleep."

"That's right, love." The term of endearment came so easily now. "Dr. Martins says that your arm was making you very ill, but you're going to be all right. He made sure of it."

She hadn't believed it until now, but with Bobby's voice so steady and rational and his eyes so clear, relief crashed through her like a wave. A sob escaped her. She raised her hand to her mouth to stifle it, but then more of them came, and she couldn't stop them. The weeping overwhelmed her.

"Oh, Nora, don't cry." Bobby weakly gripped her arm. "Please don't cry."

"I'm sorry," Nora gulped through the tears. "I'm just… it's to hear your dear voice, Bobby. You were so ill, but you'll be all right now. You're better now."

"Hush, darling." Bobby rubbed her arm.

She sank, lowering her head to his chest. She knew it wasn't proper, but then again, none of this was proper; all the same, it felt right to press her ear to his chest and listen to the steady, unrelenting thump of his heart.

A few fresh tears escaped, but her shaking breaths calmed at that steady sound.

"I'm here," he murmured.

"Don't leave," Nora whispered.

"Never. I'm right here."

She gripped his shirt, pressing her face into his chest. She could lose anything, she thought, but not him.

"Nora… where's the cart?"

She raised her head. "Oh! The cart. I sold it."

"Nora—why?"

"I had to. For the doctor. It's all right. I'd do it again, seeing you mending like this."

Bobby's brow furrowed. "You shouldn't have had to."

"There wasn't any other way."

He looked at her, pain and gratitude mingling in his eyes. "You loved that cart."

She hesitated, then gave a small, unsteady laugh. "I did. But I—" Her voice faltered. "I love you more."

The words seemed to hang between them, fragile as a flame.

Bobby reached up with his good hand and touched her face. His fingers were still warm from the fever, but gentle, so gentle.

"Nora," he whispered. "I've wanted to tell you for so long. I've loved you since the night I found you on that doorstep. Since before I even knew what love was."

Her heart pounded so hard she was certain he could hear it.

"I thought I'd lost you," she said. "When the fever was at its worst, I thought—"

"I know." His thumb traced her cheekbone. "I'm here. I'm not going anywhere."

She didn't know which of them moved first. Perhaps they both did. But then his lips were on hers, soft and warm and tasting faintly of the broth she'd fed him, and Nora felt the world fall away.

It was not a long kiss. He was still weak, and she was trembling. But when they drew apart, something had changed between them. The unspoken thing that had hovered in the air for two years had finally been given a name and a shape.

"When I'm well," Bobby said quietly, "I'm going to marry you, Nora Ellis. If you'll have me."

Tears blurred her vision. "I'll have you," she whispered. "I'll have you in a palace or a cellar. I don't care where we are, Bobby, as long as we're together."

He pulled her close, pressing his lips to her forehead. "Together," he murmured. "Always."

She stayed curled against him until his breathing deepened into sleep, his heartbeat steady beneath her ear. The fire crackled low. Somewhere outside, a church bell chimed the hour.

Nora closed her eyes and let herself believe, for this one perfect moment, that everything would be all right.

It was getting late.

Nora moved quickly, her basket bouncing on her shoulders. She had repaired the holes in the bottom, and it worked all right now for the handful of fish she could afford to purchase every morning. The amount was pitiful compared to what she used to bring to the market square in her cart, and she had had to watch as her customers dwindled to a trickle, wandering off to find other fishmongers who had the stock to accommodate them.

Never mind that now. She had sold her few fish, and better yet, she was just in time for the rubbish heap behind the inn.

Candles sparkled in the inn's windows below rows of bunting and paper chains. Even the back door had a modest little wreath, still swaying from the force with which the maid had slammed it.

Nora didn't look at the wreath. Instead, she focused on the rubbish heap. The maid had just dumped out the best of their scraps: great heels of bread, a pot full of bones that still held a little marrow, and... yes! Several carrots that were only slightly wrinkled.

Nora cautiously scooped them into her basket, then swung it onto her back. A few carrots and the bones would have to be enough for tonight's soup. The heels of bread would work with those. She had to keep every penny she'd earned to pay back Dr. Martins; it had been a week, and Bobby was back on his feet, but she still owed him.

She dreaded to think what would happen if Bobby were to fall ill again before she had paid the doctor back in full.

Head down, Nora hurried through the streets. She dodged around the millinery, even though it was a thing of beauty on this cold night, with candles and cards in the windows and its Christmas tree all lit up and aglow with ribbons in the corner. A few children passed her, ribbons in their hair, singing Christmas carols in tune to their skipping.

Even the square beside her tenement building still held its great Christmas tree; someone had added a few more paper chains to its decorations. Nora paused and gazed up at it, her eyes resting on the cardboard angel, which they had to replace regularly as they grew soggy.

She was hungry and cold, but Bobby was alive. For this Christmas, that was enough.

"Bobby!" Nora slipped down the stairs and pushed at their door. "I'm here!"

The door didn't give. With a jolt, Nora realized it was locked.

"Bobby?" She unlocked it with a shaking hand and crashed into the cellar.

It was cold and silent. Bobby was not yet home from lighting lamps, even though every streetlight she'd passed glowed brightly. She'd made him promise not to wait for her and walk her home as she used to do; the sooner he could get inside out of the cold as he convalesced, the better.

"Bobby!" Nora tossed the basket down on the floor and ran up the cellar steps.

Where was he? His route home intersected hers. She should have run into him. What had happened?

She ran onto the market square, snow splashing against her legs, and spun left and right in the shadow of the Christmas tree as she tried to decide which way to go.

"Nora! I'm here, love."

Nora whipped around. Bobby stood across the square from her, the candles from the shop behind him glowing on his hair like a halo.

"Bobby." She ran to him, flung her arms around him. "I was frightened."

"I didn't mean to scare you." Bobby hugged her, though his arms felt weak. "Let's go inside."

"Here, lean on my arm. Where were you?"

"Lighting lamps. I spoke to my master. He gave me a little more ground to cover every day, up in Clerkenwell."

"Clerkenwell! That's a long walk. Why on earth would you go all the way up there?"

"Because it's an extra penny a day, love."

"But isn't that near the prison? The other lamplighters say it's rough up there. All those Fenians making trouble."

Bobby shrugged, though she saw the flicker of worry in his eyes. "A penny's a penny, Nora. We need everyone we can get."

Nora helped him into the cellar and onto their bucket-chair. He exhaled, visibly exhausted, and she helped him out of his coat, still manoeuvring the sleeve carefully over his bandaged arm.

"We're having soup tonight," she said, "with carrots and bread. Fran brought a few loaves."

"And don't think you'll be snubbing me on the soup.

You'll give me my share," Fran growled from her usual corner.

Bobby and Nora both ignored her. What was there to say to that miserly old soul?

"Soup?" Bobby brightened. "My, that sounds lovely."

Nora set the kettle on the stove. "We're out of sugar, I'm afraid, but there's tea."

"Tea is more than enough," said Bobby.

She bustled around, assembling their tin cups, cutting up the wilted carrots and tipping them into a pot with the bones. Somewhere, someone was carolling, a lone voice, someone walking home from work perhaps.

Peace on the earth, goodwill to man

From Heaven's all-gracious king

The world in solemn stillness lay

To hear the angels sing.

Nora smiled as she stirred their watery soup. They would both go to bed a little hungry tonight, and there would be no sweet rolls or oranges this Christmas.

But there would be Bobby. And he was all she needed.

CHAPTER 11

Nora had one tiny little fish left. It was a pathetic thing, a herring no longer than her palm, but the fisherman had sold it to her for half price because of it.

She held it up valiantly now, ignoring the gaggle of boys who lounged on the street corner and laughed at her efforts. Jack Ketch's band had grown bored of her, knowing that they had robbed her of everything. They no longer held as much fear as before, yet their mockery still stung.

"Fish! Have a nice little fish!" she called. "Perfect to fit into a lunch tin! Dinner for one! Only a penny!"

Behind her, someone was singing in the millinery; a Christmas carol. It was still nearly two weeks before Christmas, yet the spirit of the holiday hung thick on the market square, with bunting in every window and a wreath on every door.

Nora had dreamed of buying a wreath to hang on her dear little cart this Christmas.

She forced the memory away and held the fish a little higher. "Get your fish!"

"A penny, you said, miss?"

The voice belonged to the old rag-and-bone man who sometimes frequented this corner. His shoes were badly scuffed, toes poking through broken soles, and he shuffled with painful exhaustion toward her.

"That's right," said Nora.

"I'll take it, thank you kindly."

Nora wrapped it a scrap of discarded newspaper and exchanged it for the small coin. "You look tired, Molesley. Has it been a long day?"

"Awful long, miss. I wasn't far away from the explosion when it happened."

Nora's heart jumped. "Explosion? What explosion?"

"Oh, don't look so frightened, miss. It was quite a bit away from here, don't you worry. Your home will be safe. Seems a group of men tried to break somebody out of the prison. Caused a terrible explosion, took out the wall, destroyed a few homes. They say there are many dead. I heard it, so I did. Terrifying. It shook the ground!"

"You must have been very frightened."

"It was dreadful. Oh, and the screaming. So many people hurt." Molesley shook his head. "Awful thing, that."

Something he'd said caught up with Nora as she was tucking the penny into her pocket. "Did you say it was by the prison?"

"That's right, miss."

"Which one?"

"Why, Clerkenwell Prison, of course."

Clerkenwell. The word dropped into Nora's chest like a bullet. Without making another sound, she turned around and bolted from the market square as fast as her legs could carry her.

It was a long way to run, made even longer by the fact that darkness had fallen, yet none of the streetlights in their area yet shone. With every dark lamp she passed, the terrible fear grew in Nora's chest like a cancer, eating her from the inside out.

It couldn't be. Not after everything they had survived. It couldn't be!

Her legs found strength from somewhere long after her chest began to burn. She was sucking down the breaths of frigid air when she reached the street that held the prison and found chaos and rubble.

Policemen in their black uniforms were everywhere, shouting at people to stay back from the heaps of shattered bricks and broken stone that filled the once-peaceful street. Several tenement houses lay in shambles, their wooden skeletons jutting out, floors exposed like the mangled guts of a slaughtered beast. There was blood on the street, mixing with the dust on the cobblestones, and doctors sifting through the rubble with men helping them, and it felt like a different world. Like a world at war.

"Bobby!" Nora screamed when she had the breath.

A policeman approached her. "Now then, miss..."

"Bobby!" Nora shrieked.

She leaned past the officer, her eyes searching the rubble, and then she saw it.

A knitted hat with a pom-pom on top, lying in the remnants of the wall.

"No. No! BOBBY!" Nora pushed past the policeman and ran to it, hyperventilating in ragged gulps, her chest aching with each breath. She fell to her knees, skinning them, and snatched up the knitted cap.

It was heavy, sodden. It dripped congealing blood.

"No," Nora moaned. "No, no, no..."

One of the workmen was beside her, taking her arm. "Come away, miss."

"No! He's here! He has to be here!" Nora screamed.

"I'm sorry, miss. If that was his hat, he's dead."

"No!" Nora screamed it with such force that the sound burned her throat. "Noooooooooo!" It was a keening, animal cry, coming from a place of agony so intense that she thought the sheer burning of it would kill her.

But it didn't kill her. Even when she pulled away from the workmen and scrabbled through the rubble. Even when her nails tore as she dragged them over broken bricks and shattered wood. Even when her voice vanished from her constant screaming of his name. Even when the workmen seized her again and pulled her away, saying that no one alive was left, that he was gone, and the pain grew so great that it seemed to suffocate her, she stayed alive.

Unlike him. Unlike her dear Bobby, lost forever.

SOMEHOW, Nora was back at the tenement.

She barely knew how she had gotten there. The past few hours were a confused swirl of trying to reach the rubble of that wall, trying to dig through the rubble and keep searching for Bobby. The workmen had been kind at first, taking her by the hand to pull her away, trying to explain with words that didn't seem to reach through the agonized fog in her mind. But when their overseer came and angrily told them to finish clearing away the rubble, they grew cruel.

It was two policemen who eventually drove her away. With no choice but to leave, Nora limped off, and she remembered sitting down in the lee of a doorway as the church bell chimed and chimed away the hours of the night. Hours that Bobby had not lived to see.

She couldn't tell if she then fainted or slept. When she woke, everything felt cold, down to the very core of her being.

Not knowing where else to go, she staggered back to the tenement. Morning came as she was stumbling across Devil's Acre.

She was reeling with exhaustion now as she reached the door and stumbled down the steps into the cellar. At once, she regretted it. Everything in it reminded her of him. The pallet where he'd slept, his cup and bowl on the table, his spare socks drying in front of the fire...

"Where have you been?"

Fran rose from her seat.

"The landlord came," the old woman barked. "Where were you with the rent?"

The rent? Nora laughed at the absurdity. Who could care about the rent?

"What are you laughing at, girl?" Fran barked.

"Rent! How could you worry about the rent?" Nora blared.

"Have you gone quite mad?"

"Maybe I have. Maybe I have! None of this is real! None of this can be real!" Nora's voice cracked, tears spilling over. "Bobby can't be dead!"

"The boy's dead?"

"He's—" Nora's strength abruptly left her. "He's dead."

She sagged onto the steps. "He's dead, Fran."

They stared at one another in silence for a few moments. Fran's lip twitched. It was the first and only emotion Nora ever saw on her face, and in its quiet tremor, she saw suppressed tears.

Then the moment's softness was gone. "Can you pay his share of the rent?"

Nora dropped her head onto her arms, resting over her knees. "No," she whispered. "No, I can't." They had barely been able to afford the rent when it was both of them, except for those few glorious days when she had had her cart.

The silence was frigid.

"Then you'll have to leave," Fran muttered. "The two old folks who live in that falling-down cottage have been begging to share my place for weeks."

Nora raised her head. "What? You're casting me out in a time like this?"

"We all have to live." Fran cleared her throat. "Take your things and go."

Utter numbness washed over Nora. She hardly felt the blow; how could she? It was nothing compared to losing Bobby, to losing her entire world.

She fetched her things as Fran watched, taking Bobby's with her, too. Then she left behind the cellar and the ghost of the boy she still loved.

CHAPTER 12

"Above its sad and lowly plains
"They bend on hovering wing..."

The music dragged Nora from her fitful sleep. She tried to cling to her doze, desperate for the glorious numbness that she found only when she was unconscious, but the many little discomforts conspired against her. The hard pressure of cobblestones on her hip and shoulder, barely cushioned by the pile of newspapers she used a bad; the dampness soaking through the one blanket she had managed to hold onto; the cold wind tugging at her hair, blowing little eddies of snow into her place of shelter.

When she stirred, an agony of cold and stiffness gripped her muscles. Her toes stung, half frozen.

The singing grew louder. Nora desperately wished that it would stop.

She gave up hope of a last few minutes' peace and sat up, shivering as the wind sneaked beneath her blankets. Hunger gnawed her shrinking belly. She wrapped the blankets around her shoulders and stared bleakly into the market square.

The cellar with its coal stove and its warm, dry sleeping pallets, and quiet old roommate was only a memory now. For two long weeks, Nora had survived by selling everything she had left. The basket. Her extra cup and bowl and blanket; she had kept only Bobby's. She had begged and scrounged for the rest, more desperate than she had ever been, and yet it had been two days since her last meal.

She touched the bundle that contained the last few things she owned. Bobby's things.

Grief sunk its claws into her chest and ripped. Nora bowed her head, fighting back the tears that threatened to strangle her.

Oh, Bobby. What was left in the world without him?

Every store on the square was dark and silent. The carollers Nora heard were merely passing by, holding their candles against the cold morning, wrapped in cozy robes. She watched them pass along the street and vanish into the distance.

A church bell chimed half past eight. Why were none of the stores yet open?

Then it struck her: it was Christmas Day.

The memory of that Christmas in the tenement building with white bread and the bright tree burned her chest like someone had thrust a hot poker into her.

"Oh, Bobby." She covered her face with her hands. "Oh, Bobby, Bobby!"

It had been twelve long days since the Clerkenwell explosion that took his life, but the grief still felt as red and raw as an open wound.

She wept for him, but the weeping could not last long. Her body simply had no strength for crying. She sagged onto her newspapers and might have slept again, but the measured tread of an approaching policeman stopped her.

Nora tucked herself against the silent doorway of the closed store she'd used for shelter, but the policeman saw her and loosened his truncheon from his belt.

"Oi!" he barked. "You can't sleep there. Move along!"

"Yes, sir." Nora scrambled to her feet, gathering up her last belongings into a bag: the newspapers, the blanket, and Bobby's hat. The bloodstains hadn't come out no matter how many times she washed it under the pump.

"Move along!" the policeman barked again.

Nora ducked her head and shuffled away, limping on half-frozen feet as she hugged the tattered bundle to her chest.

She missed her cart. She missed her basket. She missed her home.

She missed Bobby. His death had taken not only him, but everything.

Her strength ebbed low. Nora shuffled across the square, wishing that Christmas Day hadn't come. With all the shops closed, there was no one to beg from, no food scraps to scrounge from the rubbish heaps. She could, perhaps, try one or two of the shops that had living quarters above them. Perhaps somebody had potato peelings or bread crusts from last night lying in their rubbish bins.

The nearest shop was the millinery, its wreath on the front door tied with a bright red ribbon. The satin was shiny and beautiful, but the red only served to remind Nora of Papa's tongue protruding between his bloodied teeth, of the dark stain on the rubble where her sweet Bobby had lain. She hadn't laid eyes on her mother's corpse, but her imagination somehow conjured up far worse things than she had already seen.

The world took everything away. Nora opened the

rubbish bin and gazed inside. Bits of fabric greeted her and a few scraps of wastepaper.

No food.

Her knees gave out. She sagged down beside the bin and dropped her head onto her knees, hugging them to her chest.

What was the point of going on?

The creak of the door startled her. She raised her head, worried she would have to flee, but the milliner didn't notice her as she strode from the shop door. The sight startled Nora; she knew the milliner didn't live above her shop, only two seamstresses.

"Ready, my love?" a gentleman called from the corner.

The milliner's eyes were shining as she tucked a velvet pouch into her purse. "Ready. I'm sorry for forgetting."

"You remembered in time. We'll get to church early enough for you to give them your donation." The gentleman offered her his arm, smiling.

"I hope the workhouse uses it well." The milliner took his arm, and off they went.

Nora rubbed at the tears on her cheeks. The milliner's laughter floated across the square to her, and its warmth cupped her heart, lifting it. This woman not only had enough to keep her own shop and feed her own family: she had extra money to give to the needy.

The gentleman's smile hung in Nora's mind. He was so proud of his wife.

It was a wonderful thing to think about, and Nora had come so close.

A flicker of strength woke in her chest. She swung her bag onto her shoulders and struggled to her feet.

Bobby was always so proud of her. If she could grow to

be like the milliner, to be strong, to be secure, and to help, then he would have been even prouder.

Her shaking footsteps gained steadiness as she left the market square and headed north. Westminster's finest houses were not far away.

Bobby's death had taken everything from her, and now she had only one option left. But for the love of his memory, Nora would take it.

Everything about the great townhouse was splendid except for the servants' entrance. It was just like any other, a plain oaken door, designed for insignificant people carrying out essential tasks to come and go in quiet ignominy.

Still, to Nora, it loomed like the drawbridge of a great castle. She had knocked on many such doors today, many including the simple wreath that this one wore. None of these interactions had gone well; her cheek still stung where an angry housekeeper had slapped her for intruding upon their work.

The kitchen beyond clattered with activity. Nora could only hope that this would go better.

She took a deep breath and smoothed the front of her dress. It was wrinkled and dirty, but had not gained many holes in the week she had spent on the street. It would have to do.

Then she raised a hand and knocked.

Nothing happened at first. Nora wondered if this was a sign that she should keep walking and find a cozy ditch to sleep in; it was afternoon, the day nearly spent. But her growing hunger eliminated that possibility. She had eaten nothing yet today.

Christmas Day, with nothing to eat! She tried not to think too hard about how deeply such a thing would grieve her parents' hearts, would hurt dear Bobby, and knocked again.

When the door opened, Nora winced, almost expecting another blow to descend upon her. But it was no housekeeper standing in the doorway. Instead, a girl with a round, red face and tearstained cheeks stared blankly at her.

A glorious smell floated from the kitchen: roast goose, plum pudding, all the rich delicacies of a wealthy Christmas. Nora's mouth watered instantly.

"Who are you?" the girl demanded.

The girl was about Nora's own age and wore a plain blue dress and stained apron, not the starched uniforms of a housemaid.

Nora curtseyed in any case. "Begging your pardon, miss, I'm looking for work."

"Well, there's work aplenty here, if you ask me," the girl muttered.

"Clementine! Clementine! What are you doing?" someone barked. "You're letting in a draft!"

"It's somebody looking for work, Auntie Rachel," the girl called.

"How many times have I told you that you shall call me Mrs. Cratcher when we're at work?" A thin woman, her lips even thinner, pushed into the doorway. She wore an immaculate black dress, matching almost exactly the shade of her eyes.

"But she's looking for work," said Clementine, "and we're shorthanded."

Hope jumped in Nora's chest. She curtseyed again and

enunciated as nicely as she could. "I'm a hard worker, miss. I'll learn anything. I kept my own home; I can cook, clean, read, write, and sew, and..."

"Read and write?" said Mrs. Cratcher sharply. "Why on earth would you learn such a thing?"

Nora didn't know what to say, so she blathered out honesty. "I grew up in the workhouse, ma'am."

"Workhouse." Mrs. Cratcher glanced from Clementine to Nora. "Mmm. All right. We need a scullery-maid. Scarlet fever took Juliet and we need extra hands with all these guests. If you do well, we'll keep you on. You'll start right away."

Nora eagerly nodded. "Yes, ma'am. I can start now, ma'am. This very minute."

"You'll have to. What are you standing about out there for, girl? Get inside!"

Nora shuffled into the kitchen. The door swung shut behind her, enveloping her in the most delicious warmth she had ever experienced. The steamy heat from the stove made her toes defrost for the first time in days.

And the smells! Nora gasped as a footman hurried by, carrying a silver tray ahead of him. It contained the most beautiful gravy boat, finest china and delicately painted, with a hearty, greasy sauce within. Its smell made her aching stomach pang fiercely.

"Come! This way!" Mrs. Cratcher commanded. "You're not here to stand about!"

Nora hurried after her, wondering if she might ask for a bite to eat or when the servants would have tea.

"Get in there." Mrs. Cratcher imperiously pointed.

Nora stepped into a scullery. This place was warm, too, almost uncomfortably hot. Taps brought running water inside, something Nora hadn't seen since the workhouse. Huge metal sinks contained bubbling, frothing soapy water, and a gigantic mountain of dishes waited on the table beside her.

"There hasn't been time for a single one of these dishes all day, and we'll need half of them again for tea," said Mrs. Cratcher.

Nora blinked. It seemed like more dishes than a single person could do in a week, never mind a few hours.

"Well? Are you going to get to work or not?" the housekeeper barked.

Nora ducked. "Yes, ma'am!"

She seized the nearest plate, which still contained a delicate chicken bone, scraps of flesh clinging to it. Her stomach cried out in hunger.

A hard, cold hand descended on her arm. Nora jumped as Mrs. Cratcher's fingers tightened into a shackle-like grip.

"If I catch you doing anything with the scraps other than throwing them into the pig pail," she hissed, "I will have you out of this house before you can think, you miserable little wretch."

Nora swallowed hard. "Yes, ma'am."

"Good." Mrs. Cratcher whisked away, leaving red marks on Nora's arm where her fingers had been.

Nora shivered. Then she turned to work, and long, arduous work it was. None of the fine folks who visited this house ever seemed to finish their food. Halves of oranges, blobs of sauce, nibbled sausages, half-eaten kippers, she tipped them all into the pail for the pigs, even though the sight of each one made her shrinking stomach cramp for food. Then she plunged the plates into the steaming water, which burned both her hands and her eyes, but Mrs.

Cratcher came in periodically to check that it was still hot enough.

Scrape, wash, rinse, dry. The cycle went on, with the murmur of Christmas music playing somewhere above Nora's head. Wreaths and bunting hung even in the kitchen

But here, in this scullery, there was no feeling of Christmas joy.

Christmas for domestic servants, it turned out, only came on the twenty-sixth of December.

It was not a complete day of rest and feasting as it was for the grand folks upstairs, of course. Nora was woken at five o' clock in the morning, having finally gone to bed at midnight, by the irate Mrs. Cratcher, who told her that as the scullery-maid, it was her duty to be up and lighting the kitchen fires and making tea for the servants before anyone else. She had received a cuff on the ear for her tardiness.

The morning passed in a blur of activity. Nora had eaten her fill the night before, though, a jacket potato with a bit of beef and vegetables, a heartier meal than she'd had in many a day. Once she had lit the fires and cleaned the stove and made the tea for the servants, she was allowed a cup herself, with a few biscuits.

The work was miserable, but the food! Nora was grateful with every bite.

The kitchen bustled. Many of the guests from last night's party had stayed, and they ate a sumptuous breakfast. Then the servants had breakfast, too, eggs and kippers and toast, as much as one could eat. Nora had three pieces of toast before Mrs. Cratcher's cold eyes stopped her.

After that, the housekeeper sent up a selection of cold

meats, breads, and cheeses for the family and their guests' luncheon. Nora thought it was rather early for luncheon but said nothing; instead, she busied herself with the breakfast dishes.

Mrs. Cratcher appeared in the scullery doorway as Nora was wading through the last of the dishes. The housekeeper wore a bonnet and a brighter-coloured dress than usual, and she held a small parcel tied with a ribbon under her arm.

"You'll stay here today, Nora," she commanded. "When young Wulfric brings the luncheon dishes down, I expect you to clean them at once."

"Yes, ma'am." Nora curtseyed.

"It might be Boxing Day, but you're new, and a scullery-maid besides. You won't be going off anywhere, is that clear?"

Nora was mystified. "Yes, ma'am."

"Very good. Don't let me hear any stories of misconduct when I get back, now, or it won't go well for you." Mrs. Cratcher swept away.

Nora edged into the kitchen, confused. There was no sign of the bewildering array of servants, from the butler and under-butler to the footmen, valets, lady's maids, housemaids, and kitchen maids. The only person still in the kitchen was the cook, Mrs. Perkins. She was a comfortably padded old lady who sat contentedly in front of the fire with a book and her feet up on a stool.

"Nora, dear," she said, lowering the book. "Mrs. Cratcher wouldn't let you go either, would she?"

Nora smoothed her apron, nervous to ask, but Mrs. Perkins' smile was welcoming. "Where… where is everyone going today, Mrs. Perkins?"

THE ORPHAN'S LOST CHRISTMAS

The cook turned to her. "You haven't been in service before, have you?"

Nora shook her head, but didn't elaborate. She doubted that revealing her past life on the streets would do much to endear her to this civilized world.

"Well, dear, Boxing Day is almost like Christmas Day for us servants. The family makes do with a cold luncheon of leftovers from the Christmas Day feast and allows the servants go off and visit our families for the day. They give out Christmas boxes, too. Did you receive one?"

Nora shook her head again.

"Well, I suppose that's to be expected. You are very new here, after all. There was no time for Mrs. Cratcher to arrange such a thing."

"I'm to stay here," said Nora, "and wash the dishes."

"I'm sorry, lass. Sometimes that's the lot of a scullery-maid. And of a second footman, like Wulfric, who still has to serve the family. Can hardly expect them to pour their own tea, can you?" Mrs. Perkins chortled.

Nora didn't know what to say to that.

"Come, now. Sit." Mrs. Perkins waved her into a stool beside the fire. "I might not have anywhere to go, and you might not be allowed to go, but that doesn't mean we can't have a peaceful day here together, does it, now?"

"Yes, ma'am."

Bobby would have liked Mrs. Perkins. The thought sent a stab of pain through Nora's chest. She huddled closer to the fire, hugging herself.

"Grew up in the workhouse, did you?" Mrs. Perkins asked.

Nora didn't wish to discuss her past and revisit its many sorrows. "Yes, ma'am." She changed the subject. "May I ask you something?"

"Of course, dear."

"You said Wulfric was the second footman. Please, ma'am, what does that mean?"

"Why, it's part of his ranking here in the household, dear. He's second footman, and Charlie is the first footman. Then there's Frank, the under-butler, and Mr. Scrumpton, the butler."

Nora tilted her head. "It's the same for the women, then? Scullery-maid at the bottom, then the kitchen maids, and then?"

"Then the housemaids. Each rank gets paid differently, of course. You're at the very bottom, poor lamb, but you needn't be there always."

Nora brightened. "I needn't?"

"No, no. If you do good work as a scullery-maid, you could become a kitchen-maid. Now I do believe it won't be very long before there's a chance to move up in the world."

Nora listened intently.

"You see, many housemaids don't stay in service terribly long. They marry and go off to have babies."

Marriage and babies. Nora had never dreamed so far, but now Bobby's face flitted through her mind. He had said that he loved her, and she knew that she had loved him. Was that the future they might have had? If he had only lived, she knew it was. She knew that they would have found a way, somehow, to become Mr. and Mrs. Tibbett, and that one day she would have cradled Bobby's child in her arms...

All that was gone now. His death had torn away even the dreams she had not dared to have until now.

"When they do, there's room for promotion." Mrs. Perkins reached over and patted her hand. "You see, dear, if you work hard and you put your best foot forward, then good things can happen for you."

Nora knew that. She'd seen it before with her fishmongering business. She thought of the milliner, of her husband's pride, of her bright shop with its beautiful contents, and the hope in her heart flickered. It was burning as low as a forgotten Christmas candle, but compared with the utter darkness that had filled her before, it was as bright as the Star of Bethlehem.

PART III

CHAPTER 13

*1*868

Nora bent over the chopping board, her hand absolutely steady on the sharp knife. She held the cucumber carefully with one hand and slid the blade down its length with the other. The slice she carved off the vegetable was so delicate that she could see the blade through it. She lifted it into place, then cut another, and another.

"My, my, Nora." Mrs. Perkins was whipping together the sauce for the cucumber sandwiches. "Now those are some very fine cucumber slices!"

Across the table, Clementine was slicing the crusts off the bread and setting them aside to make pudding later. The girl's glared at Nora from a sweaty face.

Nora ignored her and continued slicing the peeled cucumber.

"Look at these." Mrs. Perkins lifted a slice and admired it in the bright gas lighting. "Absolutely perfect. If there were a prize for good cucumber sandwiches, why, my dear, we'd be winning it."

"I've done the bread, Mrs. Perkins," said Clementine

loudly. "You can put the sandwiches together when Nora finally finishes with the cucumber."

Mrs. Perkins glanced at the slices. "Mm, very good, Clementine. Try not to let the edges get so squashed next time."

Clementine scowled.

Mrs. Perkins chuckled as she placed the slices one by one on the neat bread squares. "It's work like this that gets you from scullery-maid to kitchen-maid in just a year, Nora. Why, you'll be a housemaid before you know it. Maybe even a lady's maid!"

Nora grinned. "Thank you, Mrs. Perkins."

"How old are you now, dear?"

"Sixteen, ma'am."

"That's young enough. Fifteen was quite an age to have started as a scullery-maid, but you've learned well. If you keep working like this, you'll do very well for yourself. Why, I won't be surprised to see you running a household one day."

Clementine gasped. "Oh, Mrs. Perkins, surely you can't mean that she could be a housekeeper, do you?"

"Of course I do, dear. You could, too, you know, if you would apply yourself. Why, you have your aunt to help you with that."

Clementine's scowl only deepened. "I don't need Auntie to help me in the world."

Mrs. Perkins gave an indulgent smile. "Of course not."

Nora arranged the finished sandwiches on a silver tray, her heart thumping. When Clementine went to the scullery to fetch the other serving dishes, she quietly moved nearer to Mrs. Perkins.

"Do you mean it?" she asked softly.

Mrs. Perkins smiled. "That you could be a housekeeper?"

"Yes, ma'am."

"Why, of course I do. It will take years, dear. That sort of thing doesn't come overnight. But if you keep on working like this..." Mrs. Perkins proudly eyed the sandwiches on their silver tray. "Why, nothing is impossible. Whatever position you find yourself in, keep on trying. If you can get to work upstairs, as a parlour-maid or a lady's maid, then you will be in a very good place indeed."

Mrs. Perkins hesitated, then lowered her voice. "Though I will say this, dear. If you do rise to work upstairs, you must be careful."

"Careful, Mrs. Perkins?"

The cook glanced toward the scullery, where Clementine was clattering dishes. "There are dangers upstairs that don't exist down here," she said quietly. "Not all gentlemen are gentle, if you take my meaning. Keep your wits about you, and never let yourself be caught alone with the master."

Nora frowned. "Lord Wainscoate?"

"I've said too much." Mrs. Perkins turned back to her work. "Just remember what I told you, dear. That's all."

Clementine returned, the stack of dishes in her hands. "What were you saying, Mrs. Perkins?"

"Only that applying oneself is always a good recipe for improving one's position, dear."

Nora turned her attention to her next task, fetching the shortbread from the oven for the family's morning tea.

It had been a long time since she had allowed herself to think of her old life. Mrs. Perkins' words conjured an image that felt familiar. She flinched away from the memories of the tenement and the life she'd had within it, and thought instead of the market square and the millinery.

A warm, bright place to live, with good clothes and the opportunity to improve the lives around her. That was what the milliner had stood for.

Nora smiled. Mrs. Ellis, the housekeeper.

It had a nice ring to it.

Bobby would have been proud.

Nora sat by the kitchen table, the family's silverware arranged neatly before her in orderly rows. The forks were her focus today, and she knew each one intimately: fish, salad, oyster, dessert, seafood, ice cream, cheese, cocktail, cake, every fork had its unique shape and tines and uses. They had one thing in common: their silver had to be utterly sparkling. Even the faintest hint of tarnish was a shameful thing in a household like that of the Lord and Lady Wainscoate.

She worked the polish over the silver with a soft rag, brightening every inch of the dinner fork in her hand. If she couldn't use it as a mirror, she did not consider it polished.

Giggles from upstairs preceded the arrival of the two housemaids. Sadie and Esther were sisters, twins, in fact, who had grown up in this household, coming up together from the scullery to the privileges of lighting fires, sweeping floors, and washing windows upstairs.

"You're absolutely right, Esther. It's the best time of the year!" Sadie reached the kitchen first, carrying a heavy wooden box.

"The most wonderful of all. Why, this day is almost as

marvellous as Christmas or Boxing Day itself," Esther agreed, bringing a box of her own downstairs.

Christmas. Boxing Day. Nora's stomach clenched. How could it be that the year had passed so swiftly?

Her thoughts flew to the Christmas tree on the pantomime stage, and at once she smelled blood and smoke.

"What could be better than Boxing Day?" said Clementine irritably. She sat across from Nora, polishing the spoons, though she had arranged them in the wrong order and jumbled up the salt and caviar spoons.

"Why, this day, of course." Sadie pried the lid off the box and reached inside, bringing out a fistful of bunting. "Two weeks before Christmas."

"We're decorating the house today," said Esther eagerly. "Or, at least, we're starting to make decorations, the things we can't reuse."

"The family has so many pretty things. Why, look at these baubles for the tree. The footmen are bringing it inside as we speak." Sadie lifted a pair of striking glass orbs from the box. They were beautifully coloured, each one holding the figurine of an angel inside. "Show them the tinsel, Esther!"

Esther drew a string of the flashing metallic ribbons from the box, gold and silver. "Isn't it just lovely, Nora?"

Nora returned her attention to the fork in her hand and said nothing. She didn't want to think about Christmas and all of its beauties. Each one was an equal agony for her.

The thought of a Christmas tree made her heart feel leaden, as though someone had replaced it with a ball of lead. She plucked her thoughts away from the Christmas tree at the pantomime. Instead, she turned them to the tree in the market square that first year with Bobby, the one with the bright angel at the very top. She could taste that soft white roll and hear the low rumble of his laughter as they sat in the abandoned tenement, watching the snow fall. It was far less extravagant than the pantomime, and pitiful compared to all the grandeur that would soon deck out the Wainscoate house, and yet it was the most wonderful Christmas she could remember. Her ankle had been so sore and she had been so hungry. But the light in Bobby's eyes had been brighter than the Christmas candles of an entire city.

"What about you, Nora?" said Esther.

She blinked, realizing that the other maids had been talking to her. "I beg your pardon?"

"What's your favourite Christmas decoration? The wreaths or the tree?" Sadie held up a string of red ribbon in one hand and a fistful of tinsel in the other.

Nora looked away. "Anything but the tree."

"What do you mean?" asked Sadie.

Nora gritted her teeth.

"All right, now, girls," said Mrs. Perkins evenly. "Not everyone wants to talk about Christmas."

"But why on earth not?" Esther protested.

"It is the best time of year," said Clementine. "The food is always better than anything else! It's a lot of work, though."

"Is that why you don't like Christmas, Nora?" asked Sadie. "Because of the work?"

Tears stung the corners of Nora's eyes.

"Now, now, girls, leave her be," said Mrs. Perkins. "You two have your mama and papa working right here in the same house and you've always been together. There's folks who don't get to celebrate Christmas with the people they love." She touched the wedding band on her finger. "Folks for whom Christmas is full of memories that once used to be happy, but loss has made them sad."

"Did you lose someone?" Sadie sat beside her. "You can tell us about them. Mama always says that talking makes anything a little lighter to carry."

Nora shook her head.

"Leave her be, I said," said Mrs. Perkins.

Sadie and Esther took their Christmas cheer to the other end of the table.

They were sweet enough girls, but Nora had learned her lesson. She had allowed herself to know love before.

And it had always cost her too dearly.

CHAPTER 14

The kitchen was a clatter of activity. Garlands hung from the rafters and a wreath on the door, but all of them had wilted in the frantic heat within.

"They're ready for the soup, Mrs. Perkins," Wulfric shouted, clattering down the stairs.

"By jiminy! They're not half in a hurry this evening, and it's still a full week before Christmas." Mrs. Perkins was sweating into her bonnet as she ladled the clear gravy soup into its tureen. "Go on, then, boy. Don't keep them waiting."

The two footmen seized the necessities for the soup and hurried up the stairs.

Nora kept her attention on the pastry she was rolling out. She'd spent all afternoon on that pastry, kneading and laminating it, blending butter into the dough, then rolling it out and folding and rolling and folding until it formed the perfectly elastic and golden dough that she now thinned out on the kitchen table. She cut it into even strips with a swift, practiced hand.

Something jostled her, and her hand slipped, slicing a jagged edge into one of the pastry strips.

"Oh, I'm sorry, Nora," said Clementine sweetly, brushing past her with a jar of red currant jelly in her hands. "I didn't see you there."

Nora glared at her. Across the room, Mrs. Cratcher caught Clementine's eye and nodded.

It was a good thing Nora was ready for these silly tricks. She rolled up the ruined piece of pastry and set it aside to use later; she already had enough strips at the ready for this evening's croquet of fowl.

"Nora!" Mrs. Perkins shouted. "I need that pastry!"

"Ready for you, ma'am." Nora straightened. "And here's the filling, too."

Mrs. Perkins tasted the blend of mustard, cold chicken, and white pepper that Nora had made earlier. "It'll want mustard. You girls never put enough..." She blinked. "My, that's well balanced. Good job, Nora."

Nora smiled, though she could almost hear the dismay rising from Clementine like steam.

"Now do hurry up," said Mrs. Perkins, scooping the filling onto the pastry and rolling each one. "They'll want the eels next. Put the finishing touches on, Nora. And where are you with the beginning of that blancmange, Clementine?"

The feverish bustle continued. It was the first of many dinner parties that the Wainscoates would host this Christmas season, and Nora knew that work in the kitchen would only grow more intense. Still, she took every step cautiously, staying focused as she added garnishes to the stewed eels before sending the heavy dish upstairs with the footmen.

She was at work on the last touches for the desserts,

whipping a pot of raspberry jam into a hearty bowl of cream, when a sudden hush fell upon the kitchen.

Nora looked up. Mr. Scrumpton, the butler, stood at the head of the kitchen table in all his liveried glory, his starched collar tight against the majestic diameter of his neck. He was a great, leonine man, even though his thinning golden mane was streaked with grey, with a magnificent brow and steady blue eyes.

Mr. Scrumpton had no need to say anything at all. The kitchen fell immediately silent in his presence. He hardly ever entered Mrs. Perkins' domain, marshalling his troops from the servants' hall instead.

Mrs. Perkins looked up from the pastries she was preparing. "M–Mr. Scrumpton," she managed. "Whatever is it?"

Mrs. Cratcher appeared beside him. "Is something the matter?"

"The guests," Mr. Scrumpton announced with tremendous gravity, "have requested me to pass on a message to the cook."

Mrs. Perkins clutched a hand to her heart, and a nasty sensation rolled in Nora's stomach, sending a sickly wave over her. A complaint from the guests would be nothing short of a disaster in a house as prestigious as this.

"They said," Mr. Scrumpton continued, "that the croquet of fowl was the best they had ever tasted, and wished me to pass along their heartiest compliments to the cook on the delicious lightness of the pastry in particular."

Relief swamped the kitchen. Nora laughed aloud; even Clementine was grinning. Mrs. Cratcher raised her chin, pride shining in her eyes.

"Well, well!" Mrs. Perkins burst out. "I thought them fancy folks barely knew that a real person made their food at all. Seems sometimes they think it all just shows up on their plates by magic!"

"It is a wonderful thing, indeed, to receive compliments from the guests," said Mr. Scrumpton, moved almost to smiling. "I wish to congratulate you most thoroughly on bringing honour to this house and to the family."

"Why, Mr. Scrumpton, that cheers me no end, that does." Mrs. Perkins chuckled. "But I can't take the credit for them pastries. It was Nora who laminated the dough. She did a wonderful job, sure enough."

A flush of pleasure warmed Nora's cheeks. "Thank you, Mrs. Perkins."

Mrs. Cratcher's smile had vanished. "Enough of this. We still have dessert to prepare. Get to work!"

"Aye, aye, you're not wrong, Mrs. Cratcher. Let's not rest on our laurels, girls!" Mrs. Perkins agreed.

Nora ducked her head and resumed her whisking. Mrs. Perkins came past and rested a hand on her arm, eyes sparkling.

"What did I tell you?" she said. "You'll be a housekeeper someday yet, you'll see."

Nora smiled. Despite the painful memories hanging with every wreath and candle in the kitchen, she returned to her work with more vigour than before.

She had nearly brought the whipped jam and cream to the perfect stiff pink peaks when something jostled her arm. Nora gasped and snatched at the bowl, narrowly keeping it from falling. The whisk tumbled from her grasp and clattered on the floor, spraying pink cream in all directions.

"Nora!" Mrs. Perkins barked. "This is no time to be playing around, girl!"

Nora looked up into the eyes of Clementine, the one

who had pushed her, and the fury in them told her clearly that it had been no accident.

Clementine hurried away.

Nora picked up the whisk. "It won't happen again, Mrs. Perkins." Yet she was not certain that her words were true.

The Wainscoate glasshouse was a matter of pride for both the family and the servants. Nora could hardly imagine what it had cost to build the elaborate structure with its slanting roofs and the boiler system that brought heat to the interior, let alone the price of the glass taxes that Lord Wainscoate would owe.

She was glad of it, however, and not only because fresh vegetables were available to the cooks both in and out of season. Picking vegetables was one of her favourite tasks in the dead of winter. As snowflakes tumbled on the other side of the glass, fogging it with their frigid cold, Nora worked in her dress and a light sweater. Her heavy overcoat, hat, and mittens hung on a nearby fence as she lifted fat orange carrots from the earth and added them to the basket on her arm. These would serve as the perfect accompaniments for tonight's roast peacock with stuffing, another elaborate dinner for a new set of guests.

Nora hummed to herself as she pulled up a last carrot and set her basket aside. She was donning her coat when she realized that the tune she was humming was a painfully familiar one: "It Came Upon a Midnight Clear."

The memories that came with that melody crushed her chest like a savage grasp. Nora abruptly stopped humming. She pulled on her hat, tucked the basket close to her, and hurried across the glasshouse toward the door. Here, ornamental plants grew in beautiful profusion, and Nora followed a path of paving stones between flowering bushes and exotic trees she couldn't begin to name, the pride of the Wainscoate gardens.

She was halfway to the door when she heard a masculine voice and froze.

The tone was clipped, educated. Nora slipped behind a palm tree and peered out with a hammering heart.

She had seldom seen Lord Wainscoate in the flesh except from a distance, but she recognized him, if only from the elegant cut of his brocade coat and the tall, proud bearing of his shoulders. He was a tall, thin man with beautifully trimmed and styled whiskers that ended in a sharp grey angle at his jaw. Gold-rimmed spectacles perched on his aquiline nose, framing bright green eyes.

A gentleman walked beside him, portly and straining the buttons of his own waistcoat; one of the guests.

"My dear Wainscoate, this is indeed a splendid collection," said the other gentleman. "It must be the envy of every house in Westminster."

"Now, now, Lord Bartleby," said Lord Wainscoate, smiling. "Not every house, of course."

They both laughed.

Nora held her breath, retreating farther behind the palm tree. As a lowly kitchen maid, she was not meant to be seen by the family at all, much less by the guests. In her turmoil about the song that had come so easily to mind, she hadn't noticed that his lordship and the other gentleman were touring the ornamental side of the glasshouse until it was too late.

Perhaps she could return the way she'd come. But no, the two gentlemen were nearer now. Her best hope was to remain still behind this palm tree and pray that they wouldn't see her.

If they did, her hopes of becoming a housemaid or even lady's maid in this house would be instantly dashed.

The gentlemen strolled nearer, chatting idly. Nora pressed herself against the rough bark and stay as quiet as she possibly could.

It was not quiet enough. Her dress rustled as she tried to move around the tree, avoiding the men, and Lord Wainscoate looked up sharply.

Nora's heart froze.

His pale green eyes, green as jade, found hers, and narrowed.

No, no, no! Dread soaked Nora's flesh. Would she merely be punished? Would she face dismissal?

"My dear Bartleby," said Lord Wainscoate, stopping suddenly, "would you proceed to the house without my company? I must address the gardener about that bougainvillea; it certainly needs more attention."

"Of course," said the other gentleman.

"Thank you. I will meet you in the drawing room for chocolate."

"Excellent." Lord Bartleby withdrew.

Nora knew that it wasn't the gardener Lord Wainscoate wished to address. He likely wanted to spare himself the embarrassment of his friend seeing a mere kitchen maid in this ornamental garden. He waited until the other gentleman had left, the glass door in its iron frame crashing shut behind him, before turning to the palm tree.

"You can come out now," his lordship said. "I know you're there."

Nora bowed her head, dismay flooding her.

"There's no use hiding," said Lord Wainscoate.

Nora squared her shoulders and gathered her strength. Even though her senses told her to flee, she knew that would be disrespectful, and therefore, dangerously foolish. Clutching the basket of carrots before her, she stepped out from behind the palm tree and lowered herself into the deepest curtsey of her life.

"I'm so terribly sorry, milord," she began at once. "I didn't see that your lordship was in the glasshouse or I would never have disturbed you. I understand my trespass, and..."

"Now, now, there's no need for all that," said Lord Wainscoate. "I know it was only an honest mistake; I can see that you were here performing your usual duties."

Nora dared not look up at him. "It was careless of me, milord, and I'm terribly sorry."

"Luckily I saw you before my guest did; he was sent away and there is no need for shame. Raise your head, now. It's all right. Stand up."

The unexpected steadiness in his tone eased Nora's racing heart. She stood and raised her head, risking at last a glance at the gentleman's face.

Lord Wainscoate's eyes rose quickly to meet hers. They were intense, his shoulders leaning toward her, and startled her for a moment. Then a kindly smile flooded his features, and he reached over to pat her shoulder.

"There, there. You're quite all right," he said.

"Please, sir, don't dismiss me," Nora blurted out. "I know I must be punished, but give me a chance. I'll keep working hard, sir. I'm good in the kitchen, sir."

"I'm not going to dismiss you. There's no need to worry. As I said, it was only an honest mistake." Lord Wainscoate smiled broadly.

The relief made Nora's knees feel weak. She clutched at

the tree for support. "Oh, thank you, sir. Thank you ever so much. No servant could hope for a kinder master, sir."

Lord Wainscoate's eyes sparkled. "It is a pleasure to be kind to one so hardworking and subservient. Tell me, girl, what is your name?"

"Nora Ellis, sir. I'm a kitchen maid."

"That's quite clear from your attire."

Nora brushed at the soil on her striped gingham dress, her thoughts working fast. His lordship seemed in no hurry to leave. Perhaps this was her chance to endear herself to him; while Mr. Scrumpton and Mrs. Cratcher made all the usual decisions around the running of the household, there was no denying that Lord Wainscoate himself was the ultimate authority in the house. If he remembered her now, he might recognize her later when she had reached the rank of housemaid, and perhaps that might work in her favour.

"Thank you very kindly, Lord Wainscoate," she said. "It's a great pleasure and an honour to work in a house as prestigious as yours. Why, it's my pride and joy to know that I serve a family so noble, and with a master so gracious, too."

Lord Wainscoate straightened, visibly preening. His eyes dipped up and down, taking in every inch of Nora. "Very good, very good. You work only in the kitchens, do you, Nora?"

The use of her first name was an unexpected familiarity. Nora curtseyed, hoping it was a good sign. "Yes, sir."

"Ah. A pity."

Nora cleared her throat. "If you'll pardon me, sir, I must start preparing these for your dinner."

"Of course... of course," said Lord Wainscoate.

He did not quite dismiss her, merely stood there looking at her, so Nora backed away and curtseyed a few more times to be sure she was not being rude. As she left the glasshouse and hurried across the frigid garden to the house, she found herself smiling.

Clementine could do whatever she liked. Nora knew now that she had Lord Wainscoate's approval, and that mattered more than Mrs. Cratcher and her niece's hatred.

CHAPTER 15

Nora hurried across the steaming chaos of the kitchen, carrying a bowl of finely chopped carrots, celery, and onion. "Here you are, Mrs. Perkins."

The portly woman sweated over a saucepan on the stove. "Land's sakes, are you ready with those already?"

"Yes, ma'am."

"Good heavens, child, you waste no time. Hurry and sauté those for me. In fact, you can make the aspic," said Mrs. Perkins decidedly. "I don't have the time. The collared eel is waiting for my attention. Why this family insists on filling the week before Christmas with half a dozen different dinners instead of just the one, nobody knows!"

"E-excuse me, Mrs. Perkins?" Nora blinked. "You'd like me to make the sauce?"

"Am I mumbling, girl? I need the extra hands. You've seen me make this aspic a thousand times. The gelatine's already dissolved in here with the stock broth and the herbs. Put those things in and get it to a simmer. Then..."

"Then the egg whites," said Nora, "and then I pour it through a flannel until it turns bright."

Mrs. Perkins beamed. "Go on, then."

Nora stepped up to the stove and added the vegetables to the heating saucepan. She stirred briskly, keeping it on the side nearest the firebox, where the cast-iron range was the hottest.

"What about me, Mrs. Perkins?" Clementine asked.

"What about you?" Mrs. Perkins demanded bluntly, adding spices and vinegar to the rolled and breaded eel in another pan.

"What do you want me to do?" said Clementine.

"What do you think, girl? Keep slicing those onions. We need them for the fowl. What a question!"

Clementine scowled from the kitchen table, but Nora ignored her. She was too busy bringing her sauce to the boil, feeling the texture with her wooden spoon; watery for now. The gelatine would need to simmer for twenty minutes before it took any real shape.

Small bubbles appeared in the sauce. Nora waited until it reached a steady simmer before she moved the saucepan to the cooler side of the stove to keep it from boiling. She glanced at the clock, noted the time, and left the sauce to simmer as she hurried back to the kitchen table to work on the dough for the julienned fowl. It had lain out for half an hour and was now ready to roll and pierce into small pieces for the final baking.

She concentrated, working the dough into the perfect texture, pausing only to glance at the clock from time to time and ensure she didn't boil the aspic for too long. Clementine and Mrs. Perkins bustled around her, silent and focused on their tasks.

Only ten minutes had passed when the sudden reek of something burning reached Nora, a heavy, bitter smell.

She spun around to see what it was and her heart

dropped into her boots. Her saucepan stood on the heavy end of the stove, directly above the firebox, and plumes of steam rose from it as it boiled violently.

"Gracious!" Mrs. Perkins cried as Nora raced across the kitchen, almost knocking her over.

"The aspic!" Nora pulled the saucepan from the heat at once and seized a spoon, stirring fast to keep the bottom from burning.

"What on earth possessed you to boil the sauce so hard, girl?" Mrs. Perkins demanded.

Panic sizzled through Nora. This aspic required time to set in its moulds before it could be sent up to the table. Remaking it wouldn't allow enough time, and to send up wobbly aspic, well, it was unthinkable.

"Answer me!" snapped Mrs. Perkins.

"I didn't, Mrs. Perkins. I had it on the other side, the cooler side." Nora met the cook's eyes. "I swear that I didn't."

Mrs. Perkins' lips tightened. They both glanced toward Clementine, who chopped vegetables with stiff, angry movements.

"See if you can save it, girl," Mrs. Perkins hissed, "and thank your lucky stars that Mrs. Cratcher or Mr. Scrumpton weren't here to see this disaster. You'll have to be more careful."

Nora nodded, trying to stifle the terror rising through her. If she couldn't save this aspic, what would they do?

There was no time to worry about it now. She had to concentrate. Nora seized a clean spoon and tasted the aspic. It was creamy, thick with lobster flavour, but not perfect: a tiny bitterness laced it. From the near burning, she was sure.

Her heart pounded. Nora reached for the sugar pot and

added a pinch. Tasting after each one, she continued to add to the pot until the aspic's flavour returned to its former delicacy.

Mrs. Perkins rushed past, sweating. "Well?"

Nora held out another clean spoon. "See what you think."

The cook tasted quickly, and her eyebrows rose. A grin spread over her features. She slapped Nora on the back. "Look at you! Good girl. Good girl! Go on with it. It's perfect."

Relief flooded Nora as she set the aspic aside to settle and started on the chopped truffles for the julienned fowl. This time, she made sure to stay near the saucepan, never taking her eyes off it.

She would not easily be turning her back in this kitchen again. That knowledge seethed in her, quietly building pressure, reminding her that whenever she began to succeed, there would be those who wished to stop her. People like Jack Ketch.

Like Clementine.

The anger built in Nora's chest all day, but she managed to keep it quiet until that evening, when they sent up the last dishes, the Venetian jelly, Imperial tartlets, and Albert cream.

As the footmen disappeared upstairs with the silver dishes, Nora tugged off her apron, flung it aside, and rounded on Clementine.

"What on earth do you think you're playing at?" she barked.

Clementine froze halfway to the scullery, her arms full of crockery.

"Nora..." Mrs. Perkins warned.

"I know what you did!" Nora shouted. "Burning my aspic, and you tried it again with the tartlets just now! What do you think you're doing?"

"I don't know what you're talking about." Clementine sniffed.

Nora's rage surged through her body. This spoiled girl might be a world away from the monstrous boy who'd sliced Bobby's arm, but they were all the same, just the same, to her mind. They wanted only to bring down those who had finally succeeded in raising themselves up in this brutal world.

She slammed her hand against Clementine's shoulder and pushed. The maid stumbled back a step with a gasp of horrified indignation.

"Nora!" Mrs. Perkins jumped up from her chair.

Clementine dumped the dishes on the table. "Don't touch me!"

"Then leave my cooking alone!" Nora shoved her again.

Clementine gave an incoherent howl of fury and charged Nora. She pushed her, sending Nora reeling back several paces.

"Enough!" Mrs. Perkins burst in between them. "Enough! Stop this right this very instant, or I swear, Clementine, I'll have you thrown from my kitchen!"

Clementine gasped. "Me? I'm not the one who started this!"

"You are indeed, you stupid girl. Don't you think I know Nora is cleverer than to overboil a sauce? I know what you're doing, and I shan't allow it."

"My aunt will hear about this!"

"I've no doubt she will, but I am the cook," Mrs. Perkins raged. "This might be Mrs. Cratcher's house, but it's my kitchen. And what's more, Mr. Scrumpton knows that."

Clementine swallowed hard.

"Now stop this, both of you," Mrs. Perkins commanded. "You're both bringing dishonour on this house."

"Yes, ma'am." Nora's anger had drained away, leaving her exhausted. "I'm sorry. I shouldn't have pushed you, Clementine."

Clementine's eyes were narrow, dangerous. "No. You shouldn't have."

Mrs. Cratcher clattered into the kitchen from upstairs. "What on earth is going on in here? It sounds like a bunch of fighting cats, not the maids in an honoured household!"

"A little disagreement between my kitchen maids, Mrs. Cratcher," said Mrs. Perkins sharply, "rooting from a bit of misbehaviour on Clementine's part, but nothing that we can't sort out. It's all over now, isn't it, girls?"

"Yes, ma'am," said Nora.

"Misbehaviour?" Clementine hissed. "Me? I'm not the one who misbehaves." She jabbed a finger at Nora. "Ask her about misbehaviour!"

"Clementine, I said that I was sorry, and I mean it."

"Ha! I don't trust a word you say, you hussy. We all know that you lived with a man before you came to this house!"

"Clementine!" Mrs. Perkins gasped. "What a terrible thing to say. Why, spreading vicious lies like this is a disgusting thing to do!"

But Nora froze, feeling drenched with ice cold.

"Nora did no such thing," said Mrs. Perkins. "Did you, Nora?"

Nora hesitated. She looked into the cook's kindly eyes

and longed not to lie to her. Not to Mrs. Perkins, the only person except for Bobby who had ever constantly been in her corner.

Besides, if she lied, she would make it as though Bobby had never existed. Was there any greater injustice she could do him?

Mrs. Perkins' eyes widened. "Nora, say something."

"Is this true?" Mrs. Cratcher demanded.

Nora had no choice. They wouldn't count old Fran as a chaperone, not truly. She was no parent or grandmother—only an old woman who had shared their tenement and proven, in the end, to care nothing at all for either of them.

Clementine's grin held nothing but savagery.

"Nora!" Mrs. Perkins cried, her voice thick with disappointment.

"No," said Nora sharply. "I never did live with a man." She felt as though she herself had killed Bobby in that sentence.

Mrs. Cratcher's lips flattened into a thin line.

"You all know Clementine only wants to gossip. It's all a story," said Nora, "and it's not true."

"It is true!" Clementine raged. "I've heard her whispering his name in her sleep when she has nightmares. 'Oh, Bobby, Bobby,' she says."

"I never lived with him! He was only a boy I was sweet on," Nora snapped, and that word, only, felt like betrayal. "I saw him on the streets, but I hardly even knew him."

The lie felt a thousand times more wrong than living with Bobby ever had.

Mrs. Perkins turned away with a sob, and Nora knew at once that the old cook knew she was lying and suspected the worst.

"She lived with a man. She's lying," said Clementine.

"She's a shame upon this household, no better than a common—"

"Clementine, enough," Mrs. Perkins barked in a broken voice.

Nora's heart shattered.

Mrs. Cratcher raised her chin. "Finish your work. Both of you. As for you, Nora, well, count yourself lucky that we cannot prove this story one way or the other. But you should know that stories like these often have roots. And if they spread..." A vicious, victorious gleam came into Mrs. Cratcher's eye. "Well, then they are very bad for a girl's future."

"Mrs. Cratcher..." Nora began.

The housekeeper gave her a glare that silenced her instantly.

"Get back to work," said Mrs. Perkins. "Both of you." She sank into her chair by the fire, chin on her chest, shoulders trembling.

Nora picked up her apron and went to gather more dishes, struggling to hold back her tears. The milliner with her proud husband and her cozy business had never felt so distant.

CHAPTER 16

Nora had never minded peeling potatoes before, yet that next morning, three days before Christmas, the task seemed as monumental as it was pointless. She sat at the kitchen table, stripping off the peels into the slop bucket, then dropping the potatoes into a basin of water to soak out their starch. They would become fondant potatoes tonight, buttery and melting. Nora knew exactly how to make them, but what did it matter now? She would never be a parlour-maid, much less a cook. Her dreams of becoming a housekeeper were shot.

Wulfric, the second footman, strode into the kitchen. "Lady Wainscoate requests tea."

"Clementine, make it," said Mrs. Perkins, not looking up from the fish she was skilfully filleting.

It was the first time the cook had spoken in hours, and she didn't look at Nora. She hadn't even said her name in the past two days since Clementine had started spreading those stories.

Everyone knew by now that Nora was dirty, degraded. Even Wulfric looked at her with a disgusted twist to his mouth as he stood by, waiting for the tea. Nor did anyone sit beside her in the servants' hall at mealtime.

She was nothing and no one, and they all made sure she knew it. No matter how much she protested that Clementine was lying, and no matter how impossible it was for them to prove the story either way, it seemed they had already judged Nora.

Measured footsteps on the stairs announced the arrival of Mr. Scrumpton. Lines of tension surrounded his eyes. "His lordship requests a presentation of all the servants to the grand hall at once."

"All the servants!" Mrs. Perkins flew to her feet. "Even the kitchen maids?"

"Even the scullery maids," said Mr. Scrumpton.

"The scullery maids! What on earth would his lordship want with a scullery maid?" Clementine cried.

"I have a fair idea," Mrs. Perkins muttered under her breath.

Mr. Scrumpton hadn't heard her. "At once. Go! Make yourselves presentable! Your Sunday best is not good enough. Then present yourselves immediately to the grand hall. Hurry, hurry! We cannot keep his lordship waiting."

Nora scrambled to her feet, half unsure if she should go, but Mr. Scrumpton met her eyes as Clementine and Mrs. Perkins ran from the kitchen.

"What are you waiting for, girl?" he demanded. "Prepare yourself at once!"

Nora's heart pounded. If Lord Wainscoate had asked specifically for the scullery maids and kitchen maids, then he must have heard the horrible stories circulating among the servants. It would not take much, the careless chatter of two housemaids dusting, a swift mention by one of the parlour-maids. She could imagine Sadie and Esther giving her away without even meaning it. If his lordship knew, his guests could know. The shame would be utterly intolerable.

Lord Wainscoate knew all about her now. Nora would be dismissed this very day, personally cast out of the Wainscoate household for bringing such appalling shame upon the family.

Nora's belly bucked with nausea. She was ruined. She would be on the streets tonight, sheltering in a doorway on a pile of newspapers again, hungry and cold and undeniably alone.

Dread turned to a slow, leaden terror in her limbs as she hastened into the only good dress she had, a starched black-and-white uniform such as the ones the parlourmaids wore. It was only for presentations, such as when the entire household stood at attention to welcome important guests (and display the Wainscoates' wealth in their vast staff).

She needed help with the apron strings, but knew no one would touch her, so she fumbled them into the neatest bow she could muster and joined the flow of servants hastening toward the grand hall.

Nora herself had never been inside the hall. When they gathered to welcome visitors, it was always outside. Its splendour was lost upon her, even with its velvet drapes, marble floor, and magnificent artworks on the walls. She had a vague impression of the enormous Christmas tree, taller than most cottages, standing at the centre with colourful parcels at its feet and ribbons dripping from its branches.

She stared at the floor, shaking from head to toe. Would they give her the last week's wage, or turn her out upon the streets near penniless? She had saved a little money, a few shillings. From experience, Nora knew that they would not last long.

She heard the thump of Lord Wainscoate's shoes on the marble and felt the other servants around her stand to attention. Nora could not bring herself to lift her head. Shame drenched her, shame at the appalling things that he, that everyone, must now believe about her. Shame at what was about to come. She knew she would now be hounded from this house, chased away like something filthy, her lies doing nothing to save her.

Oh, Bobby. Even now, Nora could find no regret in her heart. Those two years with him had been the happiest of her life.

His polished shoes, their buckles bright gold, reached her and stopped. Nora trembled to her core.

"Good afternoon," said Lord Wainscoate.

The servants curtseyed and bowed. Nora nearly fell, her knees almost buckling with the depth of her despairing curtsey.

"I have been made aware of recent events downstairs that require a change in our employment," said Lord Wainscoate, his voice flat and disinterested.

Nora fought back tears. She would not give Clementine the satisfaction of seeing her cry, she thought angrily. She would not allow that vindictive, shallow girl to feel any more victory than absolutely necessary. Her trembling stopped, and she raised her head, although she still did not dare to look Lord Wainscoate in the eye.

"Therefore, I wish to address you directly and inform you of a decision that may be considered radical, but that I have decided is in the best interests of this household," his lordship went on.

Nora was barely listening to him. She was thinking of

how she would walk from this house with her head held high. After all, she had done no wrong.

Instead, she looked at the glorious Christmas decorations covering the great hall. Huge wreaths, all holly and red ribbons, hung between the pillars. Colourful garlands and ribbons of red and green decorated the banisters of the staircase leading up to the bedrooms. Oranges, gingerbread men that Nora herself had baked, and sticks of candy hung from the Christmas tree. It was truly a magnificent spectacle.

Bobby would have loved it.

"I have been informed that Miss Baxter, my daughter's lady's maid, will be leaving shortly to get married," said Lord Wainscoate.

Nora blinked. What?

"Therefore, Lady Arabella will require a new maid. After discussion with her, we have decided on a replacement for Miss Baxter," his lordship went on.

Nora shook her head sharply, confused. Why would Lord Wainscoate choose a new lady's maid? One of the parlour-maids would be promoted. Mrs. Cratcher, too, looked utterly confused, her face furrowed.

"Your lordship had no need to make such a choice," she said. "I had prepared Daisy for..."

"I have made my decision," said Lord Wainscoate, dropping his voice an octave. "That is my prerogative, as master of the household, is it not?"

Mrs. Cratcher hastily hung her head. "Yes, my lord. Of course."

"Lady Arabella's new lady's maid will be this young woman." Lord Wainscoate extended a gallant arm.

Nora raised her head and looked around, flabbergasted.

"I believe your name is Nora Ellis?" Lord Wainscoate prompted.

The world spun. Lady's maid! They earned fifteen pounds a year, almost double what Nora did. What was more, it was a position of prestige, of tremendous trust. Nora would travel everywhere with Lady Arabella.

She could sense everyone gaping at her.

"Nora Ellis?" Mrs. Cratcher squawked. "My lord, are you certain?"

"Do you question my decision, housekeeper?" Lord Wainscoate snapped.

Again Mrs. Cratcher ducked her head. "No, my lord."

"Then see to it that Miss Ellis is provided all that she needs and reports to the Lady Arabella's service tomorrow. As for Miss Baxter, her services will no longer be required."

"Yes, my lord," Mrs. Cratcher whispered.

"Are you ready for your new role?" Lord Wainscoate asked.

The sudden gentleness of his tone forced Nora to look up at him. She curtseyed again, hardly able to believe that this was happening. "Oh, yes, my lord! Thank you, my lord. I'm ready, my lord. I won't let you down. I'll do good work, my lord, I swear it."

Lord Wainscoate stared at her as she babbled, his smile growing steadily. His eyes did not remain on hers, but took all of her in, and the approval in his expression grew.

"Yes," he said quietly, "yes, I'm sure you will do quite nicely."

Nora had never been upstairs before yesterday, much less inside the sumptuous quarters of Lord Wainscoate's only daughter. Even though she had spent the day before training in this room, her heart still caught at its grandeur when Sadie opened the door and ushered her into the bedroom.

"Here," Sadie growled. "Though what business on earth a slimy wretch like you has in a place like this, nobody knows!"

The normally cheerful housemaid's eyes were dark and filled with hatred. She kept her distance from Nora, as though the filth upon her was contagious.

Nora faced her, folding her arms. "I don't care what any of you say. I've done no wrong."

"Well, I think you're foul and that you have no business in this house at all, much less in this position as a lady's maid."

"Tell that to his lordship, then," said Nora sharply. "He chose me for this role. Will you contest him?"

"Mr. Scrumpton tried, believe me," Sadie hissed. "The mistress of the house was in floods of tears all day. I don't know what madness has come over his lordship, but all he said was that he paid no mind to silly downstairs rumours."

Sadie's voice dropped lower. "You know what happened to the last girl his lordship took a shine to, don't you?"

Nora's stomach turned cold. "What do you mean?"

"Jenny Marsh. Pretty thing, she was. Parlour-maid. His lordship started finding reasons to speak with her, same as he did with you in that glasshouse. Then one day she was gone. Dismissed without a character. Mrs. Cratcher said she'd stolen silver, but none of us believed it." Sadie's eyes glittered. "Some say she went to the workhouse. Some say worse."

"That's gossip," Nora said, but her voice shook.

"Is it? Then why did her ladyship weep for a week after

Jenny left? Why does she weep now?" Sadie stepped closer. "You're not special, Nora Ellis. You're just the next one."

"Madness!" Nora laughed, but the sound was hollow even to her own ears. "Careful, Sadie. I don't think the Lady Arabella would like hearing such opinions of her father."

Sadie's face twisted with disgust, and she left the room with a clatter of shoes.

Nora exhaled, a calming breath, and smoothed her hands over the new uniform with its perfectly starched apron and tidy bonnet.

Jenny Marsh. The name meant nothing to Nora, but Sadie's words clung to her like cobwebs. The last girl his lordship took a shine to.

She shook the thought away. Sadie was bitter, that was all. Jealous. They all were. She was determined not to reward those petty hopes. Serving as Lady Arabella's maid would be a challenge, but she would rise to it.

She racked her mind for everything she'd heard the other ladies' maids talk about and reminded herself that her job was simple at its core: she had to make sure that Lady Arabella had everything she needed. Miss Baxter would have dressed her for breakfast. What was the next step in her ladyship's routine?

Nora had had only a day's training to prepare for this role. Miss Baxter had written lists for her—with a florid hand and a dark scowl that told Nora the former lady's maid was certain Nora couldn't read. Those lists had proven useful, mostly because Miss Baxter had no idea that Nora was literate.

The rest of the day had been taken up with such a bewilderment of setting out clothes, learning to do all the intricate hooks and snaps and strings, and speeches about Lady Arabella's routine that Nora's head spun with it all.

She was well aware that Miss Baxter—that everyone in the household—had purposely set her up to fail at this new role. Perhaps they had every right to do so. Her head still reeled with the sheer absurdity of her promotion from kitchen maid to lady's maid overnight.

Her fists clenched. Perhaps she had only a tiny chance of holding onto this role, but whatever chance she had, she would take it. She would do everything in her power to prove that she could be better than those fools downstairs assumed.

Think, Nora. Think.

Lady Arabella usually took a turn about the garden on a nice day. A quick glance through the tremendous window, with its silken drapes and splendid view over the lawn, showed Nora that it was sunny enough to sparkle on the snow.

Preparation for a walk, then.

Nora pulled the drapes wide to allow the sunshine to pour into the gorgeous room with its paisley furniture and four-poster bed. There were Christmas decorations everywhere: garlands wrapped around the bed's posts, wreaths on the doors and over the fireplace, and great gold and red bows on the wardrobe doors.

She opened the doors and glanced through the dresses, trying to stifle her bewilderment. Take a deep breath, she ordered herself. She'd seen the Lady Arabella strolling about the garden all the time. She could work it out.

Nora selected garments as Miss Baxter had taught her, especially choosing things that she'd seen her ladyship wear before. She was selecting a hat and gloves when the door creaked.

Lady Arabella Wainscoate floated into the room. She was a gossamer creature, hardly real, her skin porcelain with only the faintest dusting of powder over her cheeks, her black hair piled high in complicated loops and braids on her head. Pearls at her throat matched the pins in her hair.

Nora darted out from behind the screen and curtseyed with all the grace she could muster. "Your ladyship, allow me to say what an honour it is to serve you. Whatever you need, milady, I'll do my best, I swear it."

"So you're the kitchen maid my father chose." Lady Arabella's eyes flashed. "You know I'll be the talk of London, don't you, having a mere kitchen maid attend me?"

"I know, milady. I'm awfully sorry about that. It... it wasn't my choice, but I promise I'll do everything I can to make you comfortable. I won't embarrass you, milady, I swear it."

Lady Arabella's shoulders drooped. "I suppose it wasn't your choice. It's never our choice with Father, is it?"

There was something low and dark in her tone that surprised Nora. "I suppose not, milady."

"I refuse to be dishonest with you. I tried to resist my father about this. So did Mother; she's been weeping since yesterday morning. The doctor had to bring her laudanum. Yet there's no going against Father."

Shame burned in Nora's chest, but beneath the shame, something else stirred. Why did her ladyship weep for a week after Jenny left? Sadie's words echoed in her mind. Why does she weep now?

"I'm sorry to have brought such unhappiness, milady," she managed.

"It's not your fault, I suppose. Like you say." A small smile tugged at Lady Arabella's lips. "Thank you for being kind. I'm afraid kindness was not Miss Baxter's strongest suit."

Lady Arabella turned back to the mirror, but her hands trembled slightly as she touched her pearls. "Sometimes I wonder if Father truly loves anyone at all," she said, almost to herself. "Or if we're all just... things to him. Things he owns." Her voice dropped. "Grandfather was the same, Mother says. And his father before him. They were raised to believe the world existed to serve them. That people like you aren't really... people."

She shook her head quickly, as though dispelling a bad dream. "Forgive me. I don't know why I said that."

Nora didn't know what to say to that.

Lady Arabella settled at the dressing-table. "What's your name?"

"Nora Ellis, milady."

"Nora. That's a pretty name."

"Not as pretty as yours, milady."

"Oh, please! Who wants to be called Arabella? It's so long and silly." The lady touched her hair. "Won't you take my hair down, Nora? Father wishes to see it up at meal-times, but I do so hate it. It pulls. I would rather have it in a lower bun for my constitutional."

Nora silently congratulated herself on guessing correctly that her ladyship would want a walk next. She hurried over and gently removed a few pins from the elaborate style, allowing the glossy tresses to flow over Lady Arabella's shoulders.

"Ahh, that's better." Lady Arabella sighed. "Sometimes I wish I could be like you, you know, and put my hair up all plainly under my bonnet every day without anyone complaining."

Nora doubted that the Lady Arabella would think her life quite so appealing if she had to live it. "It's certainly convenient, my lady." She gently undid a few more pins and began to bring her ladyship's hair together in a simple, single braid down her back.

Lady Arabella's eyebrows shot up. "What on earth are you doing, Nora?"

She hesitated. "I'm putting your hair down."

"I'm going for a walk around the garden, not to bed!" Lady Arabella clutched her head. "I can't go out with it looking like this! My parents and the servants will all see me. Good gracious, Nora, don't you know anything?"

Worry tingled in Nora's fingertips. "I'm so sorry, my lady. I'll do it better." She loosened the braid.

"Ouch!" Lady Arabella whined. "You're hurting me!"

"I'm so sorry. That's not... I didn't mean to." Nora grabbed a brush from the dressing table and tried to tame the black locks with it, but they only seemed to grow more tangled. "It's all right. I'll fix it for you, milady." Shaking, she drew Lady Arabella's hair back into a higher braid and pinned it up with the pearl and diamond pins as well as she could.

If she ruined her work here, then her employment at the Wainscoate house and at any great house in London was over. They would never accept her back downstairs. Not with the reputation Clementine was determined to spread for her. Her dreams of becoming a housekeeper would disappear at once, and so would her only source of survival.

"Nora!" Lady Arabella cried.

Nora jumped. "What is it, milady?"

"Why, dear, are you crying?"

Nora shakily blinked back her tears. "I'm sorry, milady. I didn't mean to get upset." She added a few more pins. "How does that feel? I'm certain it'll fit beneath your bonnet."

"Never mind that." Lady Arabella turned in her seat and took Nora's hands. "Why are you crying?"

Nora swallowed hard. "I fear I've let you down, milady."

"Oh, Nora, what a silly thing to say! I've barely known you ten minutes and already you've brought light into my room and set out my things for walking without having to be asked." Lady Arabella's smile held unexpected kindness. "You were a kitchen maid, weren't you? I overheard some of the housemaids talking about you."

What else did you overhear? Nora dared not ask. "Yes, milady."

"You've never been a lady's maid before."

"No, milady."

"That's no matter. It's strange that dear Ellie, Miss Baxter, left as suddenly as she did. I had to beg Father to let her stay even a day to train you. He wanted her to go away at once." Lady Arabella's hands fell into her lap. "I will miss her terribly. There is nobody to talk to in this lonely old house, you know."

The hollow tone in her voice surprised Nora. She had always thought that living in a house like this meant having everything one's heart could desire, yet the sudden sorrow in Lady Arabella's face seemed real.

"I had hoped she would teach you what to do, but she's not here, and that means you and I shall have to manage." Lady Arabella's sunny smile returned. "Do let's be friends, Nora."

"You're too kind, milady."

"What's the point of being unkind? Nobody likes an unkind person." Lady Arabella touched her hair. "Where is my bonnet? I had the most exciting gossip in a letter from my cousin this morning, and I can't wait to tell you everything! Do you know Lord Ferdinand, that most exotic young man from Spain?"

"I'm sure I don't, my lady." Nora grasped her walking bonnet.

"Lord Ferdinand is handsome and courteous, even if he is a foreigner, and of course everyone knows that Lady Sally Brigham has had her eye on him ever since he stepped off the ship..."

Lady Arabella prattled on, talking about people Nora had never heard of and frivolous events that hardly seemed to matter, but there was something soothing about the merry tinkle of her voice. As Nora pinned her bonnet into place, she felt the tight knot ease in her chest.

Somehow, despite all Clementine and Mrs. Cratcher's efforts, Nora felt her dream draw a little nearer. She thought of the pride she'd seen in Mama's eyes over the Christmas orange all those years ago. She thought of the love and joy in Bobby's face when she brought home every day's income from the fishmongering.

They were all gone, but in moments of victory like these, Nora felt them closer than ever before.

And yet, as she followed Lady Arabella toward the door, Sadie's words whispered through her mind once more. You're just the next one.

Nora pushed the thought away. She had survived the workhouse. She had survived the streets. She would survive this, too.

Whatever this was.

CHAPTER 17

Nora was bone-weary as she crept below the stairs, pulling off her apron and bonnet as she went. Nothing stirred in the servants' quarters. It was past midnight; the Wainscoates' brougham had only recently returned from a Christmas party that Lady Arabella's aunt had hosted. It had been a hard first day as a lady's maid.

She had almost fallen asleep waiting in the wings with her ladyship's shoes, shawl, and powder. The only thing that had kept her awake for the carriage ride home was Lady Arabella's incessant chattering about who had danced with whom and whose dress had been a veiled slight to whose mother.

After that, Nora still had to help Lady Arabella into her nightclothes and bring her the glass of milk that helped her sleep, which she had prepared herself; the other servants had long since dined and gone to bed themselves.

Now, Nora tiptoed down the stairs into the darkness of the servants' hall. It was cold here compared to the well-heated ballroom and Lady Arabella's cozy bedroom. A boiler brought a little heat to the tiny, dark room she shared with Clementine.

Afraid to light a candle and wake the kitchen maid, Nora shivered her way into her nightclothes in the dark. Her bed was narrow, its mattress crinkling straw, but she couldn't wait to ease between the sheets.

She pulled back the blankets and slipped into bed, wrapping her arms around her pillow to bury her face in...

Something filthy stuck to her skin, something sticky that reeked. Nora squealed despite herself and jerked back. Whatever it was, it had smeared over her cheeks, and the smell only grew worse when she tried to wipe it off.

She bit her scream off short and heard the rustle as Clementine woke. A gas light flared. Nora shrank back, but instead of screaming in rage, Clementine was laughing.

Horror filled Nora's belly as she stared at the brown mess on her pillow. Clementine had placed a pile of horse manure on it.

"What is the meaning of this?" Their door crashed open, and Mrs. Perkins stood in it, lantern high.

"Just showing this foul creature what she truly is," Clementine hissed.

Mrs. Perkins' eyes rested on Nora's, and her lips tightened in displeasure. Without another word, the cook turned and left.

"You're nothing but dirt." Clementine spat on the floor and turned off the lantern. "All your grand ideas and his lordship's special attentions can't change that."

Nora fought back tears as she threw her pillow on the ground, took a rag, and tried her best to clean her face. She curled up beneath the sheets with the disgusting smell still thick in her nostrils, but it was not the smell that kept her awake for long hours afterward.

It was the look in Mrs. Perkins' eyes.

―――

"Are you sure about this, milady?" Nora asked, buttoning Lady Arabella's best coat. They stood in the grand hall, both bundled up in their best clothes, although in Nora's case this meant a wool jacket instead of the mink fur that adorned her ladyship. "It's very cold."

"It isn't snowing," said Lady Arabella, "and there's hardly any wind. I can take a little cold. Oh, don't spoil this for me, Nora. I do so love to see the Christmas decorations on all the houses on Christmas Eve."

"As you wish, milady."

"You think me very silly," Lady Arabella observed.

Nora led her to the main doors. A footman opened them, and they descended the steps to the waiting carriage, drawn by a spotless pair of white horses whose breath steamed in the cold air.

"Quick, milady." Nora offered an arm. "Let's get you into the carriage before you catch your death."

"My, my! It is cold." Lady Arabella raised her muffler to her face and allowed Nora to hurry her down the steps and bundle her into the carriage.

The interior was still chilly, but far cozier than outside. Nora draped a thick rug over her ladyship's knees.

"Ah, that's lovely." Lady Arabella made herself comfortable on the velvet cushions. "Off we go, Mr. Sharpe! You know the usual route."

"Yes, milady." The coachman touched his hat and snapped the whip, and the horses clattered merrily around the fountain and down the driveway, their harness bells jingling.

It was chilly despite the carriage's thick glass windows, and Nora was grateful to slide onto the velvet cushion opposite Lady Arabella.

"Oh, look!" Lady Arabella laughed and clapped her gloved hands. "The Grighams have put up an outdoor Christmas tree! Isn't it marvellous?"

Nora wondered how much work it was for the servants to maintain the bows and tinsel and bright decorations hanging from the massive pine tree on the lawn of the magnificent townhouse, but she only said, "It's pretty, milady."

"My goodness! Look at all the matching wreaths on the Bedlingtons' windows. All silver and yellow bows. That's beautiful, isn't it?"

Nora made noncommittal noises and did her best not to look at the decorations decking out every home they passed. Each holly-covered wreath, every glittering Christmas tree was a fresh splinter of agony in her heart, reminding her over and over again of sweet Mama who roasted chestnuts so perfectly, of Papa who had somehow scrounged up that orange on her last Christmas with them, of dear Bobby with the wonder in his eyes, gazing up at that sparkling tree on the Christmas of the sore ankle and the soft white bread roll.

The knot gathering in Nora's throat was hard to ignore. She kept her eyes on the window facing the street and dried her tears quickly so that Lady Arabella wouldn't see them.

A sudden flare of golden light caught her attention. She looked up through a mist of grief and saw a scruffy form by the nearest lamppost, lowering his pole after lighting the lamp. For an instant, she thought it was him. Her hand pressed against the glass, and she gasped loudly at the sight…

Then the lamplighter turned around and Nora saw, past the sprig of holly in his buttonhole, that he had a grey beard.

She couldn't quite bite back the sob.

"Nora, my dear!" cried Lady Arabella. "Whatever is the matter?"

"I beg your pardon, milady." Nora swallowed her tears and straightened her face with an effort.

"Are you cold? What's wrong?"

"No, no, thank you, milady. All is well."

"Nora, dear, we're looking at beautiful Christmas lights, and you're crying. Something has to be the matter."

"Perhaps a touch of cold in my eyes, that's all."

Lady Arabella grabbed Nora's hand. The gesture startled her, but the lady didn't let go. Her bright blue eyes were startlingly intense.

"When I told you I wanted to be friends, I meant it," she said. "Please. Tell me what ails you."

Nora didn't want to share with this fine lady, yet the insistence in her tone made it hard to refuse, and the pressure of all she'd held inside her since Bobby's death made the words spill out. As the first snowflakes began to fall, lending their sparkling magic to the decorated homes and the jingle of sleigh bells, Nora told her everything.

Nora had heard it said among the servants that the Wainscoate Christmas Day party was the most opulent in Westminster, apart from royalty, of course, and she had always believed it based solely on the dishes they prepared for such an occasion. She doubted that even the Queen of England ate as well as the Wainscoates and their guests did at Christmas lunch, from stuffed peacock with all the finest trimmings to the best fruit cake meticulously matured for a full year before serving.

It felt strange to be upstairs, watching those dishes come out on fine silver platters touted by liveried footmen, instead of down in the kitchen's hustle. In a way, Nora missed the cooking, but she enjoyed the scowls of annoyance from the other staff as they saw her in that coveted position, waiting behind the drapes for her ladyship.

She had also never seen the ballroom decked out for Christmas before, and it was a rare treat, even though her heart ached to think how Mama, Papa, and Bobby would have loved to see this place. The Wainscoates had chosen traditional red, green, and gold for their decorations. Satin bows the size of Nora's head draped the balconies between sheets of glittering silk. Yards upon yards of garlands wrapped around pillars and banisters. The Christmas tree at the ballroom's centre was a work of art, all hung with glittering glass baubles, each one a priceless masterpiece in its own right.

The tree was fantastic, but every eye was truly on the Lady Arabella Wainscoate that night. Nora breathed a sigh of relief to see that every lady and gentleman turned to admire her passage with either lust or jealousy. Lady Arabella had had to guide her a little, but Nora had still succeeded in dressing her well. The scarlet gown made her skin seem even paler, her hair even darker. Rubies and emeralds adorned her hair and hung at her throat, and she drifted across the dance floor with a handsome young suitor as if too light and graceful to truly touch her satin slippers to the marble floor.

Lady Arabella had told Nora about the dozens of potential suitors who would be at the party. Nora had no idea if this young man was one of the ones she liked, but when they swept past, the girl's eyes found Nora's and she flashed her a quick grin.

Nora returned it, feeling a surge of pleasure on her ladyship's behalf.

"Ah, Nora." The sudden voice spoke at her elbow. "There you are."

Nora jumped and raised a hand to her throat. "Lord Wainscoate! Forgive me, sir. You startled me."

"Now, now. You know there's nothing to fear." Lord Wainscoate stood uncomfortably close. Nora smelled sweat and champagne. "I trust you're enjoying your new post in my household?"

Something about his low voice made her glance around for the other maids, but the quiet corner behind these drapes had suddenly gone empty, as though the other lady's maids had scattered at his approach. Of course, they all avoided Nora like the plague in any case, as though she might spread her sheer commonness among them. Discomfort twisted in Nora's belly. Why would his lordship approach her like this?

There was an uncomfortable tingle deep in her belly. For that matter, why had he been so bent on promoting her to lady's maid despite his wife's disgust and all social conventions? Nora realized now that her reasoning—that she had simply impressed him in the glasshouse—was mere pride.

There was some other reason why Lord Wainscoate wanted her close. Wanted her to owe him everything.

"Well?" his lordship prompted. His smile remained, but there was something flat about his eyes.

Nora curtseyed deeply. "Why, yes, milord. Her ladyship

is a most pleasant and kind mistress. I enjoy the work greatly."

"Good. That's very good." Lord Wainscoate inclined his head. "I hope you will continue to enjoy your role." He raised a hand as if to touch her shoulder, then let it fall by his side. "Good evening to you, Nora. And merry Christmas."

A breath escaped her as his lordship slipped away and vanished into the well-dressed crowd. She would have to keep a very close eye on Lord Wainscoate. Suddenly, her absurd promotion made far more sense than before.

Nora shook off the new anxiety that clung to her like a cobweb and gazed at the decorations all around her, determined not to let him ruin her night.

This Christmas might contain none of the love and laughter that she had shared with her parents and Bobby, but it held something perhaps even more important: opportunity. No matter how sinister Lord Wainscoate's purposes, she was now a lady's maid, whether society liked it or not.

Nora watched Lady Arabella twirl across the dance floor and gripped her sewing kit and second pair of shoes with fierce hands. No one would rip this chance from her.

Not this time.

Mr. Scrumpton found Nora in the servants' corridor the next morning.

"A word, Miss Ellis."

His tone left no room for argument. Nora followed him into the butler's pantry, a small room lined with silver that she had never entered before.

Mr. Scrumpton closed the door. His face was grave.

"I saw his lordship speak with you last night," he said. "Behind the drapes."

Nora's cheeks burned. "I didn't invite—"

"I know you didn't." Mr. Scrumpton's voice was surprisingly gentle. "I've served this family for thirty years, Miss Ellis. I've seen things I wish I hadn't." His jaw tightened. "Jenny Marsh was not the first. There have been others, over the years. Parlour-maids, kitchen girls. They come and go, and no one speaks of why. And I've learned that there are some matters a butler cannot prevent, no matter how he tries."

Nora's throat tightened. "Sir?"

"I cannot protect you from the master of this house. No one can." He met her eyes. "But I can tell you this: never be alone with him. Not in a corridor, not in a room, not anywhere. If he seeks you out, find a reason to be elsewhere. Do you understand?"

The weight of his words settled on her like a stone. "Yes, sir," she whispered.

"Good." Mr. Scrumpton opened the door. "That will be all."

Nora left the pantry with her heart pounding. She had thought her promotion was a stroke of fortune. Now she understood it for what it truly was.

A trap.

PART IV

CHAPTER 18

1873

Nora's fingers flew over Arabella's hair. The beautiful dark tresses lay in a complicated pattern of braids and twists over her ladyship's head, reaching an elegant pile that accentuated her features. Removed a pin from her mouth, Nora secured the last braid in place, then reached toward the dressing-table for the decorative, diamond-studded pin she would use to round off the look.

"My goodness, Nora, look at it." Arabella raised a hand to the black locks so carefully framing her face. "Do you remember that first time you took down my hair for me? It must be almost exactly five years ago now."

"I remember." Nora chuckled. "What a mess that was! You were so patient with me."

"Of course I was." Arabella's lifted hand found Nora's and gripped her fingers. "I would have been even more patient if I had known that in that moment I met the kindest friend I would ever have."

Nora found Arabella's eyes in the mirror and smiled at

them, even though she'd barely listened to that last sentence. Five years. Five long years she'd been a lady's maid, with no outlook of progress.

Would she remain there forever?

Perhaps she had been naive to think that she would ever reach beyond this position. Lord Wainscoate had achieved exactly what he hoped for when he dragged her into Arabella's service: he had trapped her here. There was nowhere else to go, not with her unconventional employment history.

Five years of dodging his lordship in corridors. Five years of making excuses, of never being alone, of sleeping with a chair wedged against her door. He had cornered her twice in the first year—once in the linen cupboard, once on the back stairs—and both times she had escaped only because another servant happened by. After that, she learned to move through the house like a ghost, always listening for his tread, always planning her escape.

Mr. Scrumpton helped when he could. She sometimes caught him watching from doorways, timing his interruptions. But even the butler could not be everywhere, and Lord Wainscoate was patient. He was always patient.

Lady Wainscoate never spoke of it, but sometimes she watched Nora with a strange, sad expression. As though she knew. As though she was sorry.

"What's wrong?" Arabella asked.

"Nothing at all." Nora couldn't break this sweet girl's heart by telling her that the position she'd so coveted had become a chore. "Except that I do believe I've made these loops crooked at the front, milady."

Arabella pouted. "Sweet Nora, surely we can dispense with that formality, at least in private."

Nora unpinned the locks she'd arranged around Arabella's face and carefully repositioned them. "Now, milady, you've persuaded me to call you Arabella instead of using your title, but I shan't be improper."

"Such a stickler, you are. Even picking up my fancy diction these days." Arabella clucked her tongue. "Why, I can't believe there were ever any silly rumours about your downstairs."

Nora chuckled. "Enough about all that. Come, there's Christmas to think of, your favourite time of the year, and of course your darling Lord Weatherby will be coming home very soon."

"He will indeed!" Arabella tucked her hands under her chin and let out a happy little squeal, like a small girl. "I had a letter from him this morning."

"I saw the envelope. I'm surprised you haven't already told me every little detail."

"Oh, I haven't read it yet, dear."

"Arabella! Why on earth not?" Nora lowered a hand to her shoulder and squeezed it. "Are you having second thoughts about him?"

"About my dear Weatherby? Never! It's just..." Arabella's lip trembled. "Oh, his journey has been so long already, Nora, and the snow is so deep. I'm afraid that his letter will say that the train is delayed and he won't be in London for Christmas after all."

"You're being awfully silly." Nora strode across to the writing desk by the window and retrieved the delicate envelope. It was composed of the most expensive paper, with flowing writing across the front in an elegant but masculine hand, and a whiff of perfume reached her as she carried it across the room. Lord Weatherby had spared no effort.

"Silly!" Arabella pouted. "What a thing to say to your mistress."

Nora laughed. "Come, come. It could be good news instead of bad; and either way, he'll be pining for your answer, don't you think?"

Arabella's eyes softened. "I suppose he will be. You're right, Nora. I'm being a coward, although I suppose I always have been."

"Nonsense."

"You know that it's true. Why, if it weren't for you, I would have married that horrible Lord Fellingham."

Nora scowled. "I can't believe no one else spoke out for you about that fool. He would have ruined you. Why, there were times when I thought he would strike you already, and you were not even engaged."

"I would have married him," Arabella repeated. "It was my mother's wish. If you hadn't called on my father to see the way he treated me that night, he and I would be wed, and I suffering under his cruelty this very minute!"

Nora stroked the girl's hair, not telling her that she feared Lord Wainscoate had had less than noble motives to put a stop to the proposed marriage. His lordship's actions were the one thing that she kept secret from Arabella. No girl needed to think such awful things of her father.

"That's all behind us now, milady. Lord Fellingham has hardly dared to show his face again in London, and you have dear Lord Weatherby now. Go on. Open it."

She brought an ivory-handled letter opener from the writing desk, and Arabella slid the envelope with it and shook out a beautiful sheet of thick, soft paper, along with a pressed violet.

"Ooh! My favourite." Arabella raised the delicate flower to her face and breathed its scent. "It signifies loyalty, too."

"Of course." Nora turned away to busy herself with preparing her ladyship's shoes for dinner, giving her a moment's privacy.

A second later, she turned back, alarmed, as Arabella let out a piercing shriek and half-rose from her chair.

"Milady!" Nora rushed to her side and grasped her arm.

Arabella looked up at her with shining eyes. Her cheeks bore no pallor; instead, they shone with rosy joy. "Nora!" She flung her arms around her and embraced her, an impropriety Nora had long grown used to. "You won't believe it!"

"What on earth is the matter, milady?"

"Nothing. Nothing at all!" Arabella laughed. "It's Weatherby. He's in London. He was able to get an earlier train. In fact, he means to come to the Christmas party at the Bedlingtons' tomorrow. I will see him soon, Nora!"

Nora clasped Arabella's hands, ignoring societal rules. "I'm so happy for you, milady. To see you this overjoyed at the thought of seeing him, why, it tells me everything."

Arabella raised the envelope to her lips and sniffed the perfume, closing her eyes, her joy complete. And even though Nora's own life remained cold and empty, she had no difficulty feeling a corresponding surge of happiness for the sake of the lady who had become her dear friend.

Evenings finished late for Nora. The family frequently dined late, even if they had only one or two sleep-in guests, as this evening in mid-December; the larger contingent of friends and family who stayed here over Christmas would start arriving over the next few days.

Even on these comparatively informal occasions, the

many courses and long conversations in the dining rooms tended to go on until late at night. It was past eleven by the time Nora had helped Lady Arabella wash, dressed her in her nightclothes, braided her hair, and tucked her safely into her sumptuous bed.

She waited until Arabella was asleep; a cruel governess had left her afraid of the dark. Once the girl's breathing grew soft and deep, Nora opened the door and stood peering down the hallway, her head high, her senses straining for any sign of danger.

In the past five years, she had learned that this moment, going from Arabella's room down to the servants' quarters, was the most dangerous of her day.

Tonight, though, she heard nothing. No heavy breathing. No doorways cast lights or shadows. The predator that stalked these halls at night, his eyes fixed upon only one item of prey, must have retired early to bed for once.

Still, Nora took no chances. She dared not carry a light, but shut the door without a sound and sneaked down the hallway in perfect silence. Where the larger rooms' fireplaces cast golden glows into the hall, Nora stayed in the shadows.

She descended the first flight of stairs without incident and exhaled in relief as she reached the lower floor where the dining room, drawing room, and great hall stood. A back hallway from the dining room would take her to the kitchen for her own dinner and then to the servants' quarters. Moving a little faster now, she darted through the drawing room and into the dining room, and that was her fatal mistake.

A door slammed in the darkness before her. Nora froze, and someone turned up the gas light, bathing the quiet room in its brilliance.

The table stood clean and empty, chairs pushed in, carpet swept clean. There was nothing in this room except for Lord Wainscoate standing triumphantly by the door that provided Nora her only escape.

She froze. She could bolt back through the drawing room, but she risked rousing the household. Not one of the servants would believe her if they heard her accusations against Lord Wainscoate. And if she raised her voice against him, she feared he would dismiss her.

He would cast her out into the unforgiving, wintry streets, and leave Arabella alone and friendless in the world.

The gas lamps flickered on the decorations that bathed the dining room in finery. The great, sparkling wreath over the fireplace; the garlands and ribbons draped on the walls; even a small tree in the corner, a lesser echo of the one in the great hall. Their cheeriness seemed to mock her. Bobby and Papa were not here to protect her now.

"Nora, my dear." Lord Wainscoate's tone was pure velvet. "There you are."

Her only chance was to brush past him, if she could, and get down the hallway to the kitchens. Lord Wainscoate would not pursue her there. Such an act would make his intentions plain to the staff, no matter how much they hated her.

She trembled, clinging to decorum, and curtseyed deeply. "I'm sorry, milord. I didn't see you here. Is there something you need?"

He took the words as the invitation she hadn't meant them to be. In an instant he was across the room, suddenly a mere foot away from her, his hand on her arm. The grip was not painful, but it was strong, possessive.

She smelled port on his breath, no less foul for its expensive aroma, and turned her face away.

"Yes, Nora," he rasped, his voice low and breathy. "Yes, there is something I need. You know it as well as I do. I've needed it for five long years, and I've been patient. Oh, I've been patient."

She trembled, seeking escape. The back door was only a few yards away. If she could find an opportunity to twist away from him, she could dart down that hallway and be gone.

But his hand on her arm trapped her, and he moved closer, his body pressed against hers, pinning her to the wall. The garlands tickled her cheek.

"Five years I've waited for you to realize that you are mine." His breath was on her cheek, his lips nearly touching his ear. His free hand encircled her waist, the fingers probing, seeking the spaces between the ribs of her modest corset. "I've given you everything. A position you coveted. A better wage than most. Come, now, Nora. You know what you owe me."

"Please, milord," Nora whimpered.

He was crushing her against the wall now, his desire unmistakable. His fingers found the strings of her apron. "Hush, hush, my dear. Why would you strive against me? Everything in this house belongs to me... as do you."

"Please, milord, release me!" Nora cried.

A sudden footstep and the creak of the door came as a saving grace. Lord Wainscoate sprang back, and Nora's hands flew to her apron strings; by some miracle he had not succeeded in untying them.

"Good evening, milord," said Mr. Scrumpton.

Nora could have wept. Why could the newcomer not have been Arabella? She was the only person Nora could think of who might have helped her, or even felt the inclination to do so.

"Scrumpton," Lord Wainscoate hissed.

Mr. Scrumpton stepped back and opened the door wider. He was still in his livery, even though it was long after dinner, and his eyes found Nora's. The expression in them was as good as a gesture. Nora stepped away, but Lord Wainscoate still held her arm. She turned back to him with a gasp of terror, and their eyes locked for a moment.

"Was there anything more you required, milord?" Mr. Scrumpton asked smoothly.

Lord Wainscoate released her arm. Nora scrambled to Mr. Scrumpton's side, her heart fluttering in her throat.

"No, that will be all," said his lordship.

"Very well, milord." Mr. Scrumpton deeply bowed.

Nora curtseyed.

Lord Wainscoate turned on his heel, sneering, and store away upstairs.

"Mr. Scrumpton..." Nora began.

The butler ushered her into the hallway and shut the door. "Has he harmed you, Miss Ellis?"

The tenderness in his voice shocked tears to her eyes. "No, sir."

"But he has tried."

Nora fought the lump in her throat with minimal success.

"Miss Ellis." Mr. Scrumpton sighed. "Come downstairs. We have something to discuss."

Nora struggled for control and managed to regain command over her emotions by the time they reached the kitchen, although she could feel her terror in her chest, like a bladder of water almost overfilled. The slightest movement could burst it.

Her dinner was, like the valet's and Lady Wainscoate's maid's, waiting on the table underneath a cover. Mr. Scrumpton ushered her into a chair. With shaking hands, Nora poured herself a cup of tea; she had been starving earlier, but now found she had no appetite.

"Miss Ellis," said Mr. Scrumpton, looming over her, "I fear that I personally, and the household as a whole, owe you an apology."

Nora looked up, a fortifying sip of tea warming her stomach, and stared at him in astonishment.

Mr. Scrumpton cleared his throat. "You were subjected to a great deal of hostility from myself as well as other members of this staff when certain, ah, most disturbing tales of your indiscretion on former days were circulated around this house. Tales that no one could verify, and that you yourself denied."

Nora set the teacup down. "You're talking about the stories Clementine told about me." She paused. "Sir."

"Such rumours can be most damaging to the reputation of a great house, Miss Ellis. In some cases, they may even touch the honour of the families we serve. You understand that this may never be allowed to happen."

Nora sipped her tea. "Whether or not those rumours are ever proven true," she said icily.

Mr. Scrumpton sighed, his majestic figure deflating. Nora had never noticed how much the past five years had aged him until that moment.

"Whether or not they are proven true," he reluctantly agreed. "The truth is, they almost always are. Where there is reason for such stories to circulate there is often a kernel of truth, perhaps exaggerated, but invariably there. I understood that you had grown up on the streets. Believe or not, Miss Ellis, I know something of the streets myself. I know that young women facing the brutal realities of London often resort to satisfying mankind's basest urges to make a way for themselves."

Nora bridled. "I beg your pardon?"

Mr. Scrumpton raised a hand. "I would not usually allow such a tone in my household, but in this case, Miss Ellis, I understand it is justified. This was my assumption. Your most unconventional ascension to your current post did little to endear you to the staff."

"Lord Wainscoate had no right to take away that position from Daisy. I understand that. He also slighted your authority over the staff with what he did…" Nora sighed. "He brought dismay to a lot of people with that, even gossip to Lady Arabella."

"It was a loathsome move, even if he is the master of the house and thus has authority over all of us. We all hated you for it, I must confess. However, over the past five years since you entered Lady Arabella's service, all of us have watched the Lord Wainscoate circle you like a hungry dog. We all knew why he did what he did."

Nora sat back, startled at the vehemence in Mr. Scrumpton's tone.

"His intentions have been clear from the start, and his insistence has been undeniable. But for five years, Miss Ellis, we have watched you evade him at every turn. Even though to submit to his advances would have proven advantageous to you in every way, you have avoided them. Your actions have left no room for doubt. Your honour, which this household so grievously questioned, has proven unimpeachable. And most recently, Clementine, to the disgust of Mrs. Cratcher, has admitted that the rumours she invented were pure fantasy."

Nora smiled. Clementine was still a kitchen maid after all these years.

"Apology does not come naturally to me." Mr. Scrumpton shifted his weight. "Nonetheless, it is what you are owed."

It was tempting to rub it in; to accuse Mr. Scrumpton of listening to the silly gossip of maids, something he despised. But, with an effort, Nora reined in that impulse. He had rescued her from his lordship's clutches, after all.

"Thank you, sir," she said. "I only wish that this revelation had come while Mrs. Perkins was still alive."

The cook had died hating her. That memory smarted fiercely.

"As do I, Miss Ellis." Mr. Scrumpton paused. "It may mean little to you in this moment, but I should inform you that should you seek employment elsewhere, you will be provided with a most glowing reference from this house."

Nora almost dropped her teacup. "Sir?"

"I will not blame you if you wish to go elsewhere. Do not allow your fears of the reference you will receive to trap you in this place of danger."

Nora sagged in her chair. A world of possibility opened before her... possibility where she would have to tell Arabella she was leaving, and see the heartache in her only friend's eyes.

Then embark into a world where no one cared for her. Not a soul.

She shook her head, reality returning. "You are very kind, Mr. Scrumpton, but even the best of references can't erase the scandal surrounding my name. I doubt anyone would hire me. Everybody knows me as the kitchen maid who somehow became Lady Arabella's maid."

The butler's face fell. "It is true. I am sorry, Miss Ellis.

Despite our best efforts, it would appear that his lordship's actions have far-reaching consequences for the rest of your life in domestic service."

He sat in awkward silence with her for a few seconds before excusing himself and going to bed, leaving Nora to stare into her teacup, touched by his forgiveness.

Yet by no means practically helped by it.

CHAPTER 19

*I*t was perfect.

Nora had made sure of it. She knew that Lord Weatherby, the tall, pale, insipid, and yet desperately kind and gentle creature who had fallen in love with Arabella, loved to take her out for a walk in the garden when the weather allowed.

On this night less than a week before Christmas, the weather had bestowed upon them a perfect evening for the Wainscoates' Christmas party. It was bitterly cold, but also perfectly still in the stretch of garden outside the magnificent French doors that adorned one end of the ballroom. Nora had spoken to the gardener, who had taken extra care to ensure that every holly bush in this garden looked its splendid best. Even without ribbons, tinsel, or glass baubles, the garden was like a Christmas wonderland with the red berries bright against the snow that lay dusted like icing sugar across the bushes.

She hovered in the doorway, watching and performing the barest duty of a chaperone, as Lord Weatherby conducted his ladylove around the garden. Technically she supposed she should have been closer to be a true chaperone; yet his hand on the girl's arm was so proper, his bearing so truly gentlemanly, that she knew it was barely necessary.

Excitement fluttered in her chest as Arabella and Lord Weatherby halted in the prettiest spot in the garden, between two great pine trees and two beautiful hollybushes utterly covered in red berries. Arabella was gazing up at them, talking incessantly, the way she only ever did with Nora.

Something fell cold on Nora's cheek. She touched it and realized that it had just begun to snow. In the gold and silver blend of moonlight and firelight from the French doors, the snowflakes fell fat and pale, each one sparkling. Arabella clapped her hands in her fur gloves and pointed up at them, laughing, her face transfixed with joy.

It had been a long time since Nora had been to church, yet she still thanked God for Lord Weatherby.

The young man sank onto one knee, heedless of the snow, and held up something that shimmered. Arabella was so busy watching the snow that she didn't notice for a few seconds. Then she turned to him, and her hands flew to her mouth.

Nora heard only the echoes of her happy squeals, but her nods and smile meant everything. Lord Weatherby slipped the ring onto her finger and rose as Arabella jumped up and down, laughing.

Her heart swelled with more than joy for her friend. She knew what this meant.

It meant freedom for them both.

After a few joyous minutes in the garden, Arabella's arms wrapped around herself, and Lord Weatherby took her elbow and steered her back to the warmth of the ballroom. Nora was waiting there with a glass of brandy and a warm fur.

"Nora! Did you see?" Arabella displayed the bejewelled band on her finger. "Oh, Nora, he asked!"

Lord Weatherby beamed, a high blush on his cheeks.

"You'll be eager to announce it." Nora held out the glass. "Quickly, drink this first, to warm you up."

"I'm not going to announce it tonight." Arabella tugged her glove back onto her hand.

"You aren't, milady?"

"No," said Lord Weatherby. "It will be only for us to know. Only for tonight." He gripped Arabella's hand and kissed the back of it with impossible tenderness.

Her eyes shone. "Go on, then," she murmured.

Lord Weatherby bowed to them both and withdrew to the ballroom.

"You're shaking." Nora wrapped an arm around the lady. "Come. The excitement and the cold have been too much for you. You need a few minutes' rest."

She conducted Arabella to a side room and arranged her comfortably on a couch with her brandy glass and fur. The girl perched there, cheeks glowing, and sipped the warming drink until her hands ceased shaking.

"I'm so happy for you." Nora sat beside her and rubbed her free hand. "Lord Weatherby is a good man."

"He's well-born and wealthy enough to satisfy Mother and Father."

"He makes you happy," said Nora softly, and thought of Bobby. It had been five long years and she was no longer the fifteen-year-old girl who had lost him, yet she knew she loved him no less fiercely than the day he died.

Arabella took her hand. After five years spent almost

constantly in one another's company, it seemed at times that they could read one another's mind, and this was one of those times.

"Nora, my dear," said Arabella softly, "one of the things dear Weatherby, I suppose I can freely call him Herbert now, spoke of was you."

"Me, milady?"

"Don't look so shocked. Did you think I would forget my only true friend in a moment like this?" Arabella smiled, tears pooling in her eyes. "Nora, dear, we want you to come with me."

Nora's heart leaped. Lady's maid to the lady of a wealthy new household? And, to add to that, a household with a master and mistress as kind as this? Suddenly, the world fell open before her. Perhaps she was not as stuck as she had believed.

"Oh, Arabella!" Nora clutched her chest.

"You don't have to, of course. Weatherby Manor is all the way out in Hampshire. If you don't wish to leave London..."

Leave London! That would mean leaving behind the majority of the gossip that had followed her all this time. It could be a completely fresh start.

She knew that Arabella wouldn't think twice about promoting her to housekeeper. With those few words, her friend had given her back the prospect of a better future.

"London has been nothing but cruel to me, and you nothing but kind." Nora clung to Arabella's hand. "Oh, Arabella, I would follow you to the ends of the earth."

Arabella squeezed her fingers. "As for me, I would not go there without you."

The next few days passed in a haze of merriment. Arabella was on cloud nine with the prospect of her marriage in the spring. Nora, too, looked forward to that golden day with high hopes. Only a few more months before she would be free of Lord Wainscoate's advances for all but the occasional visit to this home; and even then, life had suddenly become more bearable downstairs. No one spoke directly with her except, sometimes, Mr. Scrumpton, but there were no more half-portions at her meals and no more horse manure on her pillow at night.

It was two days before Christmas when Arabella spun across the room one evening before dinner, giddy with wild joy, her sky blue dinner gown swirling around her legs.

"Oh, Nora, can you imagine?" She stopped before the great mirror by her wardrobe and twirled like a little girl. "A gown like this, or maybe white, like the queen herself!"

"That is the fashion, milady." Nora smiled indulgently.

"It'll be beautiful. I'll wear lilies in my hair. No, orchids. No, white roses!" Arabella giggled and twirled again, teetering on her beautiful satin slippers.

"Easy now, milady!" Nora grabbed her arm. "Let's not twist our ankle right before Christmas."

"My first Christmas as a betrothed woman." Arabella fluttered her finger, displaying the glittering ring. "Oh, Nora, it's all so lovely."

"It is indeed, milady, but try to compose yourself." Nora gently brushed her hair back into place. "All this excitement might rattle your nerves."

"Of course." Arabella took deep breaths. "Although I have to say, Nora, my nerves have never felt less rattled in my life."

Nora couldn't help hugging her. "Let's go down."

"Of course. Oh, Nora, your apron."

Nora glanced at it. "Oh, yes, of course. That's the stain from earlier, when Wulfric knocked the coffee onto me at teatime. Let me change it quickly before dinner."

"Silly footman. I'll see you in a few minutes, then. I'll be waiting in the anteroom." Arabella headed down the hall.

Nora jogged toward the kitchen, plucking off her apron as she passed down the servants' hallway. She could hardly believe that, in a few short months, she would be living in an entirely different house. An even grander one than this, for young Lord Weatherby was very well-off.

So well-off that even Lord Wainscoate could find no fault with him, no reason why Nora couldn't leave for her new life with Arabella in her new home. Nora almost felt like singing a Christmas carol.

It had been many years since she last thought of the milliner on the market square where she'd sold fish as a young girl, but she thought of her then, of her warm and bright business, her proud husband, and the thought swelled her heart with hope.

Bobby would be proud indeed.

For the first time in five years, Nora allowed herself to relax. In a few months, she would be free. Hampshire was far from London, far from this house, far from him. She had survived. She had won.

The corridor was empty. The servants were all in the kitchen, preparing dinner. She was alone.

Too late, she remembered Mr. Scrumpton's warning.

She was passing the door of the wine cellar, her mind filled with hope for a new life without fear and dread, when Lord Wainscoate came from the dark doorway like some ghoulish phantom rising from the pits of the grave. He seized her arms and spun her into the darkness of the cellar, kicking the door shut behind them. Nora opened her mouth to scream and he clapped his hand over it. His fingers dug into the side of her face, crushing her cheek against her teeth until she tasted blood.

She struggled, but it was no use. Already his lordship, no; he was no nobility; he was a mere brute, already Wainscoate had slammed her against the shelves until the bottles rattled.

"Your time's up, girl," he hissed. "Everyone's in the kitchen, preparing my dinner. No one will be waiting for you this time." His breath was on her face, hot and intent. "No one will interrupt."

He rammed himself against her. Nora wanted to scream, but it was muffled into a groan.

"Did you think you could escape me? Did you think my vapid daughter could spirit you off without you giving me what you've owed me all this time?" he hissed. "Did you think that stupid footman spilled coffee on you by accident? You didn't see me nudge his arm, did you? Oh, no, my dear. All this was well orchestrated. There is no escape from me."

Nora kicked, aiming for his legs. Lord Wainscoate seized her hair with his free hand and slammed her head against the wall. Pain and hot blood soaked her scalp. The world spun, and she couldn't scream; she didn't have the breath.

Wainscoate let out a low chuckle. "Now you're mine."

He pinned her against the shelves of wine with his body while both hands sought the strings of her dress, tugging at them. Ripping. His breath was on her neck. Then so was his mouth.

Something deep in Nora's chest revolted. No. He would

not make her guilty of all the things Clementine had said about her.

Mama and Papa and Bobby, they would all be appalled if they knew such a thing had befallen her. So she would not let it.

Her hand found the neck of a wine bottle, and she swung it with all of her might.

Glass shattered. Wainscoate staggered back, his scream tearing through the quiet cellar. White wine dripped to the floor, turning red as it poured down the man's dinner coat.

Nora reeled toward the door, her head clearing as the sharp smell of blood mingled with the fruity aroma of the wine.

"What have you done?" Wainscoate shrieked. "What have you done to me?"

He lowered his hands from his face, revealing the ugly work that the shattering wine bottle had done. A ghastly flap of flesh hung away from his cheekbone, revealing the gleam of bone and the horrible grin of exposed teeth. Blood gushed down his neck.

"You! You witch! You harpy!" he shrieked.

Nora stumbled to the door. Her fingers found the knob, and she flung it open as the hallway filled with footsteps.

"Seize her!" Wainscoate bellowed. "She assaulted me!"

Nora bolted outside, straight into the arms of Mr. Scrumpton, who seized her shoulders with wide eyes. "Miss Ellis!"

"It was him. It wasn't me! He accosted me!" Nora shouted.

Sorrow clouded the butler's eyes. He lowered his voice. "Run. Run to her ladyship. If she supports your story over her father's, you might have a future in service somewhere.

But make haste. If he calls for the police, you will hang for this."

Nora's heart skipped. Had she escaped one deadly fate only to stumble into another?

"Lady Arabella is your only hope now. Run!" Mr. Scrumpton urged.

CHAPTER 20

*N*ora tore away from him and sprinted up the stairs, ignoring the wild state of her hair and the blood she could feel drying on the back of her neck. She staggered into the anteroom outside the dining hall.

Arabella spun around, an elegantly gloved hand to the jewels at her throat. "Nora! Where's your apron? What is all the ghastly shouting about downstairs?"

Nora seized Arabella's hands. "Milady, I beg you, if you ever loved me, you must listen to me and believe me now."

"Nora! Why are you so serious?"

"Please, listen!" Nora choked on her terror. "Your father seized me in the wine cellar. He accosted me."

"Accosted you! Whatever do you mean?"

"Arabella." Nora lowered her voice. "You understand perfectly well what I mean."

Arabella's eyes found the tears in Nora's dress and the ragged state of her hair, and she tore her hands away from Nora's and raised them to her mouth instead.

"No," she croaked. "Not Father. He would never."

"Well, he did, Arabella. Please. I fought back. I couldn't let him do that to me. Please, you have to believe me."

"You fought back!"

"I hurt him. I had to. Arabella, please, help me," Nora begged, tears filling her eyes for the first time that evening. "Please. I need you to protect me from him."

"Protect you from my father!" Arabella backed away. "Do you hear what you're saying, Nora? Do you hear what you're accusing him of doing to you?"

"It's true, Arabella! He tore my clothes! He wounded me!"

"No. Not Father." Arabella's tears spilled over. "He would never."

"Would he?" Nora's snap startled even her. "Would he never, Arabella? He brought a kitchen maid to be your lady's maid, whether you and your mother liked it or not."

"Father's a bully. I've always known that," Arabella cried through her tears, "but to do something like this to you— no! No, he wouldn't. He's a cruel, cruel man, but he — he's not—" She didn't have the words for a man who would accost a woman like this.

Nora lowered her hands. "You don't believe me then."

Arabella's face crumpled. "How could I?"

Utter cold drenched Nora's blood. She understood then, with cold shock, that she was alone in the world once more. This stupid girl, the girl she'd tended, the one she'd trusted, would betray her in this, her hour of need.

If he calls for the police, you will hang for this.

Footsteps thundered on the hallway. Wainscoate was coming, and he would see Nora hang rather than admit the horror he had committed. And the police would believe him. They would far rather hang a servant girl for assaulting her master than believe that a fine gentleman such as the Lord Wainscoate could be capable of an offense so appalling.

Nora did not pause to waste another breath upon Arabella. Instead, she seized her skirts and bolted through the other door, straight into the dining room where rows of silverware and finest china waited beneath the garlands and the ribbons. Her flying feet caught a drape, and she tugged her foot away before she could fall, bringing a sheet of ribbons and decorations crashing to the ground.

There was a scream behind her; it sounded like Arabella's. Nora had no time to look back. She crashed into the great hall and kept running, passing the splendid tree, an emblem of hope and joy and brilliance in a world that truly held only darkness and cold.

"Seize her!" Wainscoate bellowed. "Seize that villainous wench!"

Nora barged through the double doors and raced down the front steps. The night beyond was damp and cold, the wind howling, and she prayed that it would hide her swiftly. She swung hard to the left and rushed past the glasshouse, then cut to the right and scrambled through a hole in the hedge.

Hounds were baying. They were fit for the winter's hunting, and they howled for blood. Only this time it was the blood of not a hare or a fox, but a girl.

Nora ran. The night was thick with smog, so dense that she could barely see ten yards ahead, but Nora ran with all her speed. She ran until the splendid houses and Christmas decorations around her faded into the monotony of smaller homes, until the night air stank of poverty, until she was once again in the scum of Devil's Acre, only a few miles from all Westminster's splendour.

She slowed here at last, ducked into the shadow of an

empty building, and waited with her heart pounding wildly in her chest. Neither voices nor hounds pursued her. They had given up.

Of course they had. Those toffs would never dare venture into a place like this, but Nora knew its heartbeat, even though five years had passed since she last wandered these streets.

She emerged from the building's utter darkness and crept into the street, and the effects of running through the smog caught up with her all at once. Suddenly, she realized her chest had become so tight that the air wheezed in and out with audible difficulty. It throttled her. She choked on it, hands to her throat, and coughed until every inch of her body ached with the effort.

Doubled over and struggling, Nora staggered down the silent street. Between the thick, reeking smog and her streaming eyes, she didn't see the heavy thing at her feet until she tripped over it.

Her knees struck the half-frozen mud with a squelch. Nora looked around in the dark, trying to work out what obstacle had tripped her, and in the sullen gleam of a distant streetlamp, she saw a hand.

An arm.

Her gaze followed it, horrified, to the face, bluish and mottled, the eyes flat and glassy.

She had tripped over a corpse.

A shriek escaped her, triggering a fresh wave of coughing and retching. Nora stumbled to her feet and staggered down the street, striving toward the lamp, the only light she could see. She grasped the lamppost like a lifeline and clung to it, her head swinging left and right, struggling to orient herself in the thick grey curtain that surrounded her with its stench.

A bell-tower helped her gain her bearings. She was in a street not far from the market square where the milliner once had her shop and Nora once sold fish from a cart and went home every night to a boy who looked at her as though she held the whole world together.

She pressed her cheek against the frigid metal of the lamppost. Someone had hung a Christmas wreath on it; a sad approximation of the glorious ones that used to be at the Wainscoate house. Its leaves were tatty, its berries shrunken. It had no ribbons.

Her hopes felt as sad and shrivelled as that wreath.

The world spun around her. Nora leaned on the lamppost, sucking in painful breaths that stung her chest, wondering how much poison she had inhaled in this smoggy air as she sprinted. Did it matter? Did anything matter, anymore?

If she might not live to see another Christmas, perhaps that was a mercy. This time of year had never been good to her.

"Miss?"

Nora didn't open her eyes. The faint voice was kind, but it felt far away.

"Miss, are you all right?"

Something touched her arm. Wheezing, the world spinning, Nora raised her head.

She knew then that she was close to death, for the face looking earnestly into hers was warm and familiar, dusted with freckles, the smile filled with crooked teeth, the eyes as dark green as a Christmas tree.

Bobby. Bobby had come to take her to heaven with the angels.

His eyes widened. "Nora?"

She reached up and her fingertips fluttered on his warm cheek, and then darkness swallowed her.

CHAPTER 21

A fire crackled, and the air smelled of hot milk.

Nora was confused. Mama was the last person who'd told her about death and what came after, and she'd never mentioned warm milk or a hearth fire. Then again, Mama had not told her many details about heaven. Nora barely even knew if she believed in it.

Where else could she be?

She stirred, and a fierce pang of pain ran through her chest.

She was alive, then.

Her eyes snapped open. How could this be? She could have sworn she saw...

Bobby.

He was standing at the door to the tiny room where she lay on a narrow cot against the wall. Two more cots followed the other walls, one containing an old man who snored loudly and drunkenly. The fireplace and a tiny table with a rickety chair, where a bowl of something that steamed stood, completed the little place's furnishings. Even though Bobby had his back to her, even though five years had grown him and made his shoulders broader, Nora knew his silhouette as immediately and certainly as if they had never spent a day apart.

She sat up, finding herself still fully dressed, though her hands and face had been wiped clean.

"Bobby?" she whispered.

He spun around, shutting the door quietly behind him. Nora guessed that whatever lodging-house this was, it would of course not approve of her as his guest.

His face was unreadable, but it was him. Nora had no need of pinching herself. Her legs, feet, and chest hurt far too intensely for this to be a dream.

"Bobby." She leaned forward. "It is you!"

She stretched her hands out, not knowing how this could be possible, but desperate to pull him into her arms. But Bobby didn't come to her at once. Instead, he went to the table, retrieved the cup, and brought it to her.

"Your throat sounds so raw," he murmured. "Drink."

Nora clutched the cup. It was raw, but far more painful was the strange reservation in his shoulders.

If he wasn't dead, where had he been for five years?

"Drink," he said again, more softly.

Nora sipped. The milk gloriously soothed the agony in her throat.

"You're lucky to be alive," said Bobby. Time's passage had done nothing to change his voice, though Nora noticed a knotted scar at the top of his left temple. His hand, too, was scarred as he placed it on her elbow to steady her arm. "Many folks have died in this awful smog. Almost seven hundred, when I last heard."

Twelve. That was the number of people who had died in the Clerkenwell explosion. Bobby was one of them... or so Nora had thought.

Where have you been? she wanted to demand of him, but the hand on her arm was just as she remembered. Absolutely steady.

He couldn't be a ghost.

She lowered the cup. Her voice felt better, and sounded stronger. "You're alive," she said again.

"Of course I'm alive." Bobby's voice cracked, and he looked away. "I've been alive all these years, and alone."

Alone. He made the word sound so unutterably hollow.

"Where were you?" Nora whispered.

He raised his head, his eyes shining with emotion. "Where do you think? I was right here. Where were you?"

The sharpness in his tone stung her. She stared at him, speechless.

"I looked everywhere for you," said Bobby. "I asked everyone. Fran didn't know where you'd gone. I stopped people in the market square, but no one had seen the fishmonger in weeks. I even asked Jack Ketch's boys. No one knew, Nora! It was like you were a ghost!"

"What did you expect me to do?" Nora almost shouted.

"I thought you would look for me."

"I did!" Nora flung back the blanket he'd used to cover her and stumbled from the bed. He'd taken off her shoes. She found them nearby and pulled them on, her cheeks blazing with embarrassment. "I heard about the explosion and ran straight to the prison, and I saw the rubble. I saw a wall that'd been blown to dust. Blood on the street. I dug through the rubble until my fingernails bled, Bobby, and I never found you. Only your hat."

"You didn't think to search the hospitals?" Bobby cried. "I lay in St. Thomas' for weeks, but when I could walk again, I came straight here. And you were gone! I went to every hospital in London, Nora. St. Bartholomew's, Guy's, the London Hospital, I described you to every nurse and porter who would listen. No one had seen you. Even Fran couldn't tell me where you'd gone! You just gave up on me, there and then?"

"Of course not! But the men at the rubble told me you were dead. I saw your hat soaked in blood! What was I meant to do? I went to St. Thomas' myself, Bobby — twice! — but they had no record of a Robert Tibbett. No one knew your name. You were just another body from the explosion."

Bobby's face crumpled. "They had me down as unknown. I couldn't speak for three days. By the time I could tell them my name…"

"I'd already gone." Nora's voice broke. "We were both looking, Bobby. We just kept missing each other."

"How could you say that? Of course not!"

"I went into domestic service. Where else could I go?" Nora wrapped her arms around her body, feeling naked and stupid with her dress torn and her apron gone. "If you searched so hard for me, why didn't you find me there?"

"Because…" Bobby paused. "Because I never thought my Nora would become a maid."

He sounded so heartbroken, and somehow that was worse than his anger. All this time, she'd thought Bobby would be proud of her for her efforts.

Instead, he was ashamed.

"I'm sorry." Nora pushed past him to the door. "I'm sorry that I wasn't good enough for you, Bobby."

"I never said that!" Bobby burst out.

She pulled the door open and stood there, looking back at him, for a long moment. In those endless seconds, it felt to her as though five years of domestic work pressed down on her all at once. The cruelty she'd endured from Clementine and Mrs. Cratchet. The long hours, the utter impossibility of any real rest. The stalking darkness of Wainscoate's attentions. It all flooded her at once with its breathtaking futility.

"I wish you'd come sooner," she whispered. "I wish you'd come to find me."

Her voice broke. She turned and ran down the hallway of the boarding house, heading down the first flight of stairs she saw, and reached the front door as her tears spilled over.

They blinded her even more than the fog and the dark. Nora stumbled to a walk, realized that she was on a familiar street in Devil's Acre, and headed down it toward the market square with tears flowing incessantly down her cheeks.

She stopped twice to look back, but Bobby did not follow.

Nora slept very little that night. The beds in the servants' quarters of the Wainscoate house had been narrow, and their straw mattresses thin, yet it seemed she had grown used to their comparable comfort. Curling up in a shop doorway barely out of the howling wind was almost intolerable.

She huddled there, shivering, and slept in fitful snatches until the street began to wake. Every shop had a wreath upon the door and bunting in the window. When merry voices spoke in the living quarters above the shop door, Nora moved away, knowing the shop would soon open.

Dimly, she realized that it was Christmas Eve. The shops would be busy.

She could sweep crossings, perhaps. Fine folk would soon flock to this street seeking last-minute gifts or ingredients for sumptuous Christmas lunches the likes of which Nora had once helped to assemble in the Wainscoate house.

She thought of the little stash of coins she'd hidden in her trunk back in the servants' quarters and cursed Wainscoate and his cowardly daughter for robbing her of the only savings she had to show for six good years of work.

Nora brushed her hands over her dress, removing flakes of snow and trying to compose herself. She needed a plan if she was going to survive.

What for? The shame she'd heard in Bobby's voice felt like lead weights on each of her feet, making it impossibly difficult to move.

A candle flared in a window behind her, casting her reflection sharply in the still-curtained glass of the store nearby. The red marks on her face appeared less painful than they truly were; she could perhaps pass them off as ordinary blotches. Her dress's tears were all in the back.

She turned to face the window, her thoughts calculating. Even without her apron, Nora was still surprisingly presentable. If she washed her face at the nearest pump and smoothed back her hair beneath her bonnet, she still had a chance, even without references, of finding work... if no one recognized her as Lady Arabella's scandalous maid.

It was the only chance she had. She gathered up her skirts and squared her shoulders, her resolution coming more as a force of habit than any real determination, and strode back toward Westminster.

Nora resisted the urge to creep along the path leading to the servants' entrance of the grand house. She tried to remember the name of the family who lived here. Arabella had never been a guest here, the reason Nora had chosen this home in the first place. They had chosen pale blue and silver for their Christmas decorations.

It was a striking combination, Nora had to admit to herself.

She thought of that first Christmas in the tenement, with her sore ankle and the softness of that white breadroll, and the tree all glorious in the market square. Tears prickled her eyes as she trudged down the snowy path. She had thought all that beauty had died with Bobby.

Now he was alive, but could he ever forgive her? He was right. She should've searched harder. She should never have given up on the one she loved more than anything.

She took a steadying breath. Perhaps she could make things right later. Now, she had to survive, and that meant finding work.

Halfway to the servants' door, she stopped and looked left and right, searching for savage dogs. But the groom walking past with a blanketed horse didn't spare her a second glance. Perhaps all Westminster had not been privy to her confrontation with Wainscoate after all.

She squared her shoulders and marched up to the door.

A harassed-looking cook, her nose and cheeks patterned with varicose veins, answered it at the first door. "Land's sakes! What do you want? I thought you were the man with the goose. It's Christmas Eve! I don't have time for this!"

"Of course not, ma'am, but if you wish to have a pair of hands lightening your load, I can help you."

The cook's eyes narrowed. "You're in a maid's uniform, but where is your apron?"

Nora dodged the question. "I've worked as a kitchen maid for a year and a lady's maid for five. There's nothing in the kitchen I don't know, ma'am."

"A lady's maid..." The cook gasped. "What! It's you!" She recoiled as though Nora had morphed into a venomous snake.

"I'm the fastest dishwasher in London, ma'am," said Nora quickly, "and I chop quicker than anyone you've ever seen. I can make a good pastry, and my aspic..."

"Nora Ellis!" the cook shrieked. "The harpy who attacked Lord Wainscoate!"

Nora froze.

"The Lady Arabella made sure everyone knew all about you," the cook hissed. "Why are you here? Will you cut me up, too?"

"No! Of course not! I'm..."

"Help!" the cook shrieked. "Help! It's her! It's that horrid Ellis girl!"

Feet thundered in the kitchen. Nora felt her future fracturing around her.

Not only would there be no references, but her reputation was tarnished forever. Arabella and her father had made sure of it. No one in London would ever hire Nora again.

"There she is!" The cook pointed.

Nora had no options left. She seized her skirts, wheeled around, and ran once again for her life.

CHAPTER 22

The workhouse had changed very little in the eight years since Nora had left it, although she noticed that they had added new bricks to the wall beneath the palisades, the spot where Nora had first tried to escape.

It surprised her that no one had tried to drive her away. Perhaps she was not the first desperate and starving soul to sit here, on the edge of the gutter across the street, and contemplate the austere building rising against the quiet afternoon like a sombre threat despite the cheer.

She could not help but notice the contrast between the workhouse before her and the church behind. The church dripped with finery. Candles shone in its stained-glass windows, casting squares and triangles of colourful light on the deep banks of glittering snow that surrounded it. Strings of tinsel and bright ribbons wrapped around its pillars, and the open front doors offered a glimpse into a golden interior all shining with garlands and holly.

But the workhouse was as plain as ever, except for a single wreath on the front door, its presence barely nodding to the fact that it was Christmas Eve.

She wondered if that same cruel matron still worked there. If Felicity now lorded it over the women. If the work was truly as hard as everyone said.

But it was the only place in the world where she could have a hot meal, and she hadn't had a morsel to eat in more than a day. Nora could feel the tingle of the smog's effects low down in her chest and knew she would not survive long on these streets.

She stood up, brushing snow from her skirt, and the wind changed. It brought with it the music pouring from the church as its patrons enjoyed their Christmas Eve service.

Yet with the woes of sin and strife
The world has suffered long
Beneath the angel-strain has rolled
Two thousand years of wrong.

Sin. Strife. Suffering. It was all so wrong, and those angels had never felt so far away.

Nora stepped toward the workhouse, then stopped. The sound of humming reached her, pure and melodic and so painfully familiar.

Bobby was walking his beat. His silhouette came around the corner in the dusk. She watched as he raised up the long pole, with a speck of brilliance flickering at the end of it, and applied it to the wick within the streetlamp. It flared to life and filled the world with gold, bathing him in ethereal light.

Nora couldn't move. After all these years, her dear lamplighter had found his way back to the same old beat.

Had he done so searching for her? Had he been faithfully bringing light to these streets hoping that, one day, that radiance would shine upon her?

She thought of the friendship they had grown through

those palisades, of the love that had swelled between them in the years they'd scrounged for survival on the streets. It had been a hard, hard time, and yet the happiest of her life.

In her heart, she knew that the only magic, the only joy, the only beauty left in her world lay in him. For that, she would do anything. She only had to make him understand that.

He lit the next lamp, the golden light spilling over his face, and Nora knew then that he was everything she had ever wanted.

Strength flooded her. She rose to her feet.

"Bobby," she whispered.

He looked up. The light in his eyes was brighter than any flame. Snowflakes swirled through the air, catching brilliance in the lamplight.

"I'm sorry," said Nora. "I'm sorry for all of it. Five years we could have been together… and they're gone. Five years I missed you. Longed for you. Dreamed of your face every night, of your gentleness." Tears blurred her vision; she blinked them away sharply, determined to remember this moment. "I know I should have searched better for you, but please, understand that I never stopped loving you. Not for an instant. All this time, every breath, I've wished to be beside you, Bobby. I've loved you always."

His dark green eyes held hers, unreadable. She poured words into the silence, feeling they were her only hope.

"There's been no real Christmas in my life without you," she said, "but you… you brought light and magic to my life. You made everything worthwhile. You were my Christmas miracle. Without you… there hasn't been any of that. I'm sorry, Bobby. I can't ask you to forgive me or ever to care for me again, but I need you to know how sorry I am and how I feel about you."

"Oh, Nora." Bobby's face crumpled, and he cast the pole aside, its flame extinguished in a hiss amid the snow. "I'm the one who should have searched harder for you. I'm so sorry for all of it. For everything!"

He rushed to her, arms wide, and Nora cast herself upon his chest as he drew her into his arms. She didn't know if she was laughing or crying, only that the world smelled like him again, like lamp oil and pine needles, and he was hugging her so close that she could hardly breathe.

He didn't tell he that he had loved and missed her all those years, too, but he had no need to. That embrace said everything.

The next Christmas miracle came that very evening: the room beside Bobby's in the grimy little boarding-house had an open bunk. An older woman inhabited it in the brief hours when she was not at the factory, working, and she was content to share the grubby cubicle with Nora for a mere tuppence a week.

Of course, Nora didn't have tuppence. Bobby did.

"I'll find work," Nora said.

"Not tonight," said Bobby, and handed over the coin with a smile.

Nora slept better that night than she had done in a long time.

The next morning, Christmas Day, she woke to the hiss of snow on the rooftop and the deafening snores of her companion. A church bell somewhere was chiming seven;

Nora knew she could have more sleep if she liked, but her domestic habits died hard.

She lay in the narrow bunk, feeling the crawl of bedbugs through the thin sheets, and listened to the bell's chimes as they died away slowly. Part of her longed to get out of bed and go looking for Bobby. The other part of her feared that he had been nothing but a good dream in a mind addled by fear and exhaustion.

Nora had to find out. She rose, washed her hands and face swiftly in the water basin in the corner, and dressed. It had taken a few hours last night by candlelight to mend the rips in her black dress, but at least it felt respectable again when she donned it. She didn't miss the starched white apron. It was an emblem of a world that had rejected her.

After tiptoeing past her slumbering roommate, Nora eased the rickety door open slightly, and almost bumped into Bobby.

His green eyes shone with his smile. "Merry Christmas, my darling."

Nora giggled. "Bobby!"

"Hush! You'll wake the others." Bobby nudged the door shut and took her hand. "Come! I want to show you something."

Her fingers wrapped warmly in his, Bobby led her down the stairs between blotches of black mould and streaks of damp. They emerged onto a street bustling with early risers on their way to church services. The wind had stopped, and the snow fell steadily but not hard, so that everyone's Sunday finery could be on full display. Children had freshly-scrubbed red faces and clutched their new toys with shining eyes. Even the impoverished had a sense of gaiety about them, with stained ribbons in the women's hair and men with sprigs of holly stolen from hedgerows in their buttonholes.

Nora half expected Bobby to lead her to the church opposite the workhouse. Instead, hand-in-hand, they walked in the opposite direction, moving deeper into the slums of Devil's Acre. Even on Christmas, the ugliness of this place was fully on display. A wagon rumbled by, its canvas covering barely capable of hiding the lumpy shapes of human bodies beneath. Victims of the smog, Nora guessed.

They passed a bony old hag who huddled on a heap of stained and reeking rags. She held out a hand in mute appeal, her fingernails curved and yellowing, her eyes black pits in her face. Nora had nothing to give her.

"Bobby..." she murmured.

"Almost there."

They turned down a street that felt suddenly familiar, and Nora gasped at the sight of the market square beyond, for there it was. The Christmas tree. Logically, she knew it could not be the same as the one Bobby had shown her on that blessed Christmas five years ago, but it seemed exactly the same, from the gold star at its peak to the ribbons and tinsel that wound around it.

"Do you remember this?" Bobby whispered.

She squeezed his fingers. "Oh, Bobby. How could I forget?"

His eyes found hers. "You didn't forget?"

"Never."

His smile filled the world. When he reached into his pocket, Nora was almost not surprised to see what he drew out: two soft white rolls, steaming from the oven.

"Bobby!"

He grinned, seeing that she did remember. "Merry Christmas, Nora."

She bit into one, its fresh fragrance flooding her senses, and the five years of suffering barely seemed to matter now that she stood once more beside him.

"I'll find work," she said. "Or sell things. Maybe fish. It'll all be all right. I'll make sure of it."

Bobby wrapped an arm around her shoulders, drawing a few disgusted glances from the odd person hurrying by. Nora cared little for them. The people of Westminster already believed she had seduced that fool Wainscoat. Though she knew no one in Devil's Acre would recognize her, she had grown tired of the scandals and the rumours that had so destroyed her life.

Let people believe whatever they liked. Bobby was hers.

"You're here," said Bobby. "It's already all right."

She pressed closer to his warm presence. In her heart, she knew he was right.

PART V

CHAPTER 23

1878

The tenement floor was filthy, but Nora had nowhere else to put the baby.

She had done her best with what little she had: a scrubbing brush and a pail of cold water. There had been no money for soap this week. It seemed at times that this tenement building's dirt was ingrained in the very materials from which it had been built. As though no amount of scrubbing could ever remove it all.

Little John sat in the middle of the floor, bundled in his patched and faded shorts and tiny jacket. He seemed content enough to bang on the floor with Nora's only frying pan. She winced at the sound, but it was better than his screaming. Perhaps some would say that the child was undisciplined. Nora was only happy to see him moving about and making noise like any baby his age should do.

"Is that my good little boy?" she cooed.

John gave a chubby giggle.

Nora smiled and leaned down from her stool by the fire

to tickle his cheek. He was such a precious little child, with his papa's big green eyes and a mad tumult of black curls. She only wished she could see his cheeks grow round and rosy. They remained forever pallid, always sunken. Perhaps that was why he was so little for his age, or at least, so people told her. Nora wouldn't know.

Neither of the other two had made it to this age. Poor, dear little Emily had been born blue and unmoving, and dear George was two months old when Nora went to lift him from his crib one night and found him cold and stiff.

She pushed the memories away. They clutched at her heart like so many others, a lifetime of grief unrolled behind her, seemingly too much for her twenty-seven years. But she had little John now, and he might be sallow, but he was here and alive and laughing as he slammed the frying pan on the ground.

"There's my good little man," she told him.

She returned her attention to the shirt on her lap and worked quickly in the fire's fading light. When it grew later she could light a candle, but that was yet another expense. For now she leaned close and sewed the tiny hole in the dull glow of firelight.

When she had finished, Nora spread the shirt on the table (the only fully clean surface in her home) and folded it neatly. Then she added it to the bundle of finished mending on the table's corner and tied it with a piece of string.

The string always reminded her so poignantly of Mama. She smiled at the memory as she set the bundle aside. Somehow, her life had led her to a place similar to her mother's, doing piecework at home in a bid to keep her family fed and the rent paid. If only she still had Mama's bone-handled scissors. Nora's own were cheap and dull;

she had to sharpen them on a stone every few days. Mama's had held their edge for years.

John suddenly set down the frying pan and crawled determinedly to the door, little hands slapping on the grubby floor.

"John!" Nora jumped up from her chair and scooped the baby from the ground. "Where are you going, you silly boy?"

A moment later, the hallway creaked, a floorboard buckling under Nora's feet from the weight of someone outside. The bit of string they used in place of a door latch untied and Bobby stepped into the tenement, all smiles.

John squealed and held out his hands.

"Oh, that's why!" Nora laughed. "He knew you were coming, dear."

"Hello, hello!" Bobby shut the door, trying to keep out the bitter cold that always threatened to infiltrate their home, and planted a kiss on John's face, then on Nora's lips. "How is my beautiful wife?"

"Oh, hark at you." Nora laughed.

"It's true, my dear. The most beautiful thing in London. No, England. No, in all the world!" Bobby kissed her again, long and fervent, making Nora's heart do somersaults in her chest.

It was in moments like these that she could forget about the cold tenement and her empty stomach.

John squealed with happiness and clutched at Bobby's shirt with tiny fingers.

"You say he knew I was coming?" Bobby asked, pulling back.

"He certainly did. He started crawling for the door just a minute before you came in. He must have heard your footsteps on the stairs."

"Well, aren't you the cleverest baby in the world, as well as the most adorable?" Bobby set down his bag and lamp-lighting pole, the long brass rod with its hook for turning gas valves and the wick-holder for carrying flame from lamp to lamp, and swept John into his arms.

"Yes, you are! Yes, that's my little boy!"

Nora left him to coo over the baby while she hurried to the fire and stirred the pot hanging over the coals.

"Mmm. What's for dinner?" Bobby asked, inhaling the smell as though it was the finest aroma.

Nora grimaced. "Cabbage soup, I'm afraid."

They hadn't had meat in two days, though at least she had procured a hard-boiled egg for his breakfast this morning. If Bobby was as dismayed as she at the prospect of another bowl of unseasoned cabbage boiled to a soggy mess, he didn't show it. He was too busy bouncing the baby up and down, laughing at the child's obvious delight.

Nora smiled. Their tenement was small and dark, but when Bobby and the baby laughed together, there were moments when she felt that they were rich enough in the ways that mattered.

She served up the bowls of cabbage soup, and Bobby returned John to his spot by the hearth, where the baby merrily resumed smacking the frying pan on the floor.

They took hands, and Bobby murmured a quiet prayer before taking up his spoon. "How did your mending go today?"

The cabbage was bitter and gritty, but Nora was hungry; she'd last had a bit of gruel for breakfast. She slurped down a mouthful. "It was all right. I finished everything for the Fletchers, and I'll take it to them in the morning. Mrs. Fletcher is quite decent. I suppose they'll give me at least sixpence."

"Sixpence would be wonderful." Bobby kept his eyes on his bowl. "Do you think you might be able to get another family or two to give you mending work to do?"

"Well... I don't know, dear. I could ask the Weavers next door to them, but I'm not sure I'd have the time. I could work later, but the candles..."

"No, no. I don't expect you to work later."

Nora reached over and laid her hand on his. "Bobby, my love, what's the matter?"

Bobby didn't move for a long second, staring fixedly into his soup.

"Bobby?" Nora prompted.

Bobby inhaled deeply, then raised his eyes to hers. "My overseer came to see me today."

"My overseer came to see me today."

Nora swallowed. The Gas Light and Coke Company had been cutting routes for months now, ever since the new shareholders took over. The men who ran it had never lit a lamp in their lives, but they knew how to count pennies.

"They're taking away part of my route. They say it's growing too expensive to keep all these lamplighters."

"It's because of those new-fangled electric lights, isn't it?" Nora groaned. She had seen them on the Embankment, harsh white globes that never flickered, never needed a man with a pole to coax them to life. One switch could light a hundred of them. "You said this could happen. Oh, Bobby, what does this mean?"

"It means that they're paying me less, Nora. One-quarter less every week."

Nora closed her eyes, absorbing the blow. One-quarter less! They barely made the rent as it was; Nora's mending often stood between them and starvation. And they were in the cheapest tenement on the block. They had specifically taken the one with the leaky roof because nobody else wanted it, even though John sometimes upended the pail on himself on rainy days.

She said none of this to Bobby. She knew that he knew.

"It'll be all right," Bobby was saying quickly. "I'll find something else, I know it. We might have to be a little careful for a while, that's all."

Nora lowered her spoon, dismayed. "Bobby... we're already as careful as we can be."

"I know, love, I know." Bobby's face fell. "I'm so sorry." His voice cracked.

Nora gripped his hand tightly. "Don't be sorry. We'll work it out, I know we will."

Bobby nodded. "We will. Together, like we always do."

"Together."

He smiled, released her hand, and took another bite of his soup, but his shoulders were still stiff, his movements ragged.

Sudden tightness overwhelmed Nora's chest. "Oh, Bobby, none of this would be necessary if I'd only stayed away from Lord Wainscoate. I could have been a housekeeper in Arabella's house by now. We would have had everything we needed. If I had only..."

"No." Bobby grabbed her hand. "None of that, my love."

He very seldom spoke firmly with her, but there was steel in his tone now.

"None of this is your fault," he said. "All the evil you've suffered has been because of that dreadful man, not because of you. We'll win out in the end, you'll see. Goodness always wins. Why, it's the first of December today, isn't it? Only a few weeks before Christmas. Isn't that what

Christmas is all about? The light always wins. The darkness never can."

Nora met his eyes and smiled despite the heaviness in her chest. In moments like these, when her hope ebbed low, she could always borrow a little from her dear husband.

CHAPTER 24

John had finally fallen asleep. He had been screaming ever since Nora left the tenement and he felt the cold wind on his poor little cheeks. Try though Nora did to keep him covered beneath his woolly hat and in the sling she used to carry him on her chest, bundled in blankets, John always felt the cold more than most children seemed to. He cried, a thin, hungry wail, until slept claimed him at last while Nora hurried through the streets.

She tugged at the corner of his hat, trying to cover his little cheek, and then returned both hands to the bundle of mending in her arms. A few flakes of snow settled on the shirt on top, and Nora quickly brushed it away. The Fletchers were kind, but the Lorntons down the street could sometimes deduct a ha'penny or two from their payments if she brought the clothes back the slightest bit damp or crinkled.

Those ha'pennies meant eating or going hungry now, with Bobby's wage so savagely docked. A fresh burst of hot anger stung Nora's fingers and toes.

The fact that a man like Wainscoate could get away with the lies he'd told about her was a sick, ugly thing in this world.

A gust of wind howled past her, bringing a handful of snow. She turned her back, hunching her shoulders to protect John. The baby whimpered, nuzzling her, but didn't wake. Determined to keep the clothes dry and her child sleeping, Nora tucked herself into the nearest doorway, shielding little John with her body.

Music seeped through the cracks around the door. A Christmas carol, sung in two voices together, one deep, one pure.

"And man at war with man hears not the love song which they bring. O hush the noise, ye men of strife, and hear the angles sing!"

Nora closed her eyes. The pure voice was so pretty that it transported her back to the cottage, listening at the window with her mother, a long time ago. She cuddled John close and planted a delicate kiss on the tip of his little cold nose. If only she could give John half the love that Mama and Papa had showered upon her, then she would feel she had at least done something good in this world.

She raised her head, curious about the carollers who sang so joyfully, and looked through the window. With a ripple of shock, she realized that she was in the market square where once she'd been a fishmonger. She passed through it daily on her way to her mending clients, of course, but these days she was so hurried and so focused on John that she barely had time to look around.

Even the first time she'd passed by here, four Christmases ago shortly before she and Bobby were wed, she'd been startled at how little the millinery had changed. Still now, it was the same as it had always been: bright with decorations even this early in December, all ribbons and wreaths and a Christmas tree in the corner. Mannequins proudly displayed festive gowns for Christmas parties. Bolts of bright cloth invoked the thought of shining baubles or radiant holly berries.

And the milliner was still there, old and grey now, but laughing as she spun and danced to the Christmas carol, her husband's arms around her.

Nora knew she was fogging up the glass with her breath, but the milliner and her husband seemed far too caught up in their joy to notice some skinny street woman and her babe.

They were separated only by a few feet of space and a pane of glass, yet it seemed as though the milliner and her husband belonged to an entirely different world. A realm of light and laughter and warmth, a far cry from the cold and hunger that filled Nora's world.

She bowed her head, leaning her brow against the glass, and felt a soul-deep ache fill her. The girl she'd been ten years ago believed she would be like this milliner someday. That she would be able to provide coziness, charm, and beauty to her family and to all who came through her doors.

Instead, here she was, the ghosts of two lost babies looking over her shoulder, and the third wheezing quietly as he slept on her chest.

Her tears welled up, hiding the precious scene from view. She pulled her baby closer with one arm and, clutching the bundle of clothes with the other, hurried off down the dreary lanes of her life, leaving all those dreams behind.

The only apothecary within walking distance of the tenement was on the very edge of Westminster, perilously near the snarled streets of Devil's Acre. Nora always felt nervous and out of place there, and she walked fast, dodging the well-dressed men and women who swept along the clean sidewalks in their full dresses and handsome suits. Their lips curled as she darted by, as though her presence made her unworthy, as though the screaming baby on her chest was worth less than the children they left at home with wet nurses.

"Shhh, shhh." Nora tried to calm little John, stroking his hat. "You'll feel better when we get home. Mama's going to help you." She carried a packet of ground mustard, which she would use to make a hot poultice on the baby's chest. It cost a painful amount of money, she and Bobby would live on bread and tea for several days, but it was the only thing that brought the child any relief when he grew chesty and fussy.

She passed a jeweller's shop, its window adorned with garlands and a sign announcing a discount for anyone buying more than one sapphire bracelet ("Perfect for Christmas!"), and was about to turn down the next street when two black horses snorted up to the corner, drawing a magnificently polished brougham. Their harness bells jingled, their breath was jets of white steam, and Nora stopped quickly. She didn't want to get in the way of whoever was about to emerge from the hatter ahead; it was a surefire way to receive a cane to the shins or a curse to the ears.

She turned her attention to John, rocking and shushing him as he began to fuss again.

Someone gasped. "Nora?"

Nora's head snapped up. There, only a few feet away,

stood Lady Arabella. She had put on weight and her cheeks were rosy now, but it was certainly her, with her husband Lord Weatherby standing beside her. Her great eyes sparkled like jewels as they found Nora's face.

Nora recoiled.

Arabella raised a hand to her mouth. "Nora!" she cried.

"What?" someone roared from inside the brougham, and instantly, as if the past few years had disappeared in a moment, Nora was back in that wine cellar with his breath on her face and his hands searching for the edges of her corset.

Wainscoate lunged from the brougham, and a ripple of shock ran through Nora at the sight of him. The mark on his face was more than a scar. It was a disfigurement. It dragged the corner of his mouth upward into a horrible grin, while at the same time, his eye hung down, revealing a flash of pink membrane.

"You," he hissed.

Nora's arms went tight around John, waking him. He let out a wail, and it awoke something deep and savage in her chest, something that would have fought a tiger to protect him. She knew then that she had to do everything in her power to save her baby from that hateful man.

In a trice, she had darted down an alley, vaulted over a low wall and bolted into the dark labyrinth of Devil's Acre, the one place she knew that Wainscoate would never find her.

CHAPTER 25

The glow was cold, unnatural, white. Nora's free arm tightened around little John in his sling. She tried to keep her fingers relaxed as Bobby held her other hand, but he must have sensed the nervousness in her, for he gave her fingers a gentle squeeze as if to reassure her.

She gave him a bright smile, yet she doubted it could mask the boiling terror in her belly.

A thick crowd had gathered, and they moved through it only slowly. The air buzzed with happy anticipation. Children laughed and ran past with toffee apples on sticks or oranges in their hands, their cheeks rosy, muffled in warm coats and scarves. Here and there, the curious poor also moved among the crowd, but most of the folk here were well-dressed. They could afford to spend a cold December evening outside.

December thirteenth. There was something ominous about the date. Superstition wrapped its cold fingers around it, and as they neared the pale glow, Nora felt the world shifting around her. She felt that it would never be quite the same.

John mercifully slept against her, nuzzled into her chest, his tiny fists curled up beside his face. His breathing was better tonight. The mustard poultice had worked, even though the thought of it reminded her painfully of Wainscoate and his ruined face.

They paused on a corner to let a carriage by, and Bobby tilted back his head to look up at the streetlamp beside them. Its cheerful yellow flame danced upon the gas that fed it, sheltered by the thick panes of glass. "That's one of mine," Bobby said quietly. "I light it every evening. Have done for six years." His voice held a note of farewell.

Nora had always loved the way that golden light caressed Bobby's cheeks, bringing out the soft freckles and framing the rich curls of his hair.

The carriage passed.

"Come along, love." Bobby smiled. "Let's see history in the making."

Nora feared that history, but she returned his smile.

They crossed the street, leaving the warm glow of the gas lamps behind, and stood at the edge of the Thames Embankment.

The great sweep of stone stretched along the river, Big Ben looming over it, its glowing face like a second moon in the grey sky. A line of streetlamps followed its graceful curve like a string of pearls in the dark. Nora had visited the embankment before, sometimes looking for scraps, sometimes seeking work, and she remembered how the lamps had shone like jewels and cast their warm light on the water, softening the choppy waves and the long shadows of the people hurrying along its balustrade.

But now, those warm gas lights were gone. Instead, a white orb topped each of the lampposts, a cold and heartless glow unlike anything Nora had seen before. It held none of the warmth of the sun or fire and none of the gentleness of the moon and stars. It was harsh, brutal, alien, and when she looked up at Bobby, she could barely recognize him. The electric light cast sharp shadows beneath his cheekbones and around his eyes. Tiny John's face seemed bluer than ever, his skin tissue paper-like over etched veins.

He let out a moan, and Nora shielded his eyes. "He doesn't like it."

"No. No, I don't like it, either," said Bobby quietly.

Something in his voice frightened her. He looked more than disquieted by the eerie light. There was something real and serious about the nervousness on his face.

"Bobby?" Nora whispered.

His mouth turned down, making his face a grim white mask. "These lamps don't need lighters, Nora."

"What? How could they not?"

"I don't understand it myself, but that's what they said at the company. They said that they won't need us much longer anymore. There's no flames. There's no walking from lamp to lamp, putting them out and lighting them again. It's all to do with switches and wires. One person can light these lamps in an instant."

Nora's head spun. It all seemed like magic to her, and not the kind that fairy godmothers and benevolent wizards used in stories. This was witch magic, something dark and foul.

"Surely... surely you're not saying that there will be more lights like these," she said.

"I'm afraid so, my love. There will be more. Hundreds more. Thousands," Bobby whispered. "They'll light up all London with them if they can."

A London without lamplighters. A London illuminated by this soulless, pale glow.

It all made Nora feel sick. "Can you learn a new trade, Bobby?"

"I'll find the time," he said. "I'll have to."

But she knew that time was one thing that flexed for no one.

THE CANDLE FLAME danced upon the mantelpiece. Nora knew she had to use every second of its precious light to work on the torn dress spread over her lap, yet she found herself staring at it instead.

The flame was alive; it danced and dipped. Nora thought of the milliner's shop. It was always golden in there, and the warm light made the fabrics seem alive, the blues deeper, the reds more vibrant, the greens as bright as forests touched by sunlight. What would it look like under the brutality of electric lighting?

John gave a fussy little moan from the sleeping pallet where Nora had laid him. She tensed, hoping he would quiet down and go back to sleep, but he let out another wail.

A sigh escaped her. She set aside the sewing and went to the baby as he screamed. He was better, his face pinker, but that only meant he was all the more hungry. And with Bobby's stifled pay, Nora herself was hungry all the time. She tried to nurse the child, and he sucked lustily, but only for a few moments. Then he screamed again.

Tears stung her eyes. "I'm sorry," she whispered to him. "I'm trying." She switched him to the other side, and again he drank eagerly for a short while. It seemed that Nora's body had nothing to give him.

She laid the shrieking baby on the bed and went to the fire to warm up their last bit of gruel, telling herself that it would be all right. These few spoonfuls would tide John over until his father came home. Bobby knew the house was empty; he would bring bread, perhaps a few vegetables, enough to make a soup and pap for the baby. She only had to keep him alive a little longer before help would come.

John fussed, not wanting the gruel, spitting the precious nourishment all over his cheeks. Nora scraped it up with her spoon and tried her best to make him swallow it. He screamed, wanting milk, and she let the tears roll down her cheeks to match his.

The thump at the door surprised her. Nora raised her head, suddenly frightened. It was early for Bobby to be home. Was there an intruder? But what could anyone want from her home? She had nothing to give her baby, let alone a thief.

The door swung wide, and Bobby staggered through it, almost falling.

Nora flew to her feet. "Bobby!"

"I'm all right," he said, but his hand was on his face, and there was agony in his voice. "I'm all right."

She ran to him and grasped his shoulders. "What happened?"

"Don't be frightened, my love." His voice was so calm, yet it rippled with pain. "Everything is in hand."

Nora seized his wrists and pulled them away from his face. A horrible red swelling covered his cheek, already almost closing his right eye. She wanted to scream, but managed to gasp instead.

"Bobby!"

"It's only a bruise, love." Bobby wrapped his arms around her. "Please, don't be afraid."

She clung to him, shaking, their baby's cries echoing around the tenement. "What happened?"

He let out a shuddering sigh. "I don't know. They came out of nowhere, my love, while I was walking home. I tried to hold onto the money after they struck me, but they threw me to the ground and said they would kill me, and I…" His eyes went to John, then to her. "I had to come home."

"Bobby!" Nora hugged him again, harder, shaking fiercely. "Oh, my love, you did the right thing."

"I'm so sorry." His voice cracked. "They took everything, love. They… they took everything."

It was a Monday afternoon, and Christmas was on Wednesday. Bobby was bringing home his wage for the week. Their only income until Friday morning; even the mending Nora was working on, and would work on, until then would only be paid in days.

They had nothing.

The reality made her limbs feel weak. She sagged, and Bobby's arms tightened around her, but she forced herself to stand firm. She would not crumble in this moment. Not with her husband and baby looking to her.

"I'm so sorry, Nora." Bobby's eyes were full of tears.

"Don't. Don't be sorry." She cupped his face in her hands. "You came home."

"I came home with nothing."

"Bobby, you're not nothing." She kissed him, fiercely. "You're everything."

John shrieked louder.

"We have to do something." Bobby straightened. "I'll go down to the theatre. There's a big pantomime on tonight."

Pantomime. The word sent a shudder through her.

"I'll see if I can sweep crossings or hold horses." He seized the broom.

"I'll go to the market square." Nora grasped her sling and threw it over her shoulder, then scooped the baby off the bed. "That inn always used to have good scraps."

"Scraps." Bobby's hand lingered on her face. "Oh, my love, you deserve so much better."

Nora kissed him again. "We all do. I love you."

"I love you."

JOHN HAD GROWN USED to being hungry, a fact that felt like a lump of coal where her heart should be. As Nora threaded through the darkness of Devil's Acre, hastening from one streetlamp to the other as she sought the light, the baby's wails turned into moans and then to quiet fussing as he grew exhausted. She straightened his hat over his head and clutched him closer as snowflakes eddied around them.

Would this make him ill again? The thought made her sick to her stomach. This time, there truly was no money for a mustard poultice. Not a bent benny.

She could have been a head maid by now, perhaps even a cook. She would have had a cottage of her own. In her heart, she cursed Wainscoate. She half wanted to curse Arabella, too. Everything would have been different if only one person had taken her side, or if that meddling lord had left her alone to work her way up the normal way, or if Clementine had never spread those stories. Yet she could not find it in her to wish harm upon Arabella. She was just a silly, weak, cowardly creature. There was no true hatred in her.

Yet her cowardice might as well have been malice for its effects on Nora, and now her little family.

She kept her arms wrapped around John as she followed the lumpy streets, careful not to trip on frozen mud or slip on the iced cobblestones. Heat. That was another problem. She believed they had enough firewood for a day or two.

Would they freeze by Christmas, just days away?

No. Nora held her baby tighter. No, we will not.

She walked a little faster, cut down that dreaded alley, and reached the marketplace in one piece. The square was busy beneath its Christmas tree. People rushed from the grocer's to the baker's and then to the butcher's, hurrying to gather ingredients for whatever feast they planned over the holiday. A broad-shouldered woman hurried by Nora with a basket on her arm, shielded by a piece of cloth; the wind had blown a corner back and Nora glimpsed potatoes and beets inside.

Her mouth watered as her baby whimpered against her chest. She thought of the wonderful treats she had helped to prepare for the Wainscoates: the julienned fowl, the magnificent lobster aspic, the delicate croquets of lamb. What she would give for the potato peelings from a feast like that!

She stopped to catch her breath and gaze hopelessly at the Christmas tree, glowing in the light of the square's streetlamps. What would it look like under electric light? Would its magic all be stolen?

Her feet had carried her to the millinery. Nora peered inside through the glass window. The milliner was presenting a dress on a hanger, wrapped in paper, to a young woman whose eyes shone with excitement. While the young woman wore a snow-dusted coat, the milliner seemed comfortable in the long lace-edged sleeves of her dress. Her shop must be as warm as ever.

Nora touched the glass as though she could reach inside and grasp the hope that shone in the green garlands hanging by the window and draped on the clothing rack. A wave of cold and longing washed over her. Her baby was asleep at last, his little thumb in his mouth in lieu of nourishment.

It was so very cold out here and she doubted that the inn had thrown out its scraps yet. A few moments in the warm wouldn't hurt.

Quietly, Nora opened the door. The milliner was in animated conversation with her customer and didn't notice her coming in, even when the bells on the door's wreath jingled. She slipped into an unobtrusive corner and rocked her baby, pretending to look at fabric she would never be able to afford.

It was wonderfully warm in here. Nora's numb toes and fingers soon regained their feeling. She wandered from one wooden dummy to the other, admiring the glorious cuts of the dresses they wore. Where did anyone learn to sew like that?

She wanted to touch the seam on the nearest gown, but knew her hands were dirty, so she kept them on her sling. Never had she seen such tidy work. Not since she was a little girl watching Mama do her mending.

Her gaze drifted to the worktable by the window, cluttered with pins and fabric and spools of thread. A pair of scissors lay there, catching the firelight.

Nora's breath stopped.

They were dressmaker's shears with handles of carved bone, worn smooth from years of use. She knew those scissors. She had held them a thousand times as a child, snipping threads for Mama in the last light of the day. They were the only beautiful thing her family had ever owned.

It could not be. It was impossible. And yet her feet carried her to the worktable as though in a dream. She reached out, then stopped herself. Her hands were filthy. She had no right to touch them.

But oh, she knew those scissors.

"You're looking at my scissors."

Nora's head snapped up. The customer had gone; she hadn't noticed. The milliner stood beside her now, her head tilted with curiosity. Gray streaked her hair in its tidy bun, but the hairline was low, the bun full. Nora had never noticed that she had soft brown eyes before.

"I'm sorry, ma'am. I didn't mean to—" Nora stepped back from the table.

"No, please. You were looking at them so strangely." The milliner picked up the scissors and turned them over in her hands. "They're very old. I've had them since I was a young woman. They came from a great lady's sewing box, sold off when she died."

Nora's heart hammered against her ribs. Those were the exact words. The exact words Mama had used.

"Where..." Nora's voice came out as a whisper. "Where did you get them?"

The milliner's smile flickered with something — surprise, perhaps, or a distant sadness. "I told you, dear. From a lady's estate, many years ago." She set the scissors down gently. "But come. You look half frozen. Would you like to warm yourself by the fire? I doubt I'll have more customers today; that was my last dress going out for tomorrow's Christmas party."

Nora hesitated. Her eyes went back to the scissors. She wanted to ask more, but the words tangled in her throat.

"The fire is warm, and those streets are cold." The milliner pulled up a stool by the crackling hearth fire that lent its golden light to the shop. "Please. Have a seat."

Nora glanced at the door. The warmth would be wonderful for John, and if the milliner tried to do anything frightening, she would be through the door and outside at once. The lady walked with a slight limp; Nora could run away from her.

"Thank you very much, ma'am." She settled on the stool.

The fire's warmth baked on her sling. John sighed and snuggled closer, falling deep asleep. Nora pulled off his little hat and stroked the downy fuzz of red hair decorating his smooth scalp.

"He's beautiful," said the milliner. She sat in an armchair near Nora's. "How old?"

"Seven months now. I know that he's small. He's been ill."

"A wonderful age." The milliner's eyes softened. "I so enjoyed my daughter at that age. They laugh so much. Any minute now, he'll be crawling, and you'll have your hands full running after him."

"I'm sure." If he lives long enough, Nora added silently, and kissed the little head.

"I was going to have Susie make a hot cup of tea. Would you like one?" the milliner asked. "Perhaps a little milk for the baby?"

Denying the offer never crossed Nora's mind. "Oh! Would you? Please. He's so hungry. I don't need tea, but milk would be wonderful."

The milliner left briefly, and Nora rocked her baby gently, her eyes on the wooden Nativity scene on the mantelpiece. The Babe in the manger was smiling, but

Mary was not. Perhaps she, too, wondered how she would keep her child alive on that cold winter's night.

The milliner returned. "Isn't it lovely? A gift from my husband."

"It's beautiful, ma'am."

A maid brought them a tray with two teacups and a little mug of warm milk for John. Nora almost snatched the mug. She untied her sling, allowing the baby onto her lap, and he immediately let out a hungry wail.

"Hush, hush." Nora raised the mug to his lips. "Here."

At the first taste of milk, the baby began to drink, his small hands grabbing at the mug. Nora fought to keep from spilling a single drop. She made sure John drank every morsel, and after that, the baby put his little head on her chest and instantly fell into a deep, contented sleep.

Nora blinked away tears as she replaced the mug on the tea tray. "Thank you. Thank you ever so much."

"It's hard to see your child hungry." The milliner sat back in her chair, smiling at nothing, perhaps at memories. "I used to cry all the time when my daughter was a baby."

"You? Why?"

The milliner laughed. "Life hasn't always brought me warm fires and Christmas dinners." She cocked her head. "You have a familiar face. I thought so the other day, when you were watching me dance with Edmund, but now I'm sure of it. You used to sell fish from a cart on the corner by my shop."

"I'm surprised you noticed me, ma'am."

"Oh, how could I not? You were always so very determined. I loved listening to you cry your fish, you were so good at it. I would have bought it from you all the time, but fish doesn't agree with my husband, so we never have it in the house."

"I learned to sell my fish by watching you sell your dresses."

The milliner laughed. "And I learned to sew dresses from doing piecework at home, and to sell them from selling rags or old cigarette butts on the street."

"I do piecework, too. It's a pity it's not enough... never enough." Nora sighed.

The milliner gave her a questioning look.

Nora didn't know why, but her story spilled out of her before she could think twice. "My husband... he's a lamplighter for the Gas Light and Coke Company. All these newfangled electric lights are causing trouble for him, and a lord I used to work for has spread so many cruel rumours about me that no one will hire me and few folk will give him the time of day, either. Then he was mugged on his way home today. We have nothing." Nora stopped. "I'm sorry."

"London can be a cruel place, especially to a woman. I'm glad you're married. That makes everything easier. I was alone for a long time."

"Alone but for your daughter, I suppose."

"No... no, I'm afraid not. I lost my little girl and my first husband on the same night."

"I'm sorry. That must have been so hard." Nora kissed John's sleeping face. "I lost both my parents on the same night, too."

"That's awful. How old were you?"

"Six." Nora sighed. "We were at the pantomime at the Royal Victorian on Boxing Day. Twenty-one years ago now, but I remember it as though it were yesterday."

The milliner listened, her face suddenly very still, her eyes intent.

"People were shouting 'Fire! Fire!' but I never saw the

flames. I found out later that there were none that ever hurt anyone , but many people died in the panic. They trampled one another. Crushed them. I only lived because my father protected me. He gave his life for me, and my mother died that day, too."

"Boxing Day, 1858." The milliner whispered the words in a harsh, low tone. Her face was absolutely white.

"That's right." Nora hesitated. "Are you all right, ma'am?"

The milliner leaned forward and seized her arm in a strong hand that startled her. She cried out and tried to pull away, but the milliner's eyes held her.

"Tell me your name," she rasped. "Tell me now."

"N-Nora Tibbett."

"Your maiden name."

"Please, ma'am, you're hurting me."

"Tell me!"

"It was Ellis!" Nora cried. "My name was Nora Ellis."

She could not be prepared for what happened next. The milliner's teacup dropped from her hand and bounced on the hearth rug. With a cry, she flew across the space between them and flung her arms around Nora.

"Little one!" she cried. "Oh, my sweet, sweet baby girl, it's you! You're alive!"

CHAPTER 26

The world spun. John woke up and squalled, but still the milliner didn't release Nora, weeping into her neck as she hugged her.

"What... what..." Nora managed.

The milliner drew back, clutching Nora's hand in both of hers. "Of course you don't recognize me, little one. No more than I recognized you. We've been apart for so many years!"

Nora's breaths came quickly. "But how can it be? The name on the door... it's C. Whitmore."

"Catherine Whitmore now, my love. I remarried in the end, once I had had my shop for a little while. He's a widower, a good man, but we could never have children. But Nora, my sweetheart, there can be no doubt."

Nora shook her head. "It... it can't be."

"It is. Tell me. What did we have for dinner that Christmas Eve?"

Nora swallowed. "Soup. I remember it so well. We only had vegetables, but you said you'd make a lovely soup, beef..."

"Beef or no beef."

Nora's free hand flew to her mouth.

"And the scissors," Catherine whispered. "You recognized them. I saw it in your face the moment you looked at them. You used to help me snip the threads."

"Every evening," Nora breathed. "In the last light of the day."

"It is so, my love. My husband, your father, dearest John, he died in that crush protecting you. So they told me later. I was thrown to the ground and knocked cold; I only came to in the hospital a week later, and everyone thought you had died along with John."

"But my body wasn't there."

"There were no real funerals for the paupers unless someone came forward. I couldn't; "All those years," Nora whispered. "I was right outside your window, selling fish. Why didn't you see me?"

Catherine's eyes filled with fresh tears. "I looked for you, darling. For years, I looked. But they told me you were dead, buried in a pauper's grave with your father. I had no reason to search the streets for a ghost."

"Papa ended up in a mass grave?" Tears suddenly filled Nora's eyes.

Catherine squeezed her hand. "Don't be sad, my love. I saw your papa go down with his arms around you. You're quite right. He's the only reason you lived... and all these years, I didn't know. All these years I longed for you and you were right outside my window."

The realization brought a flood of tears, which poured unstoppably down Nora's cheeks. "Mama," she whispered.

"Yes, darling. Yes." Catherine was crying, too. "Your mama is here."

Nora cradled John in one arm as she wrapped the other

around Catherine, and the tears flowed freely. How had she never known? Mama had always filled the world with pure magic, and in all these tough years, Nora had always known that the milliner held the same magic. But she had never dreamed that she would get to be near it again.

"I've loved you every moment. I've missed you so much," Catherine cried. "Look at you! You're grown and so beautiful, and you have a husband, and I... I have a grandson!"

"His name is John, Mama."

"John." Catherine bent and kissed the baby's head. "Oh, hello, my sweet baby. Hello, John."

Nora didn't know whether she was laughing or crying. "It's a miracle."

"A Christmas miracle!" Catherine kissed Nora's hand. "Darling, I'll take you home with me at once. We have more than enough. You'll never be hungry or cold again a day in your life, and nor will dear John." She stood. "I'll close the millinery right now and call a cab to get us home into the warm. Drink your tea."

Never hungry or cold again! Nora could hardly imagine it. She looked down at her sleeping baby and wanted that for him more than anything in the world.

"Mama, wait." Nora brushed her hand over her face. "I can't come now."

"What on earth do you mean, darling?"

"I need to bring Bobby."

"Of course." Catherine sat again. "Your husband. Can't we send him a message?"

"He's out looking for food, Mama. He was mugged on the way home from work today. I don't know when he'll get back. I have to get to the tenement and wait for him."

"A tenement." Pain crossed Catherine's face. "Oh,

darling, I hate the thought of you spending one more night away from me."

"I won't be parted from Bobby. Never."

"Of course not." Catherine smiled. "Of course. Then you must go home as you say, and bring Bobby here tomorrow. And I... I suppose I've been hasty. I must speak to my husband first, too."

Nora's heart jumped. "You think he won't approve."

"Darling, how could he not? I've told him so much about you. Let us both go home and speak to our husbands, and then tomorrow, I'll bring him here to meet you." Tears filled Catherine's smile. "You'll be home for Christmas, Nora. Truly home."

"Oh, Mama!" Nora fought her tears.

"Come." Catherine rose. "I have many old coats in the back. I'll give you plenty for yourself and Bobby, and then I shall take you around the shops and we'll buy everything you need for dinner. Tomorrow, I'll be here. Oh, say you'll come, Nora."

"Of course, Mama." Nora hugged her again. "I never want to leave your side again."

The shop bell chimed as Nora left, her arms full of parcels, Bobby steadying her elbow. Catherine watched them through the frost-rimmed window until they disappeared into the crowd.

That evening, she could barely eat.

Catherine set down her fork. The roast chicken sat untouched on her plate.

"Eddie," she said. "There's something I haven't told you about Nora."

Edmund looked up from his wine. "Go on."

"The lord she worked for. Lord Wainscoate." Catherine's hands trembled slightly as she folded them in her lap.

"He didn't just spread rumours about her. He cornered her in the wine cellar. He meant to force himself on her."

Edmund's glass stopped halfway to his lips.

"Arabella stopped him. Threw a mustard poultice in his face, burned him terribly. But Eddie..." Catherine met his eyes. "He's still out there. And he's been looking for her. That's why she's been hiding in Devil's Acre. She's been running from him for years."

The silence stretched between them. Edmund set down his glass with deliberate care.

"This man," he said quietly. "He knows she's in London?"

"He knows she's alive. He knows she has a husband and child. And he's mad with rage over what was done to his face."

Edmund was quiet for a long moment. "Then she is not safe," he said. "Not while he knows where to find her."

THE TENEMENT HAD NEVER SMELLED this good.

Nora sang as she worked. John lay on the pallet, fast asleep, lulled by her voice as she brought out their tin bowls and spoons. The savoury scent of hearty soup filled the tenement from edge to edge.

Nora had never seen her pot full before, but she had had to put the lid on to keep the simmering soup from splashing on the fire. Best of all, a loaf of bread and six glorious eggs stood on their rickety table, ready for breakfast.

Breakfast! It was a meal they often had to miss, but not again. Never again, all thanks to Mama.

"For lo, the days are hastening on," Nora sang, "by

prophet bards foretold, when with the ever circling years shall come the age of gold!"

A familiar step on the stair made her laugh. She filled the bowls to the top and still had soup left over.

"Nora, darling! It's me!" Bobby pushed the door open. "Why, someone in this tenement thinks it's Christmas already, by the smell of... what?"

Nora grinned, enjoying the shock on her husband's face. The bruise had turned purple and his right eye was swollen shut, but the left was wide open. He carried half a loaf of stale bread in one hand. Such was his shock that his fingers dug into the crust.

"What?" he managed.

"Sit down, my love." Nora pulled out a chair. "You must be so hungry."

"S-starving." Bobby placed the half-loaf beside the fat, fresh one Catherine had bought for them.

Nora placed the full bowl of soup before him. It was a thick soup, too, with carrots, parsnips, and potatoes floating amid the shredded chicken. The smell of salt, pepper, garlic, and rosemary curled from the bowl as steam.

Bobby stared at the food, then up at her. "How?"

Nora sat down opposite him. "Because of a Christmas miracle, Bobby. A real, true Christmas miracle. I had stopped believing in them. I had even stopped believing in Christmas itself. But not anymore." She laughed. "Not anymore."

Bobby held out his hand. She grasped it, and he said a quick grace, then seized his spoon and swallowed a hearty mouthful of soup. Nora enjoyed watching him eat so much that she didn't lift her own spoon, just watched. Her husband hadn't had a morsel since a scrap of dried fish and a baked potato for supper last night.

He only paused for breath halfway through the bowl. "Aren't you hungry, love?"

"Not really. Mama gave me a ham sandwich before I came home."

"Mama!" Bobby's jaw dropped.

Nora laughed. "Keep eating, my love, and I'll tell you the whole story."

And she did. She told him about the warmth of the shop and the kindness of the milliner. She told him about the milk for John and the tea and the Nativity scene on the mantelpiece. But most of all, she told him about the scissors.

"I saw them on her worktable, Bobby, and I knew. I knew. They were Mama's scissors, the bone-handled ones she treasured so. I used to hold them every evening when I helped her with the mending." Nora's voice cracked. "All these years, Mama has been right there, and I never knew."

Bobby set down his spoon and took her hand. "A Christmas miracle," he said softly.

"The scissors were the first thing I recognized. Before her face, before her voice. I looked at those scissors and something inside me just... remembered."

THE HOUSEKEEPER HAD CHOSEN roast chicken for supper; she would be sparing the goose for Christmas Day. Catherine loved chicken, but she barely picked at hers, watching instead as her husband ploughed through his plate.

The grandfather clock in the corner ticked sonorously. Heavy drapes and a warm carpet muffled the sound of cutlery and crockery. Catherine sipped her wine, trying to soothe her nerves.

She'd personally put up the Christmas decorations in this room, and she gazed at them as she waited for Edmund to eat. He had had a long, hard day's work at the office, and she wanted to give him a moment to breathe before she told him the news that bounced around inside her chest.

Merry bunting hung all around the room. Several candles sparkled on the mantelpiece, lighting up the ribbons and holly on the wreath hanging over it.

"All right, Cathy." Edmund set down his fork. "Out with it."

Catherine jumped. "I beg your pardon?"

He laughed gently, his blue eyes tender. "You've been fidgeting instead of eating, and acting so odd since I got home. Tell me what it is that's on your mind."

Catherine let out a girlish little squeal of excitement that was most unladylike. Edmund laughed.

"Eddie, you won't believe it." Catherine seized his hand. "I found Nora."

Edmund almost choked. "What?"

"I found my little girl, Eddie."

"But how? She's... she's been dead for years."

"She hasn't! She got away! While I was in hospital, there was no one to look for her, so we all thought she had died. But she hadn't. Someone took her to the workhouse. She's all grown up now, with a husband and baby, and she's alive, Edmund. She came into the millinery today by chance... no! Not by chance. By a wonderful miracle!"

Edmund clutched her hand. "Oh, Cathy, this is the most glorious news!"

"It's a miracle, a true Christmas miracle. I never thought I would see my baby again, but here she is!"

"Why didn't you bring her home?"

"She had to go back to her tenement to get her

husband, but they'll meet me at the millinery first thing tomorrow morning."

Edmund hesitated. "Tenement?"

Catherine's insides knotted at the hesitation in his voice. "That's right. I thought I would buy them clothes tomorrow, and blankets and toys for the baby, and then bring them home after closing the shop."

"Catherine, are these people..." Edmund lowered his voice. "Are they poor?"

Catherine raised her chin. "Yes, my love. Did you think a child who grew up in the workhouse would be rich?"

"How poor?"

"Darling, they don't have food or a safe home to live in."

Edmund passed a hand over his face. "And you wish to bring them here. Paupers."

Catherine fixed him with a glare. "That's my daughter and her family. I don't care if they're paupers or not."

"I know! I know." Edmund took her hand again. "But Cathy, darling, do they have to come here?"

"She's my daughter. Of course I want to bring her home."

"Yes, love, but you know how people talk." Edmund glanced around nervously as if someone might hear him at that very moment. "Don't you understand that they already sneer at us?"

"I understand that you've always tried to keep my own past as a pauper quiet, and that you married me when I was already successful."

"Cathy, you know that is not the reason I married you. I would have married you in rags."

"Then you must accept my daughter in rags, too," said Catherine sharply.

"Cathy, she won't know how to behave."

"Then I'll teach her."

"Don't you understand? Our guests consider us barely middle-class as it is. We only have a housekeeper and one maid, for goodness' sake! If we bring her to this house, do you know what that could do to my reputation? To my paper? To your millinery? Why, they barely accept the fact that you have a shop at all." He raised his hand. "I know you won't be parted with it, and that's not what I'm saying. All I ask is that you consider that we are already dangerously close to scandal."

"Edmund…"

"Let me speak, Catherine. Have you considered the implications for Nora herself?"

Catherine frowned. "What do you mean, implications?"

"Well, if she suddenly finds herself in a house like this, how will she feel? She doesn't know how to talk to people. She wasn't raised that way. If she embarrasses herself, or makes herself an object of scandal or ridicule, that would be a disservice to her."

Catherine stared into her wine glass for a few moments. "Learning how to navigate these social circles was hard for me, too."

"You see?" Edmund visibly relaxed. "Of course we will help them, Cathy, but I feel it would be better for everyone if we set them up with a nice cottage in the city. I could give the husband work at my newspaper. Then they would be comfortable and you could visit at times."

Catherine raised her head. "No. I'm not going to hide her away, Eddie. Nora is nothing to be ashamed of."

"Cathy…"

"Come with me tomorrow," Catherine begged. "We'll meet at the millinery. There won't be anything suspicious about it. Meet her, Edmund, I beg you. She was the light of my life. Please."

Edmund relented with a smile. "I'll come to meet them, but I shan't make any promises to bring them home."

"I hope you will change your mind, love."

"I doubt it," he said.

CHAPTER 27

*N*ora had never heard her child laugh so much. She had had plenty of milk for him last night, and after a hearty meal of pap that morning, he had nursed for nearly half an hour without slowing down. Feeding him and seeing him fall asleep with a full belly was the best feeling she had ever had.

Now, John didn't want to sleep in the sling. He sat in Nora's arms instead, laughing and cooing at everyone who came past. His giggles drew smiles from several pedestrians, and the baby barely coughed at all.

The effects of one night and one morning's good eating made Nora's heart soar.

"Oh, Bobby, look at him!" She laughed as she kissed the baby's head. "Isn't it wonderful?"

Bobby had barely taken his eyes off the baby since they left the tenement. "He's perfect. He's not hungry, Nora." His gaze was filled with wonder. "Neither am I."

"It's glorious. And we never have to be hungry again. Mama would never let us suffer."

"Oh, Nora, do you think so?"

"She said so. She said we could go home with her. I'll work with her in the millinery and maybe they'll know someone with a good job for you, too. Bobby, we might never have to be cold and hungry ever again."

"I can't imagine that," Bobby admitted in a quiet voice. "I don't think I've gone a week without missing a meal all my life."

"Do you know what this means, Bobby?"

"What?'

"It means Johnny might grow up never remembering cold or hunger." Nora's eyes filled with tears. "He's so very little. He won't remember these days, not at all."

Bobby seldom wept, but he looked close to it now. The tears that shone in his eyes held nothing weak, not to Nora. In them she saw love and hope and all the beautiful things that Christmas always stood for.

She could barely believe that miracles were real.

Her step quickened as they turned into the market square. It bustled even this early in the morning. Everyone rushed to the butcher, baker, and greengrocer, determined to assemble the last ingredients they needed for their Christmas feasts.

Nora pushed through the crowd until she saw the millinery, and the sight of it made her heart leap. It had always been beautiful, especially now, with its wreaths and ribbons and bunting. But today it held a special radiance, a heavenly aura, like a halo. It held all the hope that Nora had ever needed.

She strode inside. "Mama! We're here!"

Two women were already in the millinery, looking at ribbons and buttons for final changes or repairs to their dresses for tomorrow's festivities. One gave Nora a furtive glance. The other, who wore a high-collared dress studded with lace and beautiful embroidery, curled her lip and drew away.

"Mrs. Whitmore, who on earth is this creature?" she cried.

Nora's heart sank. She glanced down at her grubby, ragged dress, the only one she owned, and at the shoes splattered with mud from the streets. Even little John's clothes were oft-mended.

Catherine appeared from behind the counter. Bobby had an arm around Nora's shoulders. Her eyes lit up, but she quickly opened a door into a back room. "This way, please," she said to Nora as though she were a customer or a stranger.

Something about her brisk manner made Nora's heart stammer. Would her Christmas miracle fade away now, while it was at her very fingertips?

Silently, she and Bobby entered the room Catherine had indicated. It was a small but comfortable kitchen containing a coal stove, a few cabinets, and a little table with chairs lined up next to it. A gentleman in a pinstriped suit with a monocle and meticulously groomed whiskers sat at the table, sipping from a teacup.

"Nora, my darling." Catherine laid a hand on Nora's arm with reassuring warmth. "This is my husband, Edmund."

It was a sudden stab to the belly to see the man who was now married to her mother, but Nora knew she could hardly have been expected to remain single all these years. She curtseyed, not knowing what else to do. "A pleasure to meet you, sir."

Something in Edmund's shoulders relaxed. "You speak well."

"I worked in a great house, sir."

"Then you know your manners." Edmund gave Catherine a swift look.

Nora held up her baby. "Mama, this is little John."

"Oh... John." Sudden tears filled Catherine's eyes, and she held out a finger to the baby. "Hello, little one."

Nora's throat tightened. How many times had Catherine used that same tone and said those same words to her? The warmth in her voice swelled Nora's heart. John giggled and grasped Catherine's finger, and a tear escaped down her mother's cheek.

"And this is my husband, Bobby," said Nora.

Bobby tugged at his forelock. "Pleased to meet you, sir, ma'am." He tried his best, but his pronunciation remained rough.

Edmund's smile slipped.

"Please, sit. There's hot tea for everyone. I trust you had a hearty breakfast?" Catherine ushered them into chairs.

Nora sat opposite Edmund. "Thank you, Mama. We had more than enough."

"Good. Good!" Catherine beamed.

Edmund sipped his tea. Bobby's eyes widened as Catherine added two cubes of sugar and a generous splash of milk to his; Nora didn't think they had ever had money for milk and sugar in the same teacup. Catherine dipped a rusk in her tea and gave it to John, who gleefully chewed it.

"It's wonderful to see your family, Nora." Catherine smiled at the baby. "They're beautiful."

"Thank you, Mama."

Edmund let out a gusty exhalation. "All right. I suppose I should cut to the chase."

Nora's heart turned over in her chest at the gentleman's ominous tone.

Edmund took Catherine's hand, but she pulled it away. He gave her a pained look.

"I am overjoyed to make your acquaintance, Nora," he said. "Let me start with that. And allow me to assure you that your mother has never once stopped thinking about you and longing for you. Why, every day she mentions your name and tells me stories about your life as a little girl. Finding you again is a miracle she never dared hope for, yet longed for all these years. I wish you to know that."

"Oh, Mama." Nora took her hand.

Catherine smiled, but her eyes were full of tears.

"What is more," said Edmund, "I recognize her great depth of feeling toward you and our familial obligation to you and your, ah, husband and child."

Nora's stomach felt like a cold stone.

"I understand that my dear Catherine suggested you could stay in our home."

Bobby's face turned pale. "You're saying we can't, sir? But she's your stepdaughter!"

"Ah. I suppose." Edmund cleared his throat. "The trouble is, Mr... Tibbett, is it? The trouble is, Mr. Tibbett, we are people of a certain social standing. We may not have lands or titles, but with great effort, we have worked our way up to a certain level."

"You're saying you're too good for us now," Nora snapped.

Edmund blinked, startled that a woman would dare use that tone against him.

"I'm sorry, sir." Nora hastily bowed her head.

A smile flickered across Catherine's face. "Clever girl," she murmured.

"Catherine." Edmund's voice held a chiding note. "We talked about this."

"Indeed we did." A muscle tightened in Catherine's jaw as she clenched it.

"You wouldn't know how to navigate the world we now inhabit." Edmund raised his chin. "The social world can be as cruel as the streets, Nora. However, like I said, I recognize the duty we have toward you. I hear your husband is a lamplighter by trade."

"That's right, sir." Bobby nodded.

"It's a dying trade, Mr. Tibbett. Electricity will replace it all soon. Sooner than any of us might think. Why, the Thames Embankment is proof of that."

Bobby's face fell. "I know, sir."

"I would like to offer you a position at my newspaper."

"I'm no great writer, sir."

Nora held her breath. No great writer! Bobby was barely literate.

Edmund gritted his teeth. "Not to worry, young man. We have plenty of other opportunities for anyone who will turn their hand to hard work."

"I will, sir. I'll do anything," said Bobby eagerly, "late at night, early in the morning, sun, rain, or snow... I'll do anything."

"Yes, yes. Quite. As for you, Nora, you may wish to remain at home with your child. It is, after all, the proper place for a woman."

Catherine gave Edmund another sharp look.

"For most women," Edmund amended, patting her hand.

"If it pleases you, sir, I'm not afraid to work outside the home. I would gladly help Mama in the millinery," said Nora.

Edmund's face made it clear that this did not please him at all. "No, no. That won't be necessary. I will make sure that you are quite comfortable. There are many beautiful little cottages to let on the outskirts of Westminster. You would be quite happy there, I'm sure, and Catherine could visit you as it pleases her."

Bobby took Nora's hand. "That all sounds very good, sir."

It didn't sound very good to Nora. It sounded to her that she was a problem and Edmund was ready to make it go away. But looking at the grim set of his mouth and the bitter defeat in her mother's eyes, she knew that nothing she said could change his mind.

"Very well." Nora pushed back her chair. "Thank you for your charity, sir."

"Come with me, darling." Catherine took Nora's arm. "We'll go shopping and make sure you have what you need. I've tried to get you a cottage for tonight, but I'm afraid, since it's Christmas Eve…"

"There's nothing available," said Nora. "We'll be going back to our tenement now."

Catherine's lips drew down at the corners. "I'm so sorry, dear."

Nora's heart softened. "Mama, it's all right. You're doing all you can for us."

Relief eased the tight lines of Catherine's face. "Thank you. Thank you for knowing that."

"I only…" Nora lowered her voice as they left the millinery through a back door. "I only wished that we could spend Christmas together, Mama."

Catherine gripped her arm. "Me too, Nora. Me too."

Nora and Bobby walked back through Devil's Acre in subdued silence. Bobby carried a basket full of shopping: potatoes, carrots, turnips, and a whole roast rabbit. There was even a plum pudding, ready baked, though it appeared Edmund's budget did not stretch to goose.

John chuckled. His little face was covered in rusk crumbs.

"Look at him." Nora kissed the baby's head. "He doesn't care one bit, does he?"

"I suppose he's right," said Bobby. "Look at all this, Nora. We won't be hungry this Christmas. She even gave us money for firewood. Why, this will be fine. Better than any Christmas we've had before." He smiled. "We'll get the fire roaring and we'll roast some chestnuts and we'll have lovely rabbit and plum pudding, just the three of us."

Nora tried to smile. "Yes. It'll be lovely."

"Oh, my love. I'm trying to cheer you up, but I understand why you're sad. You thought we'd be with your mama for Christmas. That would have been a glorious thing."

"It's not Mama who doesn't want us."

"No. Not at all." Bobby sighed. "But Edmund is ashamed of us. That's why he doesn't want you to work in the millinery, you know. He wants to keep us a secret. He can force me to stay silent at the paper; he knows your mama would tell everyone at the millinery who you are."

"Yes. As though we'd done something wrong simply because we're poor."

"That's the way of some folk, Nora." Bobby's hands were too full to put an arm around her, but he edged nearer to her in any case. "It'll be all right, you'll see."

"A nice cottage with the three of us will still be lovely."

"It certainly will. And it'll get better. I'll be the best

worker Edmund ever had. I'll show him that I can be the son-in-law he wants. He'll have us in his house yet."

Nora gazed up at him, eyes shining. "Oh, Bobby. You're quite, quite wonderful. I do love you."

"I love you too, my darling."

Nora knew that. Despite the sting of Edmund's rejection, Bobby could always warm her heart.

They passed a sickly tributary of the Thames, its waters grimy as they rolled between sheer walls of stone. Blobs of garbage drifted in them, fouling the delicious smell of the pudding and the rabbit. Nora told herself that they wouldn't have to be in the tenement for long, even if they never saw Catherine's beautiful house.

The voice behind her was a low, ghoulish rasp. "Nora Ellis!"

Nora whipped around, clutching John so hard that he cried. Surely it couldn't be!

But she had not been mistaken. Wainscoate stepped from the darkness of a nearby alley and stood facing them. The cold morning light was harsh on his disfigured face. The wound had healed badly, a thick rope of scar tissue pulled his cheek toward his ear, and the corner of his mouth sagged where the muscle had never knit together properly. Saliva dripped from the ruined corner of his lip. He had been handsome once. Now he looked like something from a penny dreadful.

"It's him!" she cried. "It's Wainscoate!"

Bobby stepped between them. "Run, Nora!"

But Nora had run from this man too many times before. She didn't find it in herself to flee before him again.

"How did you find me?" she demanded.

"Nora," Bobby hissed.

She pushed past him. "How?"

"I've been looking for you." Wainscoate's lips drew back from his teeth. "Did you think I would stay in Hampshire forever, rotting in that country house while society laughed at my face? I came back to London three months ago. I've had men watching every market square, every tenement, every street where a disgraced maid might crawl to hide." His voice dropped to a hiss. "And then I saw you myself, you and your brat, buying fish like some common fishwife. After that, it was easy. Any beggar will search for a girl if you give him a shilling. You wouldn't bear my touch, yet you befouled yourself with this wretch!"

Nora stared at his wildly rolling eyes and knew then that Wainscoate, if he had ever been sane, had now finally gone quite mad. Whether it was with lust, greed, hatred, or all three, she didn't know.

"Look what you did to me!" Wainscoate jabbed a finger at his face. "I would have given you everything, and you destroyed me!"

"You wouldn't have given me a thing," Nora barked. "All you wanted to do was take."

"Nora, get out of here. I'll stop him," Bobby urged.

But Nora had had enough. She would flee from this spectre no longer. He was no monster; he was only a silly, shabby, wounded excuse for a man, and her fears had already given him too much power.

She thrust John into Bobby's arms. He snatched up by the baby by reflex and Nora stormed toward Wainscoate.

"Nora!" Bobby lunged for her arm.

Nora dodged him. "You fool!" she shouted. "You call my husband a wretch, but you are the lowlife here! Bobby might be poor, but in his heart, he's a king. While you are lower than the most leprous urchin lying in the gutter!"

Wainscoate roared. He lunged to grab her. He was faster

than she'd thought, and Nora jumped back with a cry. Her heel met empty air.

"Nora!" Bobby screamed.

Her arms flailed, but her balance was already gone. She fell for a stomach-churning instant, and then the water of the Thames closed over her head.

The cold snatched her breath and plunged her world into darkness. Her limbs kicked and struggled in all directions, but Nora had never learned how to swim, and the current pounced upon her like a live and predatory thing. She struck out in despair and couldn't find the surface. Her chest burned for air.

Something warm wrapped around her and propelled her through the confusion of the current. Then her head broke the surface, blindingly cold, and she sucked down air that stung her chest and made her splutter.

"It's all right! It's all right," a man said. "I have you. You're all right."

Nora shook her head, dispelling hair from her face. She thought for a confused moment that it was Bobby who'd saved her, but instead the face had sodden whiskers and a distinguished brow.

"M-Mr. Whitmore?" she croaked.

"It's all right," said Edmund again. "Hold onto me."

CHAPTER 28

*E*dmund swam strongly, dragging Nora with him, and they reached the bank. A small crowd had gathered there. Nora heard her baby screaming.

"John!" she cried. "Bobby!"

Someone threw down a rope, and Nora scrambled out, helped by the men who had thrown it. They seized handfuls of her wet dress and pulled her onto the embankment.

She struggled to her feet at once, weighed down by wet fabric and bitter cold. "John!"

"He's all right, love!" It was Catherine, clutching the baby, who squalled desperately.

Nora looked around for Bobby and spotted him through the crowd. She pushed past the men as they hauled Edmund to safety. A cut above Bobby's eye bled profusely, and a strong policeman held him by one arm. Two more policemen stood by Wainscoate. His face was battered, and he was shouting.

"Bobby!" Nora ran to him.

The policeman stopped her with an outstretched hand.

"Her! That's her! Seize her!" Wainscoate shrieked.

"She's the one who did this to my face! She should be hanged!"

"You're the one who should swing, you brute!" Bobby shouted.

The policeman gripped his arm tighter.

"Hang them both, and their brat as well!" Wainscoate's mouth foamed with fury.

"Don't listen to him!" Edmund burst through the crowd, Catherine close behind with John. "I saw it all, officers. I saw him cast this young lady into the Thames. He meant to drown her. He is a murderer!"

"Murderer!" Wainscoate spat. "I am Lord Dornton, Baron of Wainscoate, and I shall not be addressed in this manner by some middle-class wretch!"

"I know what I saw, officers," said Edmund sharply.

There was a murmur of agreement from the crowd. The policemen shifted their weight, uneasy.

"He did it!" said Catherine. "I saw it, too."

"What does it matter? I feared for my life," Wainscoate burst out. "She wished to kill me. She attacked me, officers. Look! This is what she did the last time I allowed her to come close." He jabbed a finger at his face.

The policeman turned to Nora. "Miss, you'll have to come with me."

"No! She's innocent! I'm telling you, he accosted her that night!" Bobby threw himself against his captor.

"Lies. All lies. Who will you believe, officers?" Wainscoate sneered.

"You will believe this!"

The pure, high voice was unmistakable. Nora whirled around and her jaw dropped as Lady Arabella Weatherby swept through the crowd.

She was still the same in so many ways: the same pearls

in her hair, the same delicate, tissue-paper-white skin, and the same bright eyes. But there was something different about this Arabella. She seemed taller, her cheeks redder, her steps firm as she strode across the cobblestones. The crowd gave way to her as if to royalty, which she nearly was, given the rank of her husband.

Lord Weatherby was close behind her, a hand on her back, but he did not speak.

"Officers," said Arabella, "this young lady is speaking the truth. That man..." She raised an imperious finger and pointed at Wainscoate. "That man tried to do unthinkable things to her on December twenty-third, eighteen seventy-three. She lashed out in self-defence. He tried to kill her now, too, to silence her or to avenge his injuries, but certainly not because he feared she would harm him. She would never hurt a fly!"

"How do you know this, milady?" asked the officer standing by Wainscoate.

"Arabella, stop this nonsense at once," Wainscoate hissed.

"No, Father. I will not." Arabella's voice grew louder. "I will not stop. I was silent for too long when I was in your house. I allowed you to trample upon me and everyone else you pleased. To take from us and to do to us whatever you desired. But no more!"

Lord Weatherby's face shone with pride in his wife.

"No more!" Arabella repeated. "I demand in the name of my husband, the Earl of Weatherby himself, that you arrest that man and let my friend Nora's husband go!"

The senior policeman hesitated. His eyes moved from Wainscoate to Arabella — a lord's own daughter, testifying against him — then to Edmund and Catherine, to the murmuring crowd. A baron's word against an earl's wife, a dozen witnesses, and a face that told its own story.

"Do it," Lord Weatherby said quietly.

The policeman nodded. At Lord Weatherby's order, the officers rounded on Wainscoate at once.

"No!" he cried, holding up his hands. "No, no!"

The officer seized him.

"Take your hands off me!" Wainscoate cried.

"Not to worry, milord," the officer hissed. "It'll all be cleared up in a court of law."

The other officer let go of Bobby, who rushed to Nora and flung his arms around her.

"Oh, Bobby, you caught him!" Nora kissed him. "You stopped him."

"You're soaked! Darling, you'll catch your death." Bobby shrugged out of his threadbare coat and wrapped it around her shoulders. "We must get you home at once."

"No. Not to that foul tenement," said Edmund. "Catherine! Hail a cab. We must take Nora and Bobby home at once, and the baby, too."

"Sir?" Nora gasped.

Edmund laid a hand on her shoulder and met her eyes. "My wife was inconsolable after you left. She told me everything, about Lord Wainscoate, about what he did to you in that cellar. When I understood what you had survived, and that such a man still walked free..." Edmund's voice hardened. "I saw that I was wrong all along."

"No social standing is more important to me than my wife, and I should follow her example in unconditional care for my family, which you are. Forgive me, Nora. You will come home with us at once, you and your family. That is why we were here; I made up my mind that we must stop you from going back to that dreadful tenement, and we followed you. We were about to call out to you when we saw that fool Wainscoate attack you."

"Cabbie!" Catherine was shouting. "Come to the road, Nora! We must get you out of the window."

"Come, love." Bobby pulled her away.

"Wait." Nora turned to face Arabella.

The two women gazed at each other for a long few moments. There was so much Nora wanted to say. Part of her wanted to apologize, but in the end the words that came out were the only ones that mattered.

"I'm so proud of you, Arabella."

The lady held out a silk-gloved hand. Nora understood this could not happen again. The social chasm between them was too vast. But here, in this strange and fragile instant, she wrapped her soaked and grubby hand around Arabella's, and their eyes met.

"Be well, Nora," said Arabella.

Then Bobby took her hand and whisked her off to the warm carriage and to a whole new life.

That Christmas was like a happy dream, only every detail about it reminded Nora that it was real. The warmth of the great yellow fire leaping in the hearth. The smell of the roast chestnuts that the housekeeper brought in on a silver tray. The brilliance of the Christmas tree in the corner, with its paper chains and ribbons and the golden angel at its peak. Those decorations enchanted little John; he lay wrapped in a cozy new blanket at its feet, like a gift himself, and stared at the dancing candles and glistening baubles. Their lights were all the brighter in his wide eyes.

Bobby wore Edmund's clothes; they were too big, but

he was warm and laughing. He made Edmund laugh, too, and Catherine's hand never strayed far from Nora's.

They had everything. Plum pudding. Eggnog. A great goose, roasted to the richest gold, with all the trimmings and stuffing that anyone's heart could wish for. Nora suggested that the housekeeper use a touch more thyme in the stuffing, and the housekeeper curtseyed to her.

They played parlour games late into that night until little John fell fast asleep in the crib Catherine had borrowed from a church friend for him. Eventually even the men went up to bed, worn out from laughter, and it was just Catherine and Nora sitting by the fireplace, listening to the baby's quiet coos as he slept.

"I have something for you," Catherine said.

Nora lifted her head. "Mama, you've already given me, well, everything."

"I have one more thing." Catherine reached into a basket and pulled out a whole orange.

She handed it to Nora, who raised it to her lips and breathed its sharp citrus scent. The memory that flooded her made her eyes sting. She remembered the pride in Papa's eyes as she'd doled out the orange on their last Christmas together.

"He would have been so proud of you, you know," said Catherine softly.

"I know," said Nora.

"You're a good girl."

Nora met her mother's eyes. "No," she murmured. "I'm a clever one, just like you taught me."

Catherine smiled, her eyes shimmering with emotion. Outside, a few late carollers passed by their window, and a snatch of their song drifted into the house.

When peace shall all over the earth

Its ancient splendours fling
And the whole world give back the song
Which now the angels sing.

They listened until the last chorus died away, and then Nora peeled the orange, broke it in half, and shared it with her mother.

EPILOGUE

1881

Nora stood on tiptoe on the stepladder, stretching up to hang the wreath on the millinery door. It was a large and heavy one, so weighed down with ribbons and holly and little silver bells that it was unwieldy, and she had just found the nail to hang it on when something crashed into her stepladder.

"Mama! Mama!" a little voice piped.

Nora grabbed at the door as the ladder teetered.

"Land's sakes, Johnny!" Catherine rushed over and steadied it. "You'll knock your mother's teeth out!"

Nora laughed and descended the ladder. Catherine's cheeks were flushed with cold and merriment; the first flakes had just begun to fall, dusting the market square as if with sugar.

"What are you doing up there, Nora?" Catherine chided. "There's no reason for you to be climbing about in your condition."

Nora ran a hand over the half-concealed curve of her belly. "I wanted the place to be all beautiful for you when you came back. How was your shopping?" She glanced at the brown paper wrapped parcels in Catherine's arms. "Looks like it was good!"

"We got presents!" a tiny voice piped up beside Catherine.

Nora laughed and held out her arms. "Did you now, Roberta?"

Her two-year-old daughter stuck out her little hands, and Nora swept the girl into her arms and showed her face with kisses.

"We got so many presents, Mama!" John, almost four and giddy with life, bounced around at Nora's feet. "We got presents for everyone! Even for you! We found you a…"

"Now, now, John." Catherine ruffled his hair. "No spoiling the surprise."

"Oh, yes." John giggled.

"Let's go inside. It's freezing out!" Catherine swung the door open.

They entered the millinery; closed today, as they only did half-days on Saturdays, but nonetheless warm inside with the leaping fire reflecting on all the colourful bolts of cloth. Nora had used offcuts to make the bunting that hung all around the place, brightening it all the more.

On the worktable by the window, in their usual place, lay Mama's bone-handled scissors. Nora had used them just this morning to cut the ribbon for the wreath. They were hers now, Catherine had pressed them into her hands last Christmas, and she treasured them as Mama always had.

"Where's Bobby?" Catherine asked.

"Right here!" Bobby emerged from a back room, eyes shining. "Nora, don't tell me you hung that wreath."

"There's no telling me what to do, love. You should know that by now." Nora planted a kiss on his cheek.

Bobby tutted, but he was smiling.

"Looks like we're all ready for Christmas," said Catherine.

"Not quite all ready." Bobby scooped his daughter from Nora's arms. "There's one more thing."

"Oh! Is it ready?" Catherine asked eagerly.

Everyone looked up at the bulb hanging in from the ceiling. It was made of perfectly clear glass except for the two little metal rods and the strange, twisting filament at its centre.

"Let's see if it works," said Bobby.

"This is exciting!" Catherine clapped her hands. "We're to be one of the first businesses in London to have these."

"Well, we are one of the biggest millineries in the city, Mama," said Nora.

"Ready?" Bobby reached for the switch.

"I don't know. You're sure the light won't be all harsh and cold like it was on the embankment that day? Perhaps we should stick with gas." Nora shuddered.

"This is an incandescent light bulb, darling. The light is warm yellow, like a fire. I promise," said Bobby.

Nora met his eyes and smiled. She knew that this man kept his promises.

"All right," she said. "Let's see!"

Bobby grinned. And with the flick of a switch, as he always did, he lit up her world.

The End

JOIN MY NEWSLETTER

I hope that you enjoyed this book.
If you are willing to leave a short and honest review for me on Amazon, it will be very much appreciated, as reviews help to get my books noticed.

Would you like a FREE Book?
Join Iris Coles Newsletter

BOOKS BY IRIS COLE

CHRISTMAS BOOKS BY IRIS COLE
The Christmas Pauper
The Stone Picker's Christmas Promise
The Little One's Christmas Dream
The Forgotten Match Girls Christmas Birthday

OTHER BOOKS BY IRIS COLE
The Daughter's Silent Promise (Shadows of London Book 1)
The Lost Son Of London: Beneath The Smoke (Shadows of London Book 2)
The Forgotten Daughter of London (Shadows of London Book 3)
The Widow's Hope (Book 1 in Victorian Family Saga)
Little Jack (Book 2 in Victorian Family Saga)
The Lost Mother's Christmas Miracle (Book 3 in Victorian Family Saga)
The Waif's Lost Family
The Lost Daughter

BOOKS BY IRIS COLE

    The Workhouse Girl's Despair
    The Pickpocket Orphans
    The Wretched Needle Worker

Printed in Dunstable, United Kingdom